W llergic to

?

Rachel Berger is widely acknowledged as one of Australia's finest stand up comedians. Her dynamic presence and engagingly sharp observations have made her a popular performer both live and on television, across Australia and overseas.

Rachel has performed four times at the Edinburgh Festival in Scotland. While in Britain she has made numerous television appearances and performed extensively on the London comedy circuit.

'It is the offbeat observation, the incisive knack of showing up everyday events for the ludicrous pantomimes they really are that separate the women from the girls. In this department Rachel Berger is a real Star . . .' ***The Guardian, London***

'An uninterrupted high-octane monologue, delivered at breathtaking speed . . .' ***Elle Magazine, Britain***

'Berger fires on all 50 cylinders . . . she generates more heat than Battersea Power Station on a winter's night.' ***Sun Herald, Sydney***

'She is one of the sharpest comedians of either gender or hemisphere.' ***The List, Scotland***

Further information about the author may be found at **www.rachelberger.com**

Whaddya Mean You're Allergic to RUBBER?

Rachel BERGER

PENGUIN BOOKS

Penguin Books Australia Ltd
487 Maroondah Highway, PO Box 257
Ringwood, Victoria 3134, Australia
Penguin Books Ltd
Harmondsworth, Middlesex, England
Penguin Putnam Inc.
375 Hudson Street, New York, New York 10014, USA
Penguin Books Canada Limited
10 Alcorn Avenue, Toronto, Ontario, Canada M4V 3B2
Penguin Books (NZ) Ltd
Cnr Rosedale and Airborne Roads, Albany, Auckland, New Zealand
Penguin Books (South Africa) (Pty) Ltd
24 Sturdee Avenue, Rosebank, Johannesburg 2196, South Africa
Penguin Books India (P) Ltd
11, Community Centre, Panchsheel Park, New Delhi 110 017, India

First published by Penguin Books Australia Ltd 2001

1 3 5 7 9 10 8 6 4 2

Design by Susannah Low, Penguin Design Studio
Author photograph by Peter Rosetzky
Typeset in 10/14 Sabon by Post Pre-press Group, Brisbane, Queensland
Printed and bound in Australia by McPherson's Printing Group,
Maryborough, Victoria

National Library of Australia
Cataloguing-in-Publication data:

Berger, Rachel.
Whaddya mean you're allergic to rubber.

ISBN 0 14 026617 8
I. Title
A823.4

www.penguin.com.au

For my parents, Markus and Rose

If your enemy is laughing,
how can he bludgeon you to death?
Mel Brooks

PART ONE

CHAPTER ONE

Do not let your tongue lead you into sin.
– The Book of Ecclesiastes

the FIASCO

'Are you –?'

'Am I what?'

Christopher wouldn't use a condom.

'What?' I spat. 'What, what?'

He rolled over and slid further down the bed, onto his side. He was looking up into my face: puppy-eyed and wet-nosed. Clever move.

'Angry?'

'Why would I be angry? I love the itching sensation that's making me want to fuck . . . the doorknob! I don't believe you . . . unfuckinprotected sex! Why would I go there . . . the doorknob's got more fucking brains.'

'But you *know* me. I'm not stupid, I make great antipasto. I'm clean – you're wearing my socks, aren't cha? I'm *no* stranger.'

He wasn't listening.

Why should he? He had the biggest shlong I'd ever squared up to in my life. Not so much a piece of meat, but a mixed grill. Not that I'd laid eyes on it, I could feel it . . . using up all the oxygen.

He turned his head and made a coughing sound so I could barely hear him.

'There's no doorknob . . . it's a sliding door.'

'Some other horny bitch probably got there first.'

I was twelve again and back at summer camp, behind the dining tent with lust-mad Morris, the furrier's son, my first boyfriend. He: short, voice just breaking, hairline prematurely receding, clumsily pushing my clenched fist onto the lump bulging out of his permanent-press shorts. Me: taller, desire-soaked, limp puff-pastry, dying to touch *it*, confused, pulling away.

Every drooling gland in my body knew that Christopher would not be a disappointment the way Morris had been. To be fair, Morris had underestimated the velocity with which he'd grabbed at my hand. He spent the next thirty minutes writhing and moaning in his sleeping bag like a smacked puppy in a basket. For years I believed this was a normal response. My early marriage did nothing to alter this belief.

'Listen, I'm OK with this outcome, really . . . relax. I'm comfortable with things just as they are –'

'Fuck you, Christopher . . . what are we doing here . . . fuckin therapy? *I'm OK with this outcome.* What about me? What am I, the invisible woman?'

Christopher certainly was not Morris.

'There's something about me you should know,' he said, as if closing a deal. Then reassuringly, in samba tempo, he put my hand around it. From the bottom to the top, over it, under it, along it and around it, again.

'So you're circumcised. Why couldn't you just say so?'

His dirty laugh filled the space.

This was no lump, this was all the sealed sections I'd ever peeled apart and collaged together. I gasped. Which in itself is amazing because in the new millennium, women do not gasp. They exhale, they inhale, they take in deep breaths full of good thoughts and exhale the negative ones. They do goddess workshops, dominatrix classes, creative dance and Ashtanga yoga. They celebrate, connect, reaffirm, nurture, honour and reawaken deep relationships with the self.

I was ready to sit on a dick for three days.

What would you do? I'd been celibate for three years. When you work late at night you don't meet loads of eligible men. Christopher was the first man I'd met in a long time who wasn't lying face-down in the gutter.

'Lola, you're trembling?'

I sizzled. My corporeal ozone layer disappeared, my nose and mouth melted into one gooey blob. My face was a living Rorschach test that not even Rorschach could interpret. My heart pounded, my pelvis throbbed. I wanted to have a bowel movement. Was this lust or was I having an anxiety attack? The symptoms seemed exactly the same.

'Is this some kind of bionic device, Christopher? Does it come with instructions or is there a 1800 number I should call?'

I tried to ride the wave, but the swell was too much. My body slopped and sloshed and finally got dumped by an oestrogen white-cap. Tears all over the pillow.

'Shit, what is it with vodka . . . '

'You mean gin. Vodka is an upper. Quit talkin or you'll choke . . . you sound like Minnie Mouse on helium.'

I exhaled through my nose and made an ugly snotty mess.

'Is it cool to give you a hug?' he purred, trying to console me with the illusion of intimacy. As I recall it, he was ambitiously tender. I expected him to say, *Will there be fries with that?* but he was silent and attentive, drawing my body closer to his, shifting my head onto his chest.

My face, poached with perspiration and tears, slid into his armpit. I couldn't be sure if he was being affectionate or trying to smother me, which only made me more anxious.

'I can't wear condoms – they're too snug. I lose my erection.'

My vision was obstructed by one of his nipples and the spirally seaweed of chest hair. In the semi-darkness I could just make out his face. But his smile was like a lighthouse beacon, dental work so dazzling it should have warned all women-ships to steer away from the treacherous rocks ahead.

In hindsight, it's so screamingly obvious: he was handing me the gun and ammunition, gambling on the hope that I'd pull the trigger.

the CLOSURE

'Welcome, ladies and gentlemen. Look around and you'll notice the tables decorated with rococo candelabras. Are they there to create an ambience of Renaissance Europe? I don't think so! The Premier sold the State Electricity Commission and we don't know where our power is coming from any more. Uganda maybe? Why did he sell it? He probably got more for it than he was offered for his mother!'

The Premier, James Cefn Dupleix . . . I sniffed him in the crowd like a dead rat under the floorboards the moment I stepped out on stage. I watched him register my appearance with the blink of one scaly eyelid. With Dupleix you're either in or out, there's no in-between. He gave me the ya-gotta-give-it-a-go head-tilt and smile through chicken-arse lips. But the straight-backed military posturing spelt out his position. Dupleix sees himself as the centre of the political universe, attentive only to those who can keep him elevated there. This man's favourite sport is close-range hog hunting. 'Grog, guns and ammo are all I need to have some *real* fun'.

It was an art teachers' function to celebrate the success of an exhibition of the work of final-year secondary students, a formal dinner at the Victorian Arts Centre. Dupleix was special guest. I was combustible, looking for sparks. The audience was in tune, their laughter and clapping blocking out Dupleix's rattle. The function organiser, Bridgitte, a peerlessly pony-tailed Frenchwoman, kept punching her Chanel-lacquered fist against her chest.

I changed direction for a nanosecond. 'I'm trying to be politically correct, but it's just *too* hard. I think I'm profoundly politically challenged.'

Dupleix's mouth twitched into a smirk. He's a short man but seems taller, especially when he's standing on the dismembered bodies of those who questioned his authority. After a landslide victory for his party, he became Premier and removed any potential obstacles. No more Freedom of Information legislation, no more Equal Opportunity Board and no more open government. The facts came back to me like a spoiled lamb curry and I had no control of what came out of my mouth.

'Welcome to Despot World, where you, too, can experience oppression, domination and all the thrills and spills of a virtual dictatorship.'

I glanced at Bridgitte. She was the colour of yoghurt. I deepened my voice and played ring-mistress. 'Tremble through the Iron-hand Parlour, ride the Big-stick Carousel, scream your lungs out through the Tunnel of Bureaucratic Red Tape. Roll up, roll up . . . have a go on the Victoria X-Press, it spins you round and round till all the money falls out of your pockets and you learn to live without public transport and an adequate ambulance service.'

Strutting across the stage, I shot Dupleix a smile, imaginary whip in one hand, microphone in the other. He was bent down, leaning across behind the man next to him, whispering to the next one along in the food chain. He raised his upper body, arched back, ears flapping bottom-feeder style, called over a waiter and ordered more wine. He was hearing every word, but avoiding my gaze. I stood directly in his line of vision and continued.

'Mr Premier. I've been told you have a very good sense of humour, and the humility to laugh at yourself. That's excellent. Your hairdresser must have a good sense of humour too!'

I saw his mouth move. 'My hairdresser's funnier than you!'

Bingo, I'd got him. 'I'd like to shake your hand, Mr Premier, but I can see that it's busy!'

Dupleix slapped his thigh and laughed with the crowd. With a two-beat delay, the potato heads on his table crinkled into french fries. There was a broad-shouldered creature whose head moved forward and back. He was laughing, but kept his hand discreetly over his face. He looked familiar, but a waitress stepped in front of him before I could focus properly.

I had to concentrate on Dupleix. 'You're very handsome for a politician. I hope I'm not embarrassing you. But whenever I think of politics it reminds me of being made love to by a man. Especially the part where he says, "Sorry, this doesn't usually happen."'

The audience roared, having felt first-hand the effects of Dupleix's sleight-of-hand side-show. In recent months his government had closed down several schools across the city.

Bridgitte flapped her arms about in the wings and got my attention. She was practically on her Dior-sheer knees. I backed off.

'Must be the cleansing diet I'm on, all those toxins flushing out of my mouth. I feel so guilty when I go to a health-food shop, don't you? Have you noticed how unhealthy the person behind the counter always looks? They ask me if I need any help and I want to say, No, but do you? Would you like some oxygen? I think they've probably had so many colonic irrigations they've flushed out their personalities.'

A clutch of carnivores, beady-eyed and bloodthirsty, cackled into the room. Momentarily distracted, I raised my voice, and lay in wait for the right moment to pounce on the intruders and feast on their arrogance. In a pathetic attempt at invisibility, they dispersed to different tables.

'Was the tide against you, Aquaboy?' I turned on Big Ears, with his back to me, removing a chair from the table next to Dupleix's.

I tried again. 'He-llo?'

He didn't pay any attention. 'Too much hair fudge . . . clogs up your hearing! Parking the car, were you?' The arseless one straightened, took his time to turn around, and in that moment other fauna jumped in on his behalf.

'I apologise for my colleague, Miss Finkelstein . . . he *was* indeed looking for a carpark . . . for my car.' William Lisbon, Federal Health Minister, in his as-far-as-the-eye-could-see suit, lobbying as usual. He was the familiar shape I hadn't immediately recognised. He was in Dupleix's shadow and not wearing his glasses.

I took a deep breath. 'Ex-cuse me, ladies and gentlemen, but has the intoxicating aroma of garlic prawns and cheap cologne gone to my head or did you just hear a political professional say *sorry*?'

My heart thumped like the hot-tempered heels of a flamenco dancer. Why would a Federal Minister attend an insignificant arts function? And with the State Premier? Why hadn't he told me he'd be there?

William made room for the extra chair, crossed his heart and gave me a promise-not-to-tell look.

'OK, Minister, sit down.' I pulled a mock-vomit face at the audience. Laughter.

'You're bringing a lump to my throat . . . no . . . no . . . not with your back to me, please. I'm into full-frontal abuse – it helps to see your lips move.' He turned his chair to face the stage, sat down, crossed his legs and gave me his full attention. Was he seeking approval or relinquishing something? I didn't know or care. 'You can uncross your legs, Minister . . . go on . . . trust me, you'll still have your dick when this is over.'

I moved centrestage, addressing the rest of the audience. 'How was the food? Enough . . . not enough . . . too much? I love food, I'm a food slut, I eat around! I don't understand diet products like Skinny Meals – it's not food, it's pictures of food on cardboard! But then I guess a lot of people in Victoria are developing quite a palate for cardboard, since they can't afford to eat anything else.

'There are so many genetically modified foods, we don't know what we're shoving into our gobs. Testosterone in our tomatoes so they travel better and arrive firmer. Why not try that on Barry Webster, our Minister for Foreign Affairs? We've got bread with so many preservatives it lasts longer than most of my relationships. And seedless grapes, *ohmygod* – grapes that have had vasectomies. Nobody can tell what these hormones are doing to our bodies. I'm shit-scared that I'll wake up one morning with six vaginas and two penises . . . and knowing my luck the two penises will be attracted to each other.'

Heads bobbing forward and back all over the room, the best vista for a comedian. William laughed along, clapping like a seal. Thank god I hadn't fucked him. I don't like ex-lovers in the audience, it's too much like a *menage à trois*. I scanned the audience aurally, listening from the front to the back of the room. Bubbles of conversation floated up and disappeared with the slant of a person's chin.

Dupleix had his head down, lifting pretend lint from his trouser hem. Like haemorrhoids, I was an irritation he didn't need.

I overheard one of his deputies. 'Boss, we can leave . . . you don't need this shit, the car's right outside. If you want, I'll tell the kitchen to serve dessert before you speak. So there's a break between you and this crap.'

Dupleix pushed him back with his forefinger. 'You're a bozo, Froggy. She's only getting laughs because I'm in the room. Leave it alone.' Dupleix ignored the festivity as one would ignore the high-pitch hum of a distant mosquito. Without repellent, he felt the full furious sting when I came through the tear in the flywire head-on.

'Mr Premier, before I leave the stage, I want to alert you to a strange and dangerous condition that seems to have affected several of the ministers and bureaucrats in your government. And, I believe, this information is being kept from you. Soft-in-the-head syndrome, known simply as SHIT, is rampant. Yes, I know the acronym doesn't quite work, but that's the giveaway symptom.

It's been suggested that Moron Elongatus, a virus that induces a state of manic blockhead behaviour, has been released through the air-conditioning ducts at Parliament House. Does this explain the proposed closure of Springfield Hospital?'

William's face shattered and made a mess all over his lap. Dupleix poured a glass of water and simultaneously switched off his squealing mobile without finding out who the caller was. Not fully raising his head, he gave me a quick don't-fuck-with-me look. I saw flames licking at his feet. Put it this way – if he did have haemorrhoids, I'd just wiped his arse with sandpaper.

'What have you got planned for the hospital, Mr Premier? Another casino? Ex-cuuse me . . . entertainment complex? The Fun Clinic! Where punters are encouraged to live for today because there is no tomorrow. Where losers can be trolleyed straight from the high-rollers room to the cardiac unit. Where, thanks to the latest in remote-control technology, they can be sedated and even undergo surgery but keep on gambling. Or – wait for it – the incredible heart-lung-kidney machine that doubles as a pokie.'

I was skating free-form on supermodel-thin ice.

'So Mr Premier, my Premier . . . ' I waved my hand over the audience, 'our Premier, listen to your conscience . . . I *know* that would be taking advice from a stranger. And tell the Health Minister to examine your air-conditioning system for espionage. Then the mental health of your accountants before making any cost-cutting decisions based on their book-keeping skills. Thank you, thrill-seekers, enjoy the rest of the night!'

I exited via the kitchen, then down the service lift. Comedy is not a glamorous calling.

CHAPTER TWO

It is better to know some of the questions than all of the answers.
– James Thurber

the DAY BEFORE the FIASCO

March 15th – scary shit, the Ides of March. *Veni, vidi, vice:* I came, I saw, but would I get laid?

'*Et tu*, Christopher?' I asked on arrival at the gate lounge, in the silence that felt as long as a Sunday lunch with my mother. He bent forward to kiss me. I stepped back and extended my hand. He grabbed it and pulled me towards him so he was right in my face.

'That's stretching it . . . my name's been off the Roman Secret Service files since that whole Messiah thing.'

We hadn't seen each other for two months. We'd erased our tracks and hidden ourselves, remained impenetrable to each other's doubts. A non-malignant relationship, present but not dangerous.

I moved toward the exit. 'Still driving the convertible?'

He nodded, smiling bulldoggishly.

The week before, I'd faxed him my final production sheet; he faxed it back with 'OK' scrawled across the top. Maybe he was too busy to sign off or hated not getting his way. I'd stopped feeling like a marshmallow. I had work to do. I focused on giving a good performance.

We slipped into the traffic, no dialogue, no music, only the hum of the car's air-conditioning. I perspired like a leafy vegetable in a plastic bag, limp by the time you get it home. My mobile phone penetrated the silence like a door-knocking Mormon on a Sunday morning.

'Hello . . . Lola Finkelst—'

Ramona was in full flight, all parts moving at the same time. The news had just broken that she was resigning. She was coping, but wanted the media to take the story further. For Ramona, replacing a roll of toilet paper was a potential national crisis.

'I can't prove a thing, so the press won't run with it. There's nothing I can do . . . the journos are running scared. There's a rumour that Dupleix personally rang the chief of staff at the *Herald* and told him to sack Mike Blandthorn, the bloke who did the story on babies dying in community care –'

'Ramona, I have to cut you off . . . I just landed in Canberra. I've got a gig tonight and I –'

The phone cut out as Christopher drove into the Press Club carpark. He came around and opened the door.

'Do you need help with anything?'

'No, thanks. Did you organise the sound guy to be here for a check?'

'Yes, ma'am, I followed instructions exactly.'

We came in through the back entrance straight into the kitchen. One of the chefs waved to Christopher with a tea-towel and levelled a pretend gun to his temple.

He kept walking. 'Follow me. Watch where you're going – the floor's slippery.'

I took two steps for every one of his. 'Did you speak to the kitchen crew and tell them not to throw cutlery into the sink while I'm on stage?'

He nodded, still with his back to me.

'Christopher, I don't need this shit before a show . . . how can I –'

A taskforce of waiters burst in through the door ahead of us. He stopped and gently held my forearm to step aside.

'Hi guys, howzit goin?'

A L'Oréal blonde, all legs and lipgloss, chirped past on roller-blades. He did a boy-scout salute and smiled so hard I thought his ears would snap off. 'Hey, Deb, up for a big night?'

She spun around, skated back and stopped flamboyantly, just missing my feet. Christopher's fingers held onto me like claws.

'Crikey, sorry, got ambitious . . . knew what I was doing all the time.'

She gave good bullshit.

'Christopher, are you around later? I need to go over my roster with you for next week.'

He gave me a lame smile, oblivious to his decaying credibility. 'Speak to Roger, he's fixin the rosters for next week.'

I marched ahead, down the hallway.

He caught up. I wasn't looking at him.

'You're dribbling, must be time for her to bounce on your belly.'

We'd reached his office.

'Take a seat. You want coffee?' He was calm, smiling, almost mocking.

I bared my teeth. 'I don't need coffee.'

'Water? You're probably dehydrated from the flight. I'll be right back.'

I was in his chair when he came in. He handed me the glass and kept standing, leaning on one leg, towering over me like a giant Mr Gumpy. 'The sound guys are about ready to do a check, they're sayin another ten minutes. If you like, in the meantime we can do a run-through with the lights. Oh yeah . . . nearly forgot.'

He pulled a rolled-up A4 sheet from his back pocket. 'The final floor plan gives you a clear idea of the table configuration. I spoke to the crew; they're not serving drinks or throwing a thing into the sink once you're on stage.'

'Did you organise the cheque?'

'Yes, ma'am!' He stepped around between me and the desk, his groin vulnerably close to my head. He handed me an envelope from the pile of papers directly under my nose. 'I'll give it to you now, if it makes you feel better?'

I moved his hand away. 'Bad luck getting paid before the gig. I'm going through my basic professional requirements. No distractions on the floor, a good microphone and payment on the night. Have you got a problem with that?'

He sat, single buttock on the desk, facing me. 'Man, is this your regular trip before a gig?'

'If you'd responded to the production sheet I wouldn't be worrying about this shit now.'

'Jesus Christ, I did respond!'

'*OK*? Is that a response?'

'Ex-cuse me, I figured you'd have worked out by now that my head is screwed on the right way. I'd gone through everything . . . it was *OK*. What else?'

I pushed past him. 'Where's the toilet?' It was a stand-off.

I did the sound check and left for the hotel in a cab. He stayed, to be postgraduate anal with the kitchen crew. 'I'm gonna hang here, make sure the food's out, plates cleared on time, direct the traffic so there's no stalling. Then I'll go home . . . shower and pick you up on the return trip.'

'Sure, seeya later.'

He'd booked a room at the Hyatt. I presented myself, like a grunting warthog, at the reception desk of what had once been the prestigious Hotel Canberra. Built in the 1920s and more recently extended corporately skyward by Mr Hyatt. The sultry Duty Manager inhaled my name and smiled at my jewellery.

'Ms Finkelstein, welcome to the Hyatt. Mr Pillar confirmed your booking this afternoon. We've upgraded you to the Bruce Suite. Please fill in these details and Jasper will bring your bag up to the room.'

I did as I was told. Jasper appeared from behind the desk. The Duty Manager was Persephone, queen of the Underworld, and he was Cerberus, the three-headed dog that guarded her queendom.

He took my bag, stepping away from me as if I was contagious. I moved toward him. 'I hope it's a quiet room? I don't care if they give me the shed out the back, as long as I get some sleep.'

Jasper didn't respond till we turned two corners and passed an exit door. Nose tweaking, he put down my bag and reached for his keys.

He curled his lip and swung open the giant oak door. 'It certainly is *not* the back shed, Ms Finkelstein. You'll find it's very quiet, I guarantee you of that.'

He was giving me the shits. Breathing was giving me the shits. I had a funny taste in my mouth, probably the airline's faux food.

'I'm so fucking sleep-deprived, the sound of a pin dropping into shag pile could drive me to bite a chunk out of somebody's ankle.'

He squirmed. 'Quite, Ms Finkelstein.'

I glared at him. 'I can be woken up by the sound of earthworms meditating.'

'May I suggest earplugs?'

'I plug my ears with enough foam to float Hong Kong.' I was working myself up into a lather when I stepped into a beige cloudland.

The Bruce Suite was not so much a hotel room as the Art Deco equivalent of an L-shaped caravan. A come-hither foyer that lured you into the jumbo bedroom and Royal Family–sized bed. A separate en suite, kitchen, dining and loungeroom, exotic enough to stage a coup. These were not the anonymous walls of a hotel room. No plastic potpourri spray lurking in these corners, only the mustiness of the wood in the bookshelves. A sweetness collected in the open pores of its grain that guaranteed my sleep. The air-conditioning didn't quite filter the hint of camphor and cigars.

'Who books a room like this? It's obscene.'

Jasper was efficiently turning on every switch. 'Usually it's reserved for dignitaries. Presidents, statesmen, discreet plastic surgeons, that sort of thing. Mr Pillar is a friend of the Manager's. We try to look after his guests.'

'How long has it been here?'

'It's one of the original suites of the Hotel Canberra. As you can probably tell, it's been through several incarnations. It's thoroughly refurbished but nevertheless, we don't have occupancy too often.'

He gave me a look that suggested nothing less than vomit on Axminster carpet.

'Thanks for the background. I'll leave a trail of female scent in case I get lost. You'd better come looking if you don't see me by lunchtime tomorrow.'

Jasper's fumes irritated my eyes. 'Madam, there's a bottle of vodka in the smaller bar fridge in the bedroom. Mr Pillar had it sent up. Lemon slices over here on the side table . . . Tonic water, soda, mineral water, you'll find them all in the refrigerator in the kitchen. Is there anything else?'

'Where's the bathroom, through the courtyard to the second wing?'

His laugh was a grating nasal howl. A chihuahua with a cocaine habit. He recovered his land-legs and swung open the bathroom door. 'I hope you enjoy your stay with us.'

Jasper evaporated, leaving me to stand staring into the mirror, too stunned to move. A short, fake-tanned, crumpled woman, half her face covered by a gigantic pair of fake black Gucci sunglasses, stared back. Face it, you're trashed. Twenty consecutive performances in Adelaide. You produced the show yourself, planned the marketing and publicity and got on stage every night to deliver. You need help but you're too tired to identify the pests from the predators.

I made it to the bed in time to crash . . . boots and all.

I revisit an old recurring dream. I save my parents from the gas chambers by offering myself instead. But it's a scam.

There's no time to tell them. I appear dead, without being dead. No breath, no pulse, no life. The temporary effect of a secret formula sprayed into my eyes, like a topical anaesthetic. My organs on pause, until an antidote kickstarts the wheelworks again. In all of this there is a *me*, inside the me who's dead, who knows what's happening, who can see and hear but is immune to feeling. This internal me knows, as one does in dreams, that the antidote has been sold on the black market. I wait passively, already dead.

The phone rings . . . half-awake, the me inside me, speaks. 'When do I die?'

'You're gonna be great. The place is full and they're kickin! Just a friendly ETA call, to let you know where I'm at . . . do you need anything?'

He was exquisitely talented at doing thoughtful and considerate. I was in that shallow ditch between dreamscape and the real world. Where forms don't yet correspond to functions. I sat up straight, between fear and familiarity.

'Thanks, I . . . was dying . . . driving . . . I mean . . . sleeping. I was dreaming.' I couldn't open my eyes. 'I don't think I've touched down yet. What time is it? I never do this . . . how long before you're coming?'

The voice was all oven-baked, home-grown and paternal. 'Relax, it's only 7. I'm coming at 8.15, you've got plenty of time. This is exactly what you needed, you were a total wipe-out this afternoon.'

It was a struggle to move my mouth. 'I'd better get my shit together, I'll see you in an hour.'

The curtains were open, my eyes blinked open to twilight time. Headlights veiled, subdued through muslin sheers. The mellow Nat King Cole semi-darkness that croons day into night. I threw off the blanket and lay naked to the tune. I had no recollection of undressing. Dodgy stuff.

My brain escapes into a kind of pre-performance chamber roughly an hour before I go on-stage. I don't remember the pick-up or arriving at the venue. I surround myself with a high-voltage force field to prevent others getting in and to dam my energy from leaking out. Not even NASA could penetrate this.

Paul Furphy, political correspondent for the ABC, introduced me. 'Ladies and gentlemen, please give a warm and long overdue Canberra welcome to Yasser Arafat's pin-up nightmare, Lola Finkelstein.'

Applause.

It was a hard room. The geography of it – very broad, with the audience from wall to wall, across it. I had to play the space from left to right, to scan consistently, to connect with everyone.

'Welcome to AustraliaWorld, a giant theme-park just like Euro Disney, but not quite as financially successful. To our north, Queensland, a virtual tropical paradise where the only genuinely Australian experience is to be an Aboriginal in custody. And even that's not fair dinkum. The private prisons are owned by international companies, so guess what . . . the profits don't stay here. Wake up, Australia, your chicken is ready!

'CanberraWorld, aka The Improv Club, where you can *feel the power*! Especially while you're standing in the dole queue. Described in one brochure as a "thriving centre of sights, smells and taste sensations". Sounds like a trailer for an X-rated porn video set in a cheese factory!'

A tightly shickered woman down the front, dangerously rigged out with nail extensions and mascara, heckled me. 'Whas the matter with porn videosh?'

I placed her in the audience, raised an eyebrow and kept going. No point responding – she could barely get her verbs and nouns in order.

'Canberra, where there are more sightings of Elvis than our Prime Minister, the man who has no people skills. But that's no surprise . . . to have people skills you have to be a person.

'Democracy? How do you spell that? Is there a dollar sign in front of it? He says there's no link between mortgage interest rates and our foreign debt. What medication is he on? Next he'll be proving there's no link between poverty and lack of money!'

It was a dream show. The audience and comedian wedded under a canopy of laughter. Faces, swollen with pleasure, leaving all those involved euphoric, but listless. When at last I could surrender to sleep and the sense of feather-lightness that success promotes, Christopher offered to drive me back to the hotel. That was all he offered.

'You did a great job.'

I wanted him to gush, to worship at my feet. I wanted him to come back to my room, but how to ask? Would you like to come in and get laid?

He was playing theatre critic. 'You sure kicked butt.' He made a fist and punched at an imaginary jaw.

I couldn't be bothered talking. The carnal urge is overwhelming, it annihilates all other urges. He changed gears. His voice accelerated, his breathing was shallow and controlled. He was talking more to himself than to me. 'Private prisons aren't about rehabilitation. They're about meeting budgets and covering their arses so they can justify their existence.'

We stopped at a red light. He looked up, but not quite at me and continued. 'Victoria's heading to place 45 per cent of its prisons in the hands of private operators. Do you realise this is the highest proportion in the world? Dupleix is one phantom piece of legislation away from signing a deal to sell off Springfield Hospital to Shackles Inc.'

'It's not finalised,' I was too exhausted to ask him how he got this information. His intensity amplified my own paranoia. 'It's 2 a.m., I don't need fodder for nightmares.'

The spurt of adrenalin reminded me that I hadn't phoned Ramona. Maybe that's what the call was about. She'd been trying to establish an independent inquiry into why there'd been forty-one cases of self-mutilation and two suicides since the newest private prison opened six months ago.

I chewed at my cheek, keeping time to the syncopated psycho-billy of tyres on tar and Christopher's asthmatic wheezing. At the hotel, he kept the engine running and didn't get out. I'd used my quota of words for the day and could only manage to glance at the blur of him and pretend to wave.

'Call me when you wake up, I'll drop you at the airport.'

All power was down to zero. I plunged into sleep like a para-chutist into air, full body weight, willingly, with no thoughts of dangerous ground ahead.

CHAPTER THREE

Never do with your hands what you could do better with your mouth.
– Cherry Vanilla

the DAY of the FIASCO

In my dream, I was Marlene Dietrich.

My eyes unzipped to the sauerkraut flapdoodle sounds of an oompah band outside, beyond the hotel gardens. No matter how quiet the room is guaranteed to be, when I'm aboard there's sure to be a block of flats being demolished next door. Chainsaws will shred through my bones and the penetrating sound of drilling will pulverise every inch of my flesh into chewable chunks. Trombones, tenor tubas, trumpets and a big drum. A brass band was charity.

Flat on my back, like a frittata in a non-stick frying pan, I slid into a rubber-band stretch, arms and legs pulling away from my body. I needed something, a treat, a dip into the desire slush-fund for the last few weeks of non-stop solid effort.

What did I want? French toast, pancakes with maple syrup, fluffy cheese omelette?

I wanted Christopher Pillar. If he says, *Didn't you understand the first time? I'm a conquest junkie, I made my advance, you retreated, hasta la vista baby,* I can hang up, redial room service and go the French toast option.

The ring made me jump roughly three paperbacks above the mattress. Habit led me to lift up the handset but I forgot what to do next.

'Hello, is that the Bruce Suite?' His voice sprinkled through the teensy holes in the handset and splashed my face.

'Christ . . . Christopher?'

A confused pause, the insightful chuckle. 'I thought it was pretty safe to call, it's almost 2.'

I swung my legs around and sat over the edge of the bed. 'I never sleep in.'

'Your body's tellin you somethin. What've you got planned for today? Three performances, a radio interview and two hours at the gym?'

The wind was fierce at ego level. If I wanted to scale the insecurity summit, this was my golden opportunity. 'I thought I'd stay in Canberra, play tourist?'

I rolled my bottom lip over my top lip, gripping it with my teeth. My shoulders were scrunched up in the vicinity of my eyebrows, one leg tucked under my buttocks, the phone cord coiled around my waist. This protective wrapping had taken place unconsciously in two sentences. If I continued, my next call would be to a chiropractor.

He didn't hesitate. 'One condition.'

I tugged at the cord like Quasimodo at his bells. 'Like what?'

'Like you let me take care of you for the next twenty-four hours.'

'I don't need you to look after me, I'm not an invalid. Let's kick back . . . together . . . you've been flat out as well. I noticed you sucking pretty hard on your puffer last night.'

'I'll pick you up in an hour, we can have lunch and grab some supplies. If we're gonna hunker down we need a load of edible merchandise.'

'I don't have hunkering-down wear, leisure is not one of my regular destinations.'

'See ya in an hour.'

'Oy! This is not about you playing nursemaid –'

'Nursemaid is not one of *my* regular destinations. Ciao.'

I ordered coffee to help my body follow instructions. I showered, then systematically gathered and packed mascara, lipstick, hair-spray, sequinned dress, big jewellery and stilettos, the heavy machinery of stage performance. I checked for anything left behind and stumbled across a previously undiscovered guest bathroom. My flow was interrupted by Mr Hyatt's whoopee-doodle doorbell.

'Your coffee, madam. Where would you like it?' Yawning, I stepped aside to let the nothing-to-remember-her-by room service person slink in.

'Pardon me . . . put it on that pouf thing, please.'

'The ottoman?'

I lifted the newspaper and an envelope off the floor just outside the front door. 'Yeah, the ottoman.'

'Could you sign here, please?' She stifled a smirk. 'Enjoy your coffee.'

'How come they leave the account at the door?'

'Excuse me?'

I showed her the envelope.

'It must be personal. We don't generally leave . . . '

'It's handwritten on the outside, you're right . . . I didn't notice . . . sorry to hold you up.' She pranced out the door.

A snap chill floated in from the passageway as she disappeared. Habit indicated that I look outside for clues, but beyond the scrim there was only dishwater sky and slimy fog. I'd associated a brass band with sunny skies but autumn in Canberra delivered sorbet temperatures. The handwriting on the envelope was neat, carefully elongated, pointy, almost gothic letters. A fan, making a good impression in gold texta calligraphy. The note was a cut-and-paste masterpiece.

Miss FUNNY LaDY
A WORNING
MIND your own BISness.
STOP Trashing privITE PRISONS
or you MIGHT FIND
yourself IN shackels

Far from conveying a sense of threatening menace, it had a quirky cartoon quality. Collage is so benign, totally wrong for this kind of message. Each word had been individually cut out of magazines and newspapers, in a range of colours, sizes and fonts and finally, meticulously, glued. No smudging, no fingerprints. I was impressed. As a starting point, I knew my wannabe intimidator had great flair for colour and a demonic touch with clag. Tragically, he or she had a literacy problem. I'm not sure which was more menacing, the threat or the bad spelling.

I looked to the phone for guidance.

Who should I call? Ramona, shit, I still hadn't called her.

She was a cool customer. 'Go ahead, I'm listening.'

'Ramona, it's Lola.'

'Lola who?' She was coughing.

'You wanna get rid of the furball first?'

'What's your story?'

'You rang at the worst possible time. I had a gig and I've been asleep until about an hour ago. I apologise, I'm sorry. Has it ever happened before?'

'No.'

'Exactly. What's up?'

Ramona Madden, as of yesterday ex-Commissioner of the now defanged Equal Opportunity Commission. Rambo to those she allows in her compound. We'd collided roughly two years ago, in the mirror of the ladies' toilets at the Universal Theatre. Each knew who the other was. Ramona broke the ice through lips like two red planks from years of being held in place.

'I think you're bloody funny, keep up the good work.'

'Thanks.'

She poked me in the shoulder. 'He can't take our sense of humour away, can he?'

It was a rhetorical question. She was referring to Dupleix. Since he'd become Premier, her staff had been reduced, her resources diminished and two of her dogs poisoned. She pulled clumsily at a cigarette from a Glomesh cigarette case.

'I didn't think you could buy Glomesh any more?'

'My mother buys them for me, reckons it's more lady-like.' She exploded into a wicked attack of the giggles. Her whole face scrunched and contorted like an overloved child's toy. As she hunched over to deliver the nicotine to her mouth, her head slid down between a laundry basket full of unfashionable shoulder pads. Around her neck, she wore a thick gold choker like an oversized watchband. It looked tight. Crowned with a feast of black frizz, from the neck up, she *was* the human cigarette butt. A grand Nefertiti honker she had too, but not big enough to inhale her enemies. We exchanged phone numbers before leaving the ladies. The gabfest was to be continued, whenever possible, at more salubrious venues.

The last time we had dinner she was acutely paranoid, insisting we sit in the dimmest corner of the restaurant and that our conversation be carried on in whispers.

'Lola, swap seats with me, I don't want to be facing the door.'

When I hesitated, she practically pulled the chair out from under me. 'Move it, will ya.'

Eventually I distracted her with red wine, two desserts and salacious gossip about a fading Lothario we both knew.

'How did that sleazebucket meet a gorgeous twenty-five-year-old from Ghana? He only leaves the house to visit the shrink.'

'He advertised for an exotic model for his life-drawing classes.'

'Un-fucking-believable. How did you ever let him near you?'

'Who knows? Attention deficit disorder. He's got great hands.'

Until yesterday I hadn't spoken with her for a month. A week ago, she'd faxed a media release stating that she was being forced to resign. I'd tried to get in touch at her office, at home and left voicemail messages. I figured she was OK, just laying low. Now I was getting the full picture in sensaround. She was in a rage, but the defeat in her voice was more terrifying. She'd been teetering right out there on the twig of human rights; Dupleix had succeeded in snapping it off.

Characteristically, she spoke point blank. 'Dupleix's absolute majority in both houses means any legislation including routine constitutional amendments can be shot through. Are you with me or do I have to connect the dots?'

'Chill. I'm on your team, remember?'

'That scumbag has underhandedly removed any potential obstacles to his government's economic objectives.' She sucked recklessly at her cigarette. 'He's decimating independent statutory offices: the Public Advocate, gone; the Ombudsman, gone; the Director of Public Prosecutions and the Coroner, gone – all bloody gone. He torpedoes anything and anyone that gets in his way.'

'He's locked into it now, isn't he?'

Ramona needed to mouth off. 'He's selling off all the assets – public transport, ambulances, education, his sperm – not that it's worth much. Anything to get capital flowing into Babylon. He's not even pretending to cover up the delivery of construction contracts and event management deals to his mates.'

'What deals?'

'The new government offices, the Grand Prix, the casino, the transit authority. The new women's prison in Wonthaggi. His slimy fingerprints are all over it. He loves that one . . . prison on a for-profits basis.'

She coughed, paused, then let out a long penetrating sigh. 'There've been four suicides now at the Port Bass prison and more disturbances. A few days ago they authorised the use of straitjackets. There are no more rules. The legal system is no longer accessible to anyone who doesn't own an American Express card.'

'What about the media? How did they respond to your press release?'

'Two-thirds of fuck all, that's how. Zilch, zip. They know there's shit going down but the information's not in the public domain. Dupleix's made sure of that. They're shit-scared of defamation.'

'What happened to informing the public?'

'Grow up. The editors don't give a rat's. The day's leader stories come straight from Dupleix's office; he calls the tune, they mambo.'

Still more fitful coughing. 'I'll phone you later.'

The fog was inside the room. She didn't say why she'd called yesterday. I was still staring at threatening artwork. If only I could get my right eye to stop twitching and the clotted cream out of my head.

CHAPTER FOUR

The lion and the calf shall lie down together . . .
but the calf probably won't get very much sleep.
– Woody Allen

the KICKOFF

Jasper lunged, cheeks sucked in, hand outstretched to grab my bag.

'Ms Finkelstein, please, why didn't you call?'

I stepped back, chin up slightly like a fake witness, and didn't hand over my accessories. 'Thanks, but it's only a frock and some fake pearls.'

'Will you be wanting a taxi to the airport?'

He was beginning to depress me. The smell of goanna oil and whatever cologne he'd squirted on was a body-snatching combination.

'I'm being picked up.'

Why was I telling him? These sort of passive interrogators usually live at the Department of Social Security. It was best to head him off at the pass. I walked towards the door. He followed.

'Did you injure yourself playing rugby, Jasper?' Judging by the size of his thighs and muscle mass, a sports injury was never on the cards.

He stood silent, arms by his side, lonely without his baggage. 'I don't play rugby.'

'I can smell ligament.'

'Liniment.'

'Whatever.'

He knitted his fingers together, perhaps as a learned gesture of control but more probably the maddening itch of dermatitis. 'It's my neck, I woke up stiff on my left side. I hope the smell isn't too overpowering?'

He was worried. Good, it might occupy his brain stem for long enough for Christopher to arrive.

I gave him a bigger bone to chew on. 'Actually, it's kind of erotic. It gives you an aura of thwarted energy, but . . . virility at the same time, like . . . like a gelding.'

I sidestepped around him, veering left. I could see Christopher's car. 'See you next time Jasper, ciao!' I fled through the self-opening doors of perception.

Christopher came American: faded Levi's, navy T-shirt, irony-proof, nylon bomber jacket and joggers. He was not-long-out-of-the-shower moist, vanilla-white face, ice-cream on the verge of melting. The fog was thicker with a light shake of drizzle. Away from the hotel and Jasper fumes, the brisk air set off my uncertainty switch. Christopher heard the click and noticed the tight fist shoved under my thigh.

'Am I driving too fast?' He grinned at me like a child at a popcorn machine.

'No, this is my normal level of anxiety.'

He steered with one hand and tugged at my wrist with the other. The fist slipped out; he sliced it with his fingers and held on.

'This is an expectation-free zone. All *you* have to do is eat, drink and watch trashy videos. What's to be freaked over? I'll move the video into the spare bedroom. Hang there if you want to or we can eat together, whatever you like.'

The arrangement was clear: separate rooms, separate beds. A grubby swell of mistaken conclusions and shredded prospects swished around my ankles. We were in a suburban shopping centre carpark. I paddled for safety. 'I haven't had pizza for yonks, what's your favourite?'

'Anything with hot salami – JESUS!' He dodged one feral trolley and slammed on the brakes as a mutiny of trolleys led from the rear by a crumpet-faced boy took siege from the left.

I wound down the window and spat my anxiety all over him. 'What's your other gig? Driving trucks through playgrounds? Get a fucking life –'

Christopher winched my head back into the car. The trolley-controller raised a finger. I responded in Italian, with my fist.

We used wire baskets to cut our way through the orgy of fresh produce. Christopher led the way. I can never decide what to buy in the galaxy of choices that is *the s*upermarket.

'Why don't *you* grab some rice?'

Right away I was struggling. 'White rice, basmati, long grain, short grain, brown rice, jasmine rice, rice imported from a country I'm boycotting . . . mock-rice for people with rice-intolerance . . . '

'Forget it!'

I strolled at his side, carrying the glamour items: spices, sun-dried tomatoes, extra-virgin olive oil. He'd stood authoritatively in front of the chaste bottles, his jacket zipped right to the collar like some culinary mark of respect.

'You know why it's *extra*-virgin olive oil?'

'No.' I folded my arms under my breasts, ready to receive classified information.

He checked the aisle conspiratorially. '*Very* ugly olives.'

A display stack of baked beans further down the aisle, in the no-man's-land between personal hygiene and perishables, in slipped a packet of condoms with the extra-virgin olive oil. What were you thinking? That Christopher would momentarily fade to black and not notice? Then you brushed by like a cat around his ankles. Damn stupid, damn horny and damn bloody obvious.

He stretched his face into a gawky grin that threatened to unzip his jacket. When he spoke again, it was in his telephone-prompt voice. 'How'd you go gettin back to whoever it was that called yesterday when we were drivin to the club?'

Why would he remember that? Maybe he thought it was another man. I played it straight.

'I remembered this morning. Lucky . . . almost lost a friend.'

'That bad?'

'You know how it is, sometimes you want someone to be there, immediately. Just for you. Yesterday that wasn't possible, so they were pissed off.'

'Who did you say it was?'

He wanted to know. It made no difference to me.

'Ramona Madden.'

'She's got a mighty chip on her shoulder.'

'She's ferociously competent. Some people find that difficult.'

'She's got no real power. She's nose-distance away from people who do, but she can't really effect any change. I'd say that'd be pretty damn frustrating, wouldn't you?'

'She's got a lot of respect.'

'Sure, why not? She's smart, good instinct, but nevertheless, she's got no real power.'

He suddenly had the look of a man experimenting with food poisoning. His dilated pupils peeled ahead towards the deep freeze. I hadn't recognised her – Deb, the rollerblading slut, right in my face.

'Hey, Lola, didn't think we'd meet up again.'

'You remember Deb from the club?' Christopher bleated.

'I met someone called Kate, didn't I?'

They laughed. I maintained I was into riddles.

'What are you two up to?' she said with a grin that could snap-freeze a herd of beef.

'I'm showing Lola around Canberra.'

'No supermarkets where you're from?' She was silhouetted against the glow of a fluoro sign that read CHEAP MEAT.

The beast in me wanted to sink my teeth into her arm and spit out each knuckle of every filleted finger.

'I'd love to chat, Kate.'

'Deb!'

'But we're on a tight schedule, loads to see . . . '

'Canberra's not *that* big.'

'No, but we've only got an hour. Then we're going back to my hotel room and fucking ourselves senseless. Bye, Kate.'

Christopher gave me a pissed-off look and waved goodbye to Deb with his keys.

Back in the car he slumped deep into the bucket seat. 'I don't believe you did that.'

'*You* . . . turned into jelly. What is it with you and her? Did I just screw up a happy marriage?'

'No! She's a teenager.'

'Yep. She is and you've been playing grown-ups. Didn't you say it was OK to stay at your place?'

'Correct.'

'So, I'm presuming this is not a serious thing and that whatever you and that creature have been doing, you're not doing it now. Not this weekend anyway?'

He sat up again, tall in the saddle. 'We had dinner a few times, she sees me kinda like a big brother.'

'Oh *pah-lease.*'

'I think you were a little heavy-handed.'

I rolled my eyes at him. 'She's a pain-in-the-arse.'

We arrived at his place as dusk fell. I fell first. As so often happens, my brain knew that I didn't need as much adrenalin tonight so it went AWOL. A total neural hijack. I went as droopy as a game-show display model sprawling over the prizes. I took hold of a bunch of plastic bags from the boot and made for the door. Only I didn't – I missed a step. There were two very low, slimy steps pretending not to be steps. You know the kind. Like a weird crossing of currents, my body spun around, probably caused by the uneven oscillation of groceries. Cold air turned to hot and like a rogue wave I splashed into the doorpost. I went hot where minutes before I was cold, damp in spots where one is reliably dry. The forecast was not cheery.

My forehead was the first point of impact. But the full domino catastrophe came to pass and I fell like a botched soufflé, lower and lower, until I limbo'd in the front door.

'Did I just did that . . . *do* that . . . did I just *do* that?'

'Not even a Chinese acrobat could choreograph that move.' He collapsed on his knees beside me like a stoned labrador begging to fetch.

'*That* is an entrance – are you safe now?'

I was on the floor looking up into his face, upside-down. 'I can see up your nose into your head. Please stop laughing so hard.'

He held onto me while I hobbled to the safety of a soft surface. I scanned for any internal damage. 'My arms and legs are fine – but my head?'

'Idiot gland . . . acutely inflamed.'

'I'm serious, I don't feel my head at all. Do I look swollen?'

Fido-man gave me an inscrutable smile. 'Don't move . . . I'll get you a glass of water.'

He pinched my cheek and handed over the glass. 'I made up your bed, it'd be smart to lie down for a while, you look pale. You passed out for a few minutes. It's the second room to your right, the blue one. I've still gotta grab a few things, I won't be long.'

I slid my hips forward to stand up.

'Take it easy, try not to do anything dumb. I'll wake you when I get back.'

I felt abandoned.

'Should I slice a couple of onions?'

He lurched away from me. 'You, near a knife? I don't think so.' He led me to the spare room and pushed me in, welfare-style, his hand under my elbow. 'Rest up till I get back.'

Frank Sinatra woke me up.

Fly me to the moon
and let me play amongst the stars,
let me see what spring is like on Jupiter and Mars . . .

Someone was cooking. Basil, garlic and tomato crept into bed with me like the Three Stooges and slapped me into the here and now. Canberra, Christopher, his place, my idea to be here.

I was conscious enough to know not to make an appearance without checking a mirror.

CHAPTER FIVE

I think, therefore I am . . . I think.
– Graffiti

UNREQUITED LUNCH

Two months before, in January, coming into view down the escalator at Canberra airport, I registered that the tall, dopey-looking guy with the distressed denim jeans and the bungled hairstyle was the man I'd been so curious to meet. It was too late to disappear. I saw him staring at me. I cut my way towards him through others embracing, shouting goodbyes and dragging small children away from strangers and said, 'Hi, I'm feeling nauseated. Do you mind driving me to the hotel? We can talk later.'

He extended four long thick fingers and a sideways leaning, flat-on-top-thumb. 'Christopher Pillar, pleasure to finally meet you, ma'am.'

I shook his hand. He took my bag.

'The hotel's only a lickety-spit away. Can I get you anythin?'

Ma'am – who did he think he was talking to, Miss Kitty at the local saloon? The word provoked teeth-grinding. But my hormones rewrote the script and without consultation my buttocks clenched. A mutiny by the lower half of my body in response to an ungainly American who was employing me to do a show at the National

Press Club. I needed a stronger vitamin B supplement.

'I'm a bit worn out . . . I think I've reached zero tolerance with flight attendants.'

He laughed outright, a deep, sexy, staccato offering of acknowledgment. His hand squeezed my shoulder. I stepped away from it and waited for him to open the car door. A neat, yellow Renault Cabriolet . . . not overly sporty.

In one professional manoeuvre, he lifted my bag, placed it in the boot, opened and held open the passenger door, while I reluctantly got in. Then, slick as lubricant, he oozed into the driver's seat. I heard him wheeze.

'Do you mind if I smoke?'

My aim was way below the belt and probably halfway up his rectum. 'I'm allergic to smoke, but go ahead.'

'Gotta have at least one vice, dontchya think, ma'am? I like inviting trouble.'

Trouble didn't RSVP, so Pillar never rode into Marlboro country.

I'd flown to Canberra to assess the voice on the other end of the phone. *That* voice had flirted with me from the moment the fibre optics connected. It began as a business call. He was intense and not the least bit frightened of rejection.

'I'm worried that a Canberra audience will be too conservative for my sort of in-yer-face stuff.'

'No way! You're funny and irreverent, that's an irresistible combo. It'll sell out. I'm confident and I'm running the venue.'

'And writing the cheques?'

'Yep, put my money where my mouth is. You wanna stay in Canberra for a few days after the gig?'

'I don't know if I can afford . . . '

'I'll do a deal with the hotel.'

' . . . the time . . . '

'I'd really get a buzz showin ya around.'

Christopher Pillar's voice was a cocktail blend of Pacific West meets New England. What a mango might sound like. It made me want to jump into his mouth and make fruit salad with his words. I've always been lured by anything to do with the mouth. I love to eat, I love to kiss, I'm a stand-up comic. I earn my living with my mouth. It follows, then, that a voice and an accent could entice me to buy an airline ticket and do some investigative lip homage.

'I won't be able to stay after the show in March, I have to be in Sydney. But a reconnaissance trip would be useful. I've never spent much time in Canberra.'

'Why dontchya come in January? I've got time then, it's quiet. You can scout around, get some background bumpf . . . go back home and have loads of time to write.'

And thus I landed, an explorer, propelled by curiosity and an ear for mangos.

There was nothing weird about Christopher Pillar that first day. Typically, like most things in my life, he didn't meet my expectations, so I hated him. I'd been having conversations with tropical fruit, and he was *only* human, unforgivably banal as a cauliflower. It's a mystery how I've managed for this long with my father's Austrian severity and my mother's Polish weakness for tragedy.

Canberra was all crisp and sunny that morning, the way it can be when it's not pissing with rain and bloated politicians. Parliament wasn't sitting, there was no mud being flung, so the air was clean. We arrived at the hotel in minutes.

'I'll pick you up at 1. Call if you need anythin.' He sped off, power-assisted steering, firm and well-controlled.

I checked in and fell asleep fully clothed as a protest.

By one o'clock it was hot. Australian hot, blowflies dawdling at low altitude. He'd chosen an open-air restaurant right on the edge of an artificial lake at the National Gallery. Embraced by a blue sky with only a machiatto-dash of white cloud, I began to relax. My napkin slipped. I bent forward and down under my chair to pick it up and felt the cooling hint of a breeze against my arm.

I looked straight ahead and saw a blob of foggy mist floating across the water.

'Could we stop at a health-food shop? I need to buy a strong magnesium supplement.'

'Sure. Is it the heat?'

'Maybe. I'm hallucinating, I could swear there's mist floating across the lake. It's the middle of the day . . . almost 36 degrees . . . and I'm not drunk.' I chuckled nervously, in the manner of TV executives when they know they've compromised noble work in the pursuit of ratings.

Christopher gave me his Colgate smile and purred triumphantly, 'No, ma'am, that's fog! It's an installation, part of the gallery's collection.'

His Coca-Cola brown eyes frothed. He relished the moment. His eyes fixed on me, on the fog and back to me. 'Are you all right?'

'I'll take my shoes off, that always clears my head.'

'I can satisfy your curiosity.'

'Whatever happened to exhibitions? I don't get installations or performance art! There's that guy who sticks fish hooks into his body then suspends himself from the ceiling. And Ivan Durrant, who dumped a dead cow in front of the gallery in Melbourne. And the German Expressionist artist, Steinlauf. He'd lie down completely naked, his arms and legs tied with ropes to pegs on the floor, then stay there for days in his own excrement, while onlookers filed by.'

'Probably got that idea from watching Australians in Bali over the Christmas holiday period.'

Bits of food shot out of my mouth across the table. I sagged forward, laughing too loud. The front of my shirt gaped open.

'Don't think you should lean over like that.' He was letting me know he could see my breasts.

I fixed on him with my brunette jerk-off gaze.

He sensed he'd stumbled recklessly beyond the boundary. 'Just lettin you know that I'm distracted.'

I had a profound visceral sense of Christopher's psychic anchor securing itself somewhere deep beneath my surface. Maybe I was hungry? I shoved two potatoes and a chunk of salmon into my mouth and chewed for as long as I could, to give myself some time. I felt exposed. Too many glasses of chardonnay. I should have sensed this desire for pleasure as a warning of emptiness to come.

I snapped back far too enthusiastically. 'Why don't we take a walk through the gallery? Check out the current exhibitions? Expand your view a little.'

His head tilted forward in a mock gesture of obedience. 'Yes, ma'am. I'm all yours.'

I waited at the entrance in Teflon-mode. He grinned, in what he must have hoped was a guileless, boyish, yearning expression. It didn't stick. Protectively, he placed his free-enterprise American hand in the small of my back, as if I might snap or go the wrong way without his guidance. We strolled through the pristine passages of the gallery without speaking but it wasn't weirdistan. I wasn't uncomfortable in his company, but I *was* anxious to see the Press Club. The sooner I could visualise the position of the stage, the sound system and lights, the sooner adrenalin would shoot through my body like an exploding cigar. Who needs an audience?

The other part of my job was more complicated. Like Psyche in the palace of Pluto I needed time to sniff around. I had to try to absorb the city, allow it to fill me up like an enema. I wanted to retain Canberra until fullness was felt, ensuring the success of evacuation *and* effective writing. Christopher gave me a syrupy head-tilt.

'You wanna size up the Press Club right now?'

I hadn't even opened my mouth. Did he know about my cavities as well?

'It's obvious you're not gonna relax till you've staked out the space and wire-tapped the facilities.'

I walked a few steps ahead, slowed down and glanced back at

him over my shoulder. 'I'm doing a comedy show, not a congressional investigation.'

He smiled a ten-year-old's 'Look, Ma, no hands' smile: pleased, but wobbly. 'I collected a bunch of tourist brochures for ya, it's all back at the club. We can scoot over, I'll show you around the place. Take the brochures with you, it'll be your homework.'

We were standing on a ramp leading out of the gallery.

'Let's do it then,' I shrugged.

'When we're done at the club I'll drop you back at the hotel so you can do some brainwork. I'll come by later to collect you for dinner.'

A sharp twitch tugged at my mouth. 'Listen, I –'

He raised both hands up in the air, surrendering. 'Part of the homework. We have dinner, you boot onto the Pillar and ask questions about Canberra. It can be an *interactive* experience.'

'My software's incompatible.'

Steam enveloped his scalp. He was manufacturing dandruff.

'You're frowning at me like I'm an ambiguous road sign.'

'If you don't mind me saying so, ma'am, I think you oughta loosen up.'

I did my best American accent. '*You oughta loosen up,* that old chestnut?'

He slinked beside me like a wolf, his teeth gleaming.

'What are you saying here?' I was talking with my hands like a social worker, palms towards him in an open gesture.

'You're a control freak.'

He grabbed my hands with both of his and squeezed hard.

I froze.

'Whaddya wanna eat?'

I rescued my manicure. 'I don't know, you decide.'

Acknowledging with his eyes that I'd taken two steps away from him, he folded his hands behind his back and grinned. He breathed out through his nose. The downrush of air fanned the coals in my groin and involuntarily my cheeks flushed with the heat.

'So *now* you want *me* to take control?'

Annoyingly, I was sticky all over. A torch job executed by a psychic arsonist. I slid my sunglasses from the top of my head down over my eyes. 'There's only so much bullshit one should look at with the naked eye.'

He puffed out his cheeks and exhaled. Without protection, the second gust turned my breasts to powder like over-baked biscuits.

I was confused, anxious and aroused, but not in that order. Perfect combo to view the National Press Club.

Pillar circled around the back of the building, bringing his ego to a halt directly in front of the back door. The designated carpark transformed him immediately to bossman of his domain.

'C'mon, there's no-one around. I'll give you the fifty-cent tour.'

We turned a corner, his hand spread over my face like a tuna steak. I stepped sideways. He tugged at my neck, I was forced to keep my head straight, four crumbed-fingers over my eyes.

'What the fuck?'

His voice deepened. He spoke in God accent. 'Pork Council of Australia. Jewish eyes forbidden to behold or you'll be turned to stone.'

'*Pork* Council! What's their slogan, *So many barrels, so little time*?' I wriggled out of his grasp. A primitive memory kept my gaze straight ahead, just in case.

The Press Club building was a buzzing hive of tenants. The Pork Council. The head office of an events company provocatively named FUN Ltd, whose psychedelic interior had me bent over with my head between my legs. And on the second floor, Babel headquarters, the American Information Service.

'Someone told me that the AIS is a front for the CIA. Is *that* your real gig? Secret Agent Pillar?'

'I don't play golf well enough.'

I registered a temperature change in his voice. Too many brass eyelets for me to unravel the information. He leapt ahead quickly, dragged open a huge tarpaulin flap and directed me through as if behind a curtain.

'The main room . . . our little house of horrors.'

'Excuse me?'

'We're in the middle of a makeover, it's not lookin its best right now. By March there'll be a fresh paint job, new carpet, superior sound system. I designed the lighting rig myself.'

'I think the rolls of cable and tins of paint add a certain rough glamour.'

Outside, the wind moaned at my sarcasm.

I don't remember much about the inspection. Pillar's single-mindedness of purpose in everything he did made more of an impression. The desk in his office gave nothing away. A clear sheet of glass, dead level, held by four blasé rubber stoppers on top of two reflective black A-framed supports. No screws, no nails, no drawers with loose staples and a cache of smoked almonds. On top, a widowed IN tray and celibate computer.

The carpet was the colour of corned beef. There were no windows. The only flora and fauna grew from the tourist poster on the wall advertising Canberra's spring-flower festival, Floriade, *a million flowering plants*. I sneezed. The poster came unstuck. No photo of a loved one or favourite object, no clue to the animal that inhabits this hollow.

'I bet you don't leave a scum line in your bath tub.'

'Baths require a time commitment. I'm a shower man.'

CHAPTER SIX

I think sex is better than logic, but I can't prove it.
– Anon

LEATHER

I'd only been gone three hours. I returned to my hotel room and four messages marked urgent from Lawrence. I was in a Catholic mood, restless with thoughts of crucifixion. I ran the bath and put in fifteen drops each of frankincense and myrrh to clear any guilt. Friday afternoon – he was at the AIDS Council. I kicked off my shoes, flopped onto the bed and dialled the number, poised to bite back. Lawrence can make me do things I'd rather not remember. He was agitated.

'Darl, where the hell are you?'

'I'm a Badedas-squirt away from getting in the bath.'

'What part of the country?'

'Canberra –'

'Right the first time – in hell.'

'*You* phoned me . . . '

'Affirmative,' he sneered and continued. 'Canberra *is* a warm bath, darl, full of live, poison jellyfish . . . urgh!'

'What gives, Lawrence? Four messages?'

'Sweetums . . . ' he started to sing and sounded like a rejected tomcat. 'You should be so lucky, lucky, lucky, luckeeeeeee!'

He was organising a fundraiser auction for the AIDS Council. I was one of the auctioneers.

'Is there a problem with the auction?'

'No problem, excluding the gnome princess and her carry-on about *white wine in the green room . . . I must have it for my voice.* She's a complete tool. But hold the phone: *why* are you in Canberra?'

'I'll be doing a gig at the Press Club in March . . . I'm snooping for material.'

'Of course you are. Well, don't scratch and sniff *too* deep. You might uncover a gang of right-wing leather queens who want to reduce GST on whips and harnesses. Why do you think they're called "Wets", darl?'

'Lawrence, I'm desperate for a bath. I've only got a couple of hours to prepare questions for this guy. Tell me *now*, why the urgent messages?'

He cleared his throat prognostically. 'It's not the auction. Nobb *woman* is talking closure of Springfield.'

Dita Nobb, the Cabbage Patch doll with a narcissistic need to be famous and a peerless history of cock-ups. Also the State's Health Minister. Her cutbacks were already crippling an overloaded system.

'Only a few weeks ago she said, "We're not in the business of closing down hospitals." What's happening?'

'Dupleix. A while back he did a grand tour of the State's hospitals and announced that his government was going to fix the hospital system. Bingo. And *fix* it they did, darl, with such thrust, the system's got anal fissures.'

'It makes no sense.'

'Since when did *that* matter?'

'But there's no other facility. Where does Nobb expect to relocate the patients?'

'No-one knows yet. They're too exhausted to fight being relocated, especially the families. There isn't enough information to be sure of what action to take next.'

I watched a clammy cloud of steam drag itself across the room like a bloated diva. 'What did she actually say?'

'That Springfield's no longer financially viable, that we don't need a specialist service. They want to carve it all up. Thirty beds here, thirty beds there. Forget beheading and disembowelling like your bona-fide barbarian, they prefer a slow torture. I doubt they've even considered that hospitals have patients. The treasurer . . . whatshisname?'

'Lloyd Ramsgate –'

'That's the one . . . only knows one word: deficit, deficit, deficit. Wouldn't surprise me if there's plenty of money in the Reserve Bank. He's such a dick he's forgotten the PIN.'

'I'm back in Melbourne tomorrow, I'll phone you then.' I hesitated. 'How did you know where to find me?'

Silence. I could hear bathwater getting cold.

'It's not a difficult question. What's the problem?'

'I have to remember where I was last night.'

'You mean you're trying to remember which sleazy venue –'

He interrupted. 'I was being significantly available. Boyzland, that's it. It's all coming back to me now. The tiny, dark cubicle, cruisy whale-birthing music, trembling shadows, and Paul. You know Paul, the one with the neck brace? *That* Paul. He's got this brain-damaging loud voice that clears your ears like Drano and I . . . stumbled upon him sleazing onto Frank.'

'Frank?'

'Frank Dixon, your ex-assistant. I couldn't help myself. I crept up on them, as you do, and caught the tail-end of Frank telling Paul that he didn't work for you any more and that you were probably in Canberra.'

'I'm surprised he repeated my name without gagging. Why would he tell Paul?'

'Paul's a stickybeak, wants to know everything. He probably asked. They wouldn't remember too much anyway. Paranoid, are we? Shall I check on you later to make sure you haven't been kidnapped by a swarm of killer bees?'

'There are no killer bees, only the one queen bee and hundreds of drones. She struts her stuff on a one-night-only ticket, no interval, no costume change. On that single outing she mates with as many as twenty-five drones –'

'Personally, I'd go for the soldier bees, but go on.'

'The drone has to explode his genitals onto the queen's body, dying in the process but leaving behind unquestionable evidence of their liaison.'

'Those drones . . . so unreconstructed.'

'Speak to you tomorrow –'

'God bless . . . gotta run. Bridge Club meets tonight at my place.'

Lawrence is tumble-down tall. Hunched do-nothing shoulders segue to the illusion of hair shaved close to his head. He wears unfashionably large, thick-lensed glasses that don't distract from his display-window, feel-free-to-browse eyes. Some people believe he minced out of the womb in a black leather vest. I've never seen him not wearing one. Most often over a T-shirt, with a deeply felt message printed on it, like 'Mr Faggot to You!' His preferred footwear is big leather boots.

'Leatherman's boots, size 12, from Rob of Amsterdam. That's Amsterdam as in Holland, darl. You know, Europe.'

And always black, *never* brown. He's a devotee of Prozac: 'Takes the edge off the other drugs, darl.'

I trust him. He's a leather queen. The once rosy-cheeked, white-collared choir-boy who got lassoed by the tug of rawhide and wore his new crown and collar with pride.

I don't understand the sexual politics of leather. Is there more risk than finger-painting? Leather is smooth and yielding. Gradually, it moulds to the shape of whatever it surrounds without ever weakening. With heat, it breathes and stretches as it embraces the host's body part. A second skin.

The first time I performed at the Bound 'n' Gagged Club, men only, I was scared shitless. I slipped in on the sweat of leather-coupling and got sucked into a cave of muscle-flexing, leather-clad brutes. A showroom of brand-new cars doused with cologne. I added my chassis to the display, knowing that it was the wrong model.

Nothing in my experience could have prepared me for the tableau I intruded on. I pushed through the crowd, copping an elbow to the chest, a glass to the back of my head. My brief giddiness quickly subsided. I was leaning on the bar, eavesdropping, my nostrils congested with the rich diversity of scents. My knees felt like two tumblers of peach-berry shake.

'His garden beds are bigger than Texas –'

'He paid enough for them. Didn't do them himself, says he tried gardening once but stubbed his toe on his wallet and couldn't continue. He hired some rough-trade socialite gardener to do them.'

'How barren would the world be without box-hedging – and golly, we do it well, don't we?'

'Giz a kiss, babydoll –'

'Are you mad, Clinton? If you get a floral design it'll look *hidd-ee-yes* bunched together . . . you have to have Roman blinds, Byron Bay white walls. Nothing else will work . . . '

'Our new babies are so beautiful . . . Italian greyhounds . . . too gorgeous.'

'What are their names?'

'Marchesa and Luzzio.'

I'd imagined a host of ghoulish, contraband thugs. Sordid sadomasochistic swap-meets and body-piercing. And here were two glistening men to my right, dressed vigorously in leather caps, leather vests, leather chaps, boots and assorted cord and string, presumably to indicate sexual proclivity, talking drapes and pets.

Lawrence spotted me through the choking glow of the dance floor. He must have sensed that I was not only out of my depth, I was part of the lost civilisation below the sea. He blew me a kiss and took three to four huge marching-type steps toward me; steps punctuated by micro conversations.

'Get over it, Russell. *Every*one knows nipple rings take a long time to heal. If it was infected you'd be squealing like a pig.'

He put a joint between my lips. I flinched, pulled it out and tried to hand it back. 'It's got lipstick all over it now —'

He plucked it gently from between my fingers and stretched his other arm in front of my face for a more formal greeting. 'Lawrence. This is so *not* my colour.'

'Lola Finkelstein.'

'I know who you are,' he said, tugging my hand back up to my lips. 'Suck on that, darl, I'll be right back with a voddie.'

I'm cursed with an over-sensitivity to most chemicals. I'm too paranoid to indulge in any artificial substances before a show. Mindful that this might be some rite-of-passage for novices, I inhaled. Before I could exhale, Lawrence was back in my face with a vodka. 'Get that interya. It'll balance your chakras.'

'But I have to go on in a minute.'

'Exactly . . . SCULL, SCULL, SCULL!'

I performed that night to my first exclusively gay audience. It was the genesis of my friendship with Lawrence and a connection with tribe. Entering the feverish world of leather bondage, role-playing and drapes turned some inner voice to full volume. I couldn't ignore it. Like Orpheus, these men preferred to focus their affections on other men. But on stage, with big lips, big hair and a big mouth, I demanded their attention, if only for the duration of my act. Perversely, I was the spectator, seduced by their provocative behaviour. The heckling was a hybrid of bitchiness and street-wise tease.

Out of the rabble a voice yelled out, 'Take off your top!'

It didn't make sense.

'You wanna see my breasts?'

'No, sweetie! We wanna try it on.'

I'd never worked so hard.

Nor had they.

This was my initiation, and thunderous applause was confirmation of membership. That first time I almost choked from the palpable sexual energy in the room. In the soup mix of my confused and demented childhood, lust had taken on a negative and forbidding repulsiveness. But here in the reddish-amber evanescence, it was a lust pageant and I ached to be a contestant. Impossible. I was the visiting female in a gaggle of male peacocks strutting their stuff. They swaggered, bumped and posed, noses tweaking and groins bulging. Cockiness is god in the double-dare realm of leather pride. So the Jewish Princess sniffs her first bacon and discovers that kosher translates as major denial.

Lawrence appeared with a goofy grin and a new leather accessory.

'What is it?'

'A harness,' he announced enthusiastically. 'It attaches around your neck and chest. Then down, down, down to that pot of gold at the end of the rainbow.'

'What happens when you need a piss?'

'Doesn't make any difference. It's attached with a cock ring.'

'What's a cock ring?'

'*Lis-ten* – it's what it says . . . a ring *a*-round your cock.'

'Why?'

'Because, darl . . . to maintain your erection. Are you with me?'

'Sort of, but . . . '

'Here's a riddle for you: what's the difference between red and purple?'

'What?'

'Depends on how tight your grip is.'

That was six years ago. The cuticle-biting voyage of discovery with Lawrence continues.

CHAPTER SEVEN

Come up sometime and see me.
Come up Wednesday. That's amateur night.
– Mae West

CROSS WORDS

I added boiling water and descended ritually, silently, into my cup-a-soup bath. Totally submerging my head and body, to flush away thoughts of Frank Dixon. Lawrence would've phoned every respectable hotel in Canberra, neatly dismissing each squishy front-desk manager until he found me, just the sort of search-and-destroy adventure Frank loved.

Frank.

My ex-PA, confidant and style counsellor for just over a year, dedicated totally to the gig. Together we were a formidable team. Frank made impressions quickly and indelibly. He hugged people easily. Everyone adored him. His laugh was volcanic. He was calculatingly efficient and he encouraged me to delegate. I moved forward when he was around, until that memorable afternoon he got the hump and flew into a paroxysm.

'*Whatever* I do is never good enough.'

I rolled my eyes. 'What's with the victim-wife script? You haven't said a thing about feeling this way before.'

'It's been building. I've been trying to only hate you after hours, but you're impossible.'

'Frank, you know you don't hate me. What's your inner voice telling you? What's *really* the problem?'

He was blotchy with rage, screeching through clenched teeth and a twisted mouth. 'You . . . *you* make me feel stupid. I don't get what you expect from me any more. You're not listening to me *now*. Fuck my inner child, *fuck* you –'

'Frank. *Frank* . . . will you chill for a minute? It's inner *voice*. Inner *child* is lifestyle-magazine, pop-psychology crap. Try breathing out the anger . . . slowly . . . Inhale, then exhale. In for four counts, out for eight.'

'Tell someone who cares. I don't work for you any more.'

'I only asked if Pillar had returned a copy of the signed contract.'

'Blah, blah, blah!' he spat. Then he strutted off in a northerly direction with more choreographed twirls, thrusts and lost feathers than a drag-show finale.

I stood alone in the gutter of a busy street in peak-hour traffic, one hand clutching a wig of cascading brunette curls, the other arm draped with a gigantic blue-sequinned mermaid's tail. The strap of my bag dragged around my neck like a noose. Not your average family squabble. I thought he'd be over it in a couple of hours. I phoned several times until he finally answered. The silence froze my fingers to the phone.

'Frank, what's going on?'

He whistled Peggy Lee's 'Fever' directly into my middle ear.

'I don't think you're clear yourself, are you, about whatever it is? We need to talk. But can we get through the photo shoot tomorrow first? It's all in place, the location, photographer and a make-up artist. I really need you there.'

More huffy whistling.

'You can't *just* quit.'

'*Fry* baby, the heat got too much. Bye-bye.' Dial tone.

The worm had turned, metamorphosed and flown away, leaving

only a crusty shell. I didn't hear from him for a week, then he called very early one morning.

'Good morning.'

I moved with early-bird agility. 'Maybe.'

'What would you like me to do with your files? Deliver or post them?'

'Post them . . . Certified.'

'Fine. Could you *post* me my reference letter?'

'You're absofuckinlutely serious, aren't you?'

'I don't know what you mean.'

'I *mean*, even if I did give you a reference letter – and I won't be – you'd have to pull it out of your waxed arse first. Sideways.'

Four months after his street-theatre performance, the skin on my wound was still chiffon-thin. I brooded on what he might think about the whole episode now and fantasised that he'd be regretting it. He would've remembered that I'd be in Canberra at this time because he'd answered Christopher's initial inquiry.

We'd speculated on what Christopher Pillar looked like.

'His voice says he's hung like a horse.'

'Grow up, Frank. How can you tell? You've only spoken to him once.'

'I'll find out.' He mimed holding the phone, thumb to his ear, little finger at his mouth.

'What size lycra shorts do you wear, doll – double D?'

'Don't bother, all the straight men have been kidnapped by buxom alien Amazons.'

'*Pah-lease,* I'm sobbing already. Get a grip. *I'll* find out what team he plays on. But my hunch is he likes girls. It's about time you got a bit dirty.'

'Go ahead, see what you can dig up. But if he's straight and there's even a remote chance I'll find him desirable, you'd better get him an ambulance subscription.'

'Go, girlfriend!'

Frank confirmed that Christopher was straight and *not* in a relationship.

'You didn't just *ask* him, did you?'

'Never you mind,' he snapped crisply, revelling in his power.

Frank worked for me from his flat. I never heard the initial conversations between him and Christopher. It was around the time negotiations first started that he became cranky and unreliable. He successfully dug up Christopher's personal details, but was hopelessly inefficient in securing information about the venue or the contract. The more information I asked for, the more restless and resentful he became.

Frank grew up in Canberra, knew people there and was familiar with the venue. I figured it would be an easy first contract for him to negotiate single-handedly. Until then, I'd continued to work with him, walking him through the booking, from initial phone call to signing.

This was his first solo ride and he'd gradually become more vague and neurotic. I wanted to take over, but offered to help him instead. He refused.

'Did Pillar agree to the deposit and payment details?'

'We didn't discuss the fee.'

'So it's not confirmed?'

He was sweating. 'Yes, it is.' He hesitated. 'I haven't confirmed the fee. Is that a problem?'

My lips crimped so tightly, it made my toes curl. 'It's best to check what sort of budget he's got. Otherwise we could get locked into a contract and then find out he doesn't have the bucks.'

'I'm on top of it. If there's a squall, I'll put out a blue alert, with plenty of time to apply waterproof mascara.'

One week after I'd signed the contract, Frank walked. More than the rejection, it was the speed of his exit that caught me off-guard.

I muttered his name under my breath, sinking for one last time beneath steamy bubbles. I enjoyed the soak. Thoughts of Pillar sloshed up in the ripples of my own body tide. I remembered something I'd read in a book on pest-repellent plants: *There are more than 400 species of cockroaches in Australia but only a few of these are pests. Those that cause problems in the house are introduced from the United States . . .*

I floated back up in time to avoid the bends, resolved that Pillar had been a menace from the start. I felt edgy, naked. I *was* naked. I stepped out of the bath. Why was I feeling like someone had used the last bit of toilet roll and wasn't about to replace it? *Cockroaches are most active at night.* At the bottom of my bag of bathroom voodoo I found a tube of peppermint foot cream. I rubbed it onto the soles of my feet and the gaps between my toes. I was in a stiletto mood. Exposing a bit of toe-cleavage might prevent me from putting my foot in my mouth.

From across the room, the remote control winked at me and set my foot tapping. The peppermint was doing its job. I pressed a button and the big black box revealed an ABC newsperson. I pushed the volume arrow and Dupleix's head smeared itself into my room, his voice like a foot crunching down on snails. He spoke condescendingly to the journalist.

'Think about it, mate, we want to give the public a sense of security, at the same time putting in place a more progressive prison system with better conditions for prisoners.' He was looking compassionately straight down the barrel of the camera, grinning right at me and millions of other voters. 'And a privatised corrections system will deliver the goods . . . '

'But Mr Premier, isn't it true that the company your representatives have been speaking with was recently criticised when twelve prisoners escaped from a prison transport van? And one prisoner was mistakenly released by prison officers who didn't understand how the bail system worked?'

'Listen, sonny. We've got the stats and they show that the escape rate is negligible compared to the number of prisoners transferred each year by that company.'

'Sir, in the UK a member of the Conservative Party was forced to resign as a non-executive director of the company because it was claimed he helped secure contracts to run jails managed by this organisation. Any comments on that, Premier?'

'Of course people from the private sector will no doubt be employed by the organisation, but we're alert to that sort of conflict of interest.'

'But how can you guarantee that won't happen? The moment you treat corrections as a profit-potential service industry . . . '

I pointed the black wand and Dupleix vanished. His face had an astringent quality that dried my throat and withered my skin. I was still only wearing my towel, not nearly enough coverage against the twister of profit in corrections. The bullshit goes that the State is trying to reduce the corrections budget by inviting private enterprise. Yeah right, but the primary goal of these companies is to maximise profits. Doesn't that mean that there's a vested interest in more prisoners and longer sentences?

The answer lay in the mini-bar. Vodka, tonic and ice – I engaged in a tete-a-tete with all three and emerged more animated but no less confused. This was cryptic crossword territory.

I loathe cryptic crosswords. Like a pessary misguidedly placed in the wrong orifice, they make me froth at the mouth.

CHAPTER EIGHT

Let's face it, the sex organs ain't got no personality.
– Mae West

WILLIAM LISBON

I came running out of the lift like an ostrich on speed, perched on high heels, legs swinging slightly apart to avoid lingerie abrasion. I strutted straight past Christopher. The man I'd had lunch with was not the man leering at me from the leather couch in front of the lifts.

'Excuse me . . . hel-lo . . . *Lola*,' I swung around to connect with someone sharper, less white-bread than the guy at lunch. 'Is there a posse out lookin for you?'

I registered the makeover but played it safe until I was sure it was him. 'No . . . '

'You wanna take it from the top?'

I took a deep breath. 'I'm sorry. The phone rang. I didn't think it was 7.30 and then it seemed like the clock hadn't moved. I wasn't ready. I wanted to call but I didn't have your mobile number.'

'You're speakin in tongues.'

The fumes of his cologne were giving me a rash.

'When did you arrive?'

'7.55. Are you OK?'

'Your aftershave's . . . punchy.' I moved to one side.

'*You* look great. Didn't know you had legs.'

He nodded toward the bar. 'We *should* have a drink first.'

I made a noise that could've been a yes or a no.

'I've booked two restaurants, Italian and Japanese. Which do you prefer?'

This *was* the same guy. 'Japanese. You didn't know that? I'd reckon you know what my oestrogen levels are today.'

He led me into the bar. I changed my mind. 'Let's go straight to the restaurant. We can have sake.'

'Sure.' He massaged his brow. 'Long as *you're* happy.'

I opened the door of his tonka-toy and slumped in. He waited till I was comfortable, closed my door then tapped on the window, gesturing for me to open it.

By the time I'd found the push button and had the window half-open, he was crouching, face level with mine, grinning. 'You're 'bout three days away from your period, going by your mood swings.'

I dismissed him with a not-so-elegant wave of my hand. He bolted round to the driver's side, jumped in and revved the engine. The night air was damp and chilly, crawling down my neck like ice-cream.

Of course he was punctual. He said 8 p.m. and was present and picking at his teeth at 7.55. I didn't come down until 8.15. I'm consistently late, a life-long objection to being born prematurely. This particular evening, a phone call sabotaged my attempt at punctuality. The phone jangled with sinister chimes while I was struggling with the plastic studs of my teddy.

'Hello there . . . William Lisbon, Minister for Health.'

For those of you not familiar with a teddy, it's a sort of all-in-one singlet and knickers creation that fastens in the gusset via plastic press studs. If you're stupid enough to put the teddy through a hot spin-drier, these plastic studs melt into lacerating blobs that never again fasten as they were created to do. This can be frustrating. In the worst of scenarios one can inflict permanent scars on oneself and any future undergarment sales-assistant that may innocently offer you a teddy. Some teddies have hook-and-eye openers. For the sadomasochists or obsessive compulsives who want to lift lint off any furniture they sit on, there are teddies with velcro fasteners.

And the Minister for Health? He's a hustler, temporarily transformed into a man of power by the spell of federal politics.

'Is anyone there, Lola?'

'Give me a minute, William. Hang on.'

'Have I called at an inconvenient time?'

'No, no . . . fucking hell . . . hold on a second.' I had the phone wedged between my chin and shoulder, both hands busy at my groin, struggling with spandex and plastic studs. I was in a rage with my lingerie and bleating like a ewe. Three days away from my period, only one spark away from combustion.

'I can call back if you're busy?'

I was on my hands and knees. 'I'm problem-solving.'

'You don't say. Can I distract you momentarily?'

'How did you know I was in town?'

William cleared the backdoor in his throat. 'I never reveal my sources.'

'You should check them. I've been tracking your comments on Medicare. Who the hell is feeding you the facts? Dita Nobb wants to close Springfield. She claims she's testing the feds' ideas on a smaller stage.'

I was flat on my back on the floor, but still not showing the white flag.

'I'm not sure I know what you're . . . '

'Nobb is closing half the beds at Springfield Hospital. So *I* reckon and so do a shitload of other people that closure of the hospital is *pending*.'

I'd received a newsletter from AIDS Support a few days before. They're a kind of fast-food approach to volunteer support. Members offer help around the clock. Nothing too small, nothing too far. They visit patients with no family, bring magazines, supply wheelchairs when someone goes home and they listen. They'd been sniffing closure for months.

'I can't be expected to have information about every small facility in the country.'

'Certainly not. But this is not a *facility*, it's a hospital. Which just happens to have the most allocated HIV/AIDS beds in Australia. If it ain't broke, why fix it?'

His voice had the remoteness of a recorded message. 'I don't know about Springfield Hospital and if I did, the topic would be out of bounds. This is a social call.'

I registered a faint tremble in William's voice. He had to know about Springfield. Why was he bullshitting? The time on the radio-clock was running out. I was late.

'Tonight's stitched up, William. I'm sorry, I have to keep moving.'

'An after-dinner drink, perhaps?'

'Maybe another time.'

He licked his lips and spoke in a choc-coated placating voice. 'I'll keep in touch.'

I met William Lisbon two years ago when his hatchet woman, Wendy Simms, asked me to perform at a fundraiser in Melbourne. At the time, I donated my services to ambitious Labor politicians who hungered for power and an excuse to wear bad suits and unsavoury expressions. I blame it on the side-effects of an acute calcium deficiency and a child-like gullibility that this was my personal, albeit small, contribution to keep Labor in power. I wanted to believe they were the guys with the white hats. I should've stuck with the tooth fairy.

The campaign launch raised big bucks. William basked in my relentless abuse. He wore a grey suit. The jacket was too narrow across the shoulders. His jaw and eyebrows were oversized for his head. Each time I noticed him he was wrestling with the lining of both. Neck forward, chin down, shoulders hunched, arms dangling helplessly at his side. Primate posturing. When he eventually lifted his knuckles off the ground and made simian overtures of gratitude, I threw him some peanuts.

I felt a hand on my shoulder and then a person pushed his way into the space between me and the bar. It was a slick move and fast.

'I've been a long-time fan, it's a thrill having you here. Thanks.'

The place was packed, much too big a crowd for a pub. I could barely hear him. 'Sorry? It's too loud —'

He cupped my elbow with his hairy knuckles and pulled me closer. 'You'd be comfortable with big crowds, wouldn't you?'

I turned sideways to avoid getting crushed by his Adam's apple. 'No, actually. I'm agoraphobic. I have trouble concentrating at close range.'

I pushed forward to rescue my drink off the bar. 'So what campaign promises will you be breaking?'

'Break a promise, break a person's heart. Most of us believe in what we're doing.'

'Can you hear that squeaky sound, William?'

'No, I'm concentrating on you.'

'It's the sound of your credibility shrinking.'

A green-eyed, oblong-headed blonde appeared at William's side. She was tall, lean and wore an expression of someone being held at gunpoint.

'You did a great job, Lola. Fantastic, wasn't it, darling?'

'My wife, Daphne. Lola Finkelstein.'

Daphne: intelligent, loyal wife of William and mother of their son. She was in place being supportive, lurking in his shadow. She held out her hand. My eye was automatically drawn to her nose.

'Thank you. Great venue, isn't it?' A mouthful of words turned to mush. Wrong combination, polite drivel and uncompromising curiosity. Daphne's nose twitched like a rabbit's. She must have had this habit for so long she was oblivious to it and everyone accommodated her denial. In seconds, the tweaking nostrils diminished her height and strength and signalled a psychic SOS.

She twitched, I blinked. Our combined flutterings created a hurricane in a remote corner of the planet.

'Are you being sarcastic?' she queried, *twitch twitch,* in spite of the static in our connection.

'Certainly not. I feel at home here. The carpet's a masterpiece of lager and vomit and the mixers are watered down, but it's authentic. There's nothing ambiguous about this place.'

She went into hyper-fidgety. 'Ambiguity . . . such a soft word, it floats off your lips, for such a hard place to be. Do you know what I mean?'

It was a rhetorical question. William had shifted a few people to the right of us. Daphne's eyes darted speedily through the room till she spotted him.

'We don't get many opportunities to spend time alone,' she whispered, motioning toward the crowd and simultaneously edging away from me.

The election came and went, and via supernatural forces Labor managed to keep running the country. William scored the health portfolio and phoned to personally thank me for my support. He didn't stop phoning.

Some women are attracted to power, I get Irritable Bowel Syndrome. He'd fax me at a venue if he was in town at the same time. The messages got bolder and more prankish. There's no question about the pleasure I got from his unflagging ego. He massaged my genitals from a distance and the stimulation was effective. The chimp squealed till he got my attention.

He was a friend of the HIV/AIDS community. He listened. Triennial funding for the federal AIDS organisations, although never enough, had been increased. Lawrence had said that William was a backroom strategist who was rarely in the headlines, but was reportedly head chef to several Labor roastings.

Why had he chosen this occasion, my first time in Canberra, to use the phone instead of fax? Maybe Lisbons migrate upstream to spawn only in isolated geographic locations.

I was curious to meet with him again. Sardines are delicious, but it's wise to check the oil in the tin to be sure they're not rancid.

Christopher spoke between gear changes. 'Did you bring your mobile?'

'No. I didn't think I'd need it. Is there a problem?'

He tried hard to convince himself. 'I guess we can rough it.'

I sat opposite him in the restaurant. Beneath bamboo and the soothing oriental light of rice-paper lanterns, I brought out a tape recorder and started asking questions.

'What's it like living in a town full of public servants and retentive gardeners?'

He reached over and turned off the tape. 'Why don't we order first?'

I turned the tape on again. 'Is talking *verboten*?'

'No, ma'am. But I'd like to recommend that we order before question time.'

'In a minute. Can you hang out for a minute?'

'Yes, ma'am.' He sat back into his chair. 'Canberra does present like one giant herbaceous border. It's true there's a law that prevents folks havin a fence across their front garden –'

'That explains all the privet.'

He saluted with two fingers. I responded with another two fingers. Things were moving along nicely. I switched off the tape recorder and focused on the menu.

Christopher spoke in a tone that was more apologetic than seductive. 'It's a bum deal that you live in Melbourne, like seein the trailer for what I know would be a fantastic movie and never gettin the chance to experience the full feature.'

I lifted my head slowly out of the menu and avoided his gaze with calculated precision. I didn't want to lose my appetite. The waitress was on standby. I got in first. 'Gyoza, a main-course sushi please and large sake.'

'Miso soup for me, please. Tempura vegetables and eel. You wanna share?'

'No.'

CHAPTER NINE

Little Red Riding Hood is a Russian contraceptive.
– Graffiti

DINNER PROBE

'Don't you get lonely? Don't you ever imagine what it would be like sharing your life with someone?'

He kept sniffing for a response.

'Yes, I get lonely, that's when I ring Mr Time . . . *at the third stroke, it will be 9.34 and 20 seconds precisely*. He's always there, reliable, constant, and if I put my ear really close to the phone I *know* he's talking *just* to me. And yes, occasionally, I think about what it would be like being in a loving relationship. That's when I know my blood-sugar levels must be down.'

He stared at me with the compassion of a gefilte fish.

'I knew at age five that I was an intensely jealous woman. This handsome guy came to stay with us, Uncle Markus. He had grey–blue eyes and square everything: jaw, shoulders, hands. He was the most exciting man I'd ever met. The smell of him came first, the scent of limes and vetiver. We were inseparable. I sailed piggyback on his shoulders like Cleopatra down the Nile. We went swimming. He taught me to sing. But the bastard met a grown-up and fell in love.

'At the wedding, everyone posed for the family portrait. I shredded my pretty powder-blue tulle dress with the knife intended for the wedding cake. My tiny fingernails clawed the ribbons from my hair. I refused to be photographed. He was thirty-five, I was about to turn four. I had no words for what was happening. I struggled to find a colour for my mood. Eggplant. I'll do anything to avoid feeling eggplant.'

Christopher's breathing was irregular. There was a brief, athletic silence. 'I had a speech impediment as a teenager.'

'Really? What – like a stutter?'

'I couldn't say no to sex.'

One of my legs toppled sideways.

'That's my foot you're stomping on –'

'I give a great foot massage –'

'Fuck off!'

He moaned like a labrador peering goofishly through a screen door.

'I don't bonk people I work with. I slept with a comedian once and fretted all night that in a moment of ecstasy I might give away my material.'

The conversation was affecting my body's chemistry. My tongue felt like a mollusc clinging to the back of my throat. The last serious boyfriend I'd had admitted in an act of vengeance that he'd slept with another woman. He didn't *admit* it. He *shared* that he'd sought out 'the uncritical warmth of a casual encounter'. On the next full moon, propelled by lunar rage, I flung everything he'd given me – books, jewellery and his drawings – off St Kilda pier.

I regretted again saying no to William and tried not to imagine him and Daphne making love.

'Canberra? So feed my curiosity already.'

'The city was built around Lake Burley Griffin.'

'An artificial lake named after Walter Burley Griffin, the American architect who designed the city. Why did they ask an American?'

He frowned, finally removing his foot off mine. 'The Minister for Home Affairs organised an international competition for the design of the capital and Walter and Marion's design won.'

'It's a bizarre design – concentric circles around a hill. It's like they got pissed one night and thought *Hmm everything is spinning, yep that's a novel idea for a national capital.*'

'It's supposed to be like a colosseum. Lots of land around it, parks for the birdlife. There's a heap of rare species –'

'It presents like a theme park. A great tree-lined, monument-filled, bird-inhabited, warm, fuzzy, Canberra experience. In the meantime unemployment is berserk. The national debt is being considered as a name for a new range of sanitation products and tourists are expected, going by the brochures, "to journey into the triumphs, tragedies and magnificent achievements of our history".'

He gestured for time-out, but I was on a roll. 'What about the Royal Australia Mint? I quote from the brochure: "You'll see more money made in an hour than most of us make in a year". The snap, crackle and pop of crisp bank notes – wow, that'll challenge my bladder control! This city is the manifestation of Australia's personality disorder. And tell me please, what's with the miniature replica of buildings and gardens of Great Britain? At one-twelfth the scale? Who gives a shit? *Gee, it's just like the real thing, only smaller!*'

'What's your beef with Canberra?'

'I'm hungry. Let's get to the Press Club story. Three lobotomised subeditors fell through a trap door in a shower of split infinitives, survived and formed the Press Club, right?'

He nodded and made a gesture of surrender with his shoulders. 'The Club was formed in 1962 to provide a forum for national and international speakers. It was founded by journalists so they could meet up and imagine themselves players in the political process. Occasionally, they'd invite eminent guests to speak and drink with them.'

'Do you think my gig will work? Aren't Press Club audiences accustomed to lunchtime speeches?'

'Yep, one hundred per cent. Everyone listens to your morning radio raves with Kevin.'

'Pity Kevin lost the gig.'

'What?'

'Kevin Hush, the presenter. They've given us both the flick. I guess too many politicians *were* listening.'

'Penetrating control headquarters right under their noses, in stereo? What did you expect?'

I shrugged. 'My father always said the difference between prostitutes and politicians was that there were some things prostitutes wouldn't do for money. Thc more I delve into federal politics, the more I want a go on every ride.'

'You think being a comedian excludes you from censorship? The very nature of what you do is isolating. It makes you an easy target. Politicians are different. They have an irrational fear of death, which defines their behaviour. They'll reschedule and repackage anyone or anything, including themselves, that threatens their political shelf-life.'

'Somebody has to occasionally pull the chain.'

'Hole-in-one, baby! Why d'ya think I booked you to do the show?'

'You're intoxicated with my juggling?'

A pale, shortish, plumpish guy in a black shirt sat down two tables away to my left. He'd made his way through the restaurant carrying a trumpet case and a black leather jacket. The waitress offered to hang the jacket for him, but he refused. He looked over and smiled at me, ordered Japanese tea and promptly spilled most of it into his lap.

Lawrence's phone call busted into my thoughts. I don't remember what made me think Christopher would be interested. 'Springfield Hospital in Melbourne is going to be closed.'

He was trying to get the waitress's attention. His body turned towards her, but his gaze was still with me. 'Is this your problem?'

I figured he was annoyed with the lack of service.

'It's an infectious diseases hospital. Health department planners are arguing that it's uneconomically small and inconveniently located.'

He spoke in the direction of the waitress. 'The government has the right, in terms of its hospital planning, to decide where specialist services should be based. That's how it works.'

'Yes, but who's making the decisions and based on what information?'

I waited till he looked directly at me. 'They haven't consulted the patients or the hospital staff.' I was talking to myself.

He blew me a kiss. 'You're real sexy when you're feisty.'

The waitress came over in a scurry of Japanese poise. He spoke to her softly, seeking redemption. 'Could we have our sake right away, please?'

I was going back to Melbourne tomorrow. In the big picture, he was just a fingerprint. 'You don't give a shit. Why should you? You're a white, middle-class, heterosexual male!'

I swerved to avoid a razor-sharp teddy-stud.

'What about Fyshwick? Porn capital, isn't it?'

'It's an industrial estate surrounded by acres of farmland. Smash repair shops, light industrial businesses, tyre distributors and smack-dab in the middle, the Pleasure Dome, Adam and Eve Boutique and Venus Bookshop.'

Sake and gyoza arrived, a soothing combination.

I avoid antagonism while eating, it's poison for the digestive enzymes. A few finger-lickin' mouthfuls and I strolled into the Christopher Pillar side-show. I prodded for a background pamphlet.

'I was born in Seattle. My father was a lay minister, he's retired now.'

'What's he like?'

'Simple, genuinely kind, decent man, spent most of his energy trying to keep my mother happy. I gotta younger sister and an older brother, we're not close. My parents relocated nearly every three years when I was very young. I wanted to believe that they'd be happier if I wasn't around. I decided to leave home when I was fourteen.'

'Have you workshopped this?'

He sucked greedily on his Ventolin. 'Don't need to. I left home, end of story. I hated the way my mother treated my father and I didn't wanna hate him for not standing up to her.'

He spoke with a detachment that betrayed his sensitivity. I didn't tap on any other doors. I had my own mother psychopathology and wanted to avoid bringing it up for dessert.

I did a U-turn. 'Have you been married?'

'Yep.' I watched him neatly remove a cigarette from the packet and rotate it between his thumb and middle finger. 'I didn't bother with trying to get a handle on what went wrong.'

'I'm hearing that you're not very reflective?'

'I avoid internal journeys . . . no frequent-flyer rewards.'

I thought then he was probably the sort of man who lost his temper only rarely but when he did, it was ugly. He never once mentioned politics or revealed personal enthusiasm for any ministers. It was hard to know whether he was being discreet or simply wasn't interested. I couldn't resist asking about William.

'Any classified information about the Minister for Health?'

'Gossip round town is that he's into boys.'

I choked on tuna. 'But he's married, with a child!'

'Sorry, Dorothy, I guess we're not in Kansas any more.'

'All the men I know are waking up next to other men.'

Green tea arrived for me, coffee for him. He offered a flat teaspoon of sugar. 'One spoon or two?'

'None. I'm weaning myself off stimulants.'

He dumped the teaspoon into his espresso and slid the unlit cigarette between his lips.

He didn't mince words. 'It's so stoopid not being able to smoke in a restaurant.'

'Excuse me, but isn't that Ventolin in your pocket?'

'Nope, I'm just glad to see you.'

I led the curiosity posse down another trail.

'It's January 28th. Fifteen years ago today, the space shuttle *Challenger* exploded 73 seconds after take-off. Do you remember the faces of the family members on the ground watching their loved ones blast into oblivion?'

'Americans don't have the best reputations as lovers, but some of us *can* keep it up for more than 73 seconds.'

It was after midnight and still not enough sake when Christopher dropped me back at my hotel. We sat in the car, illuminated by a bright half-moon. He lazily slid one arm around my waist. 'Why don't you stay for another day?'

The city was silent, except for the sound of bodies being dragged on marble floors. The night-life, if there was any, was somewhere else.

'I really need to get back.' I slipped out of the car and his grip a bit too quickly and far too strongly.

He leaned across the passenger seat. 'I'll see you in the morning. *Que suengos con los ancelitos.*'

'What?'

'May you sleep with the angels.'

'They prefer men.' I waved goodbye with the gleam of my stiletto.

PART TWO

CHAPTER TEN

Mao Tse-Tung didn't have to deal with people who were watching seven hours of television every day.
– Elaine Brown

TRICK or TREAT?

While Lola sleeps, keeping her mouth speed at zero, let's check in on Christopher. Who is he? Just another well-endowed body with a tattooed heart? Christopher Pillar had always known that the US government supplied the Contra guerillas with arms. Like many of his idealistic contemporaries, he flew to Nicaragua in the autumn of 1986 as a personal protest against the Reagan administration. He was a zealous supporter of the revolutionary cause in Nicaragua and impatient to fling himself into a moat gurgling with crocodiles. Predictably, when David Marks, a university friend who'd been living in Managua since 1983, wrote to him and asked him to come and help him build a much-needed hydroelectric plant in the northern frontier mountain area near Honduras, he didn't hesitate. He'd graduated from university with a degree in engineering and a spermload of natural stamina. The Sandinistas needed someone with his skills.

David warned Christopher of the potential dangers. 'It's not pretty. I'd be lying if I said that there isn't anything to worry about. There is. The Contras are all over the place.'

It was precisely in the region where they hoped to build the plant that former national guards, with American backing, ran the Contras. Christopher underestimated that danger, since he had nothing to compare it to. He'd left home, lived on the streets and hung out with small-time drug dealers, teenage boys with elevated testosterone levels, whose freshly-sprouted facial hair cut deeper than their knives. And then university, where danger was a public rejection by your chosen object of desire.

David was the original nerdy peacenik, a short guy who wore glasses and a plastic pocket protector to carry his pens. He didn't dance, he shuffled. His body possessed a kind of skinny, perishable frailty. Christopher never imagined him coping in a genuine hotspot.

That day on the mountain, David and a couple of volunteers climbed further up the hill to survey the location from a higher point. Christopher was directly behind them. Everything happened in a nanosecond. The speed gave them immunity from fear. He'd struggled to remember it for years, but each vignette smudged into the next like a rain-stained storyboard. A flurry of shots that he didn't register seriously till he sniffed his own burning flesh. The amplified penetrating pain, swelling nausea, heavy head . . . no head, clean slate.

He woke in the US airforce helicopter on the way back to the States, too medicated to connect the dots. He remembered asking about David and the medic not responding. Muffled voices all around. The odd sentence stayed with him, like a banana peel left behind after a garbage collection. He was weak from several transfusions.

The official State Department report was that they'd penetrated Contra territory. The Contras had called for David – allegedly uniformed and armed – and the others to surrender, but the Sandinistas reached for their guns and opened fire. The Contras fired back. David was shot dead.

Christopher knew this was bullshit. The dry-mouthed, scabby pimps in Washington were protecting their ragged arses. Only one of the men with David had a gun and, after all, the Contras were guerillas. Being polite was not part of their job description. They wouldn't have waited to be fired at. If the CIA ran the Contras, then Christopher's parents' taxes had paid for the bullets that were still lodged in his thigh. These bullets infused him with an instinctive curiosity, like a seed seeking its original soil. And from their moment of entry he couldn't resist wanting to know why David was dead. He was killed trying to give the Sandinistas some power. Power to light up the dark, to read by, to educate themselves with night classes, to refrigerate medication.

Christopher was eventually interrogated by American officials. He told them the truth, that he remembered nothing and then began to ask his own questions. In the beginning, he wanted only to know the truth about the day on the hill. He unravelled that sordid knot through a naïve patience born of bewilderment and shell-shock. By then the compost of lies had sprouted the bullet-seeds. Christopher knew that the only solution was to work from the inside. Intelligence welcomed him with open, parasitic, arthropod arms. The all-American, home-grown boy–man, compromised and wounded, displaying a healthy cynical resentment towards anti-government protesters. The dumb bastards bought it.

The State Department's account was never believable and some Sandinistas claimed that David had been shot point-blank. Had David been executed? If so, who gave the order, and why? David's friends and supporters who continued to do his work were angry and paranoid.

Christopher asked questions carefully and kept a low profile. There were many who eagerly offered help, but he chose to move alone and to speak only to those he was sure would not betray him. His tenacity ripened in the hothouse desire for revenge.

A couple of American forensic doctors who had examined David's body agreed that he had been shot point-blank. But the official autopsy report suggested 'accidental death'. The body was conveniently lost between examinations; the authorities didn't want anyone seeing the gruesome evidence.

David's family held a memorial service for him back in the US, but Christopher stayed away. Not able to offer comfort or deny feeling guilty that he was alive, he felt most useful back in Nicaragua, navigating through the official maze and helping to finish the job David had started.

Christopher spent months talking to locals in the district where the shooting had happened. By chance, he'd met a woman whose cousin had been with the Contras. It was impossible to meet with the cousin, who'd disappeared deeper into the mountains. But she agreed to try to speak with his wife. The three of them gathered in the wife's smoke-filled, dimly lit kitchen. She'd been cooking with chilli oil. Christopher couldn't stop coughing for long enough to gather his thoughts. The wife never offered her name, but told him what she knew about that day.

Finally, Christopher concluded that Nicaragua had been a pawn in the Cold War between the US and the Soviet bloc. Each had sought to fuel the highly flammable civil differences for their own end. Properly examined, the difference between the Contras and Sandinistas was wafer-thin, perfect for frying. There'd been no order to execute David, nor had he been tortured. The ambush was misguided, a bungled attempt by a bunch of locals to avenge a brother's death. He felt like an idiot. By the time George Bush was masturbating in the Oval Office, realising finally that the Sandinistas were no threat to the US, Christopher was addicted to adrenalin and diagnosed HIV-positive.

The blood that saved his life, but not really, had been contaminated plasma distributed illegally on the black market through Third World countries. Life was a game show, hosted this season, ladies and gentlemen, by the chief of middle-class smugness, that nightmare of the free world – the American president. 'C'mon down, Christopher Pillar, you've been a great contestant.'

And the fun wasn't over yet. The final schtick was a leap of faith, an irrevocable jump out of an aeroplane with Lola Finkelstein.

He lay motionless, in the green-dark of the digital clock, limp as a stick of celery on the bottom shelf of the fridge. His arms crossed behind his head, the doona pulled right up to his chin. He looked round for his puffer and felt secure once he'd identified it poking out of his trouser pocket on the floor.

A click brought his eyes up to the fluorescent numbers as 1.59 turned to 2. He told Fillet he'd call. Grudgingly he turned sideways, lifted up onto one elbow, switched on the bedlamp and picked up the receiver. Habit dictated that he listen for an irregular tone. 'Yo, filet mignon, howzit going buddy . . . just callin home like I said, so Momma won't worry.'

A gravelly post-throat-op voice responded. 'Mate . . . what's this fillet shit?'

Bruce Price was his boss at ASIO, the Australian Intelligence organisation to which he'd been transferred. Christopher fantasised that if you combined a trough-full of sheep offal and oatmeal, some seasoning and boiled it in skin made from the animal's stomach, you'd have a Bruce Price. A human haggis, all pink and lumpy and full of acid in the cavity where his personality was supposed to be.

He sneered into the phone. 'You ain't got no backbone, Brucie.'

'Jeez, you carry on like a pork chop.'

'In all the years I've been here, I never figured out what that means. How the hell *does* a pork chop carry on? Personally I've never dated a pig.'

Fillet buckjumped down the phone. 'Listen mate, Dupleix wants a report ASA-fuckin-P and I'm already flat out like a lizard drinking.' Christopher listened to the purr of Fillet's overweight breathing. 'Sniffing around a comedian doesn't make ya funny, Pillar. I'm no fuckstick. I know ya taking the piss. My advice is quit while y'ahead and get on with the job. I haven't got time for this crap.'

Fillet didn't ask questions. He had no concept of where to pause for question marks, a necessary qualification for the job.

Christopher played it like a snake in the sun, relaxed but ready to lunge. 'Don't worry, I'll handle it. She's controllable. I'll redirect her. She doesn't know jack-shit.'

'That stupid cow and her poofter mates are creating a shitload of interest around the hospital closure. Dupleix's bloody determined it gets no fucking publicity.'

'Nothin's gonna happen. She doesn't understand half of what she's sayin. She's not politically savvy and in any case who's gonna take a comedian seriously?'

'They don't have to take her seriously. Those scabs will print fart sounds if they pong enough.' He blew his nose impatiently. Christopher had the spontaneous impression that Fillet was scratching his balls.

'She's got an opinion on everything, a bloody talkback radio show on legs. Dupleix reckons she's trouble. If she starts spurting the bullshit those faggots have fed her it might encourage some nosy journo to poke his snout in the wrong trough.'

'Yessiree, Captain Fillet! Over and out, uh be de, uh be de . . . that's all, folks!'

'Give it a break, Pillar, ya septic idiot!' Fillet hung up in his ear.

Christopher clicked down the handset. In a low whisper he repeated 'septic tank, yank, wank-er' to his doona. He sat in his bed, propped up by two cross-examined pillows. Like a surgeon removing debris from a flesh wound, his face twisted in effort as he recalled the facts. He was neither reflective nor philosophical; the end would justify the means. Lola was hard-nosed, determined, had no romantic entanglements, no pets. She maintained contacts, not intimate friendships. She hated wearing knickers.

The child of Holocaust survivors, they had insisted she trust no-one and early on she discovered they were part of the package. She was no-one's property, but at the frequent disposal of her demons. She was paranoid. The combination of hard-headed stubbornness and utopian idealism made her appear adolescent at times. He chuckled to himself, something he didn't often do.

By controlling the flow, he could dispatch selected information as he felt she needed it. He was certain she'd ask a thousand questions and make her conclusions despite what he said. He was agitated, but didn't over-analyse, which probably explained the more frequent asthma attacks. The spy in him detected that she touched his vowel parts, but Christopher rejected these sensations. He'd long ago lobotomised that part of his brain – or possibly it had worn thin and split apart like the overused hole on a watch band.

She annoyed the fuck out of him. She was high maintenance, extracted coal-mines of energy, had to be in control and was breathtakingly girlish when it came to politics. Precisely why he believed she was perfect for his plan.

His brief was to expertly distract Lola from anything to do with Springfield Hospital. To keep her uninquisitive, to deny rumours if necessary, to offer her false confidential documents. But his shadow observed without being observed, spied her gathering the information, listened in behind the tree of counter-espionage. Waiting for the opportunity to jump out ahead of her, ignite her curiosity and vanish again.

Lola Finklestein was the opportunity he'd been waiting for since Nicaragua. This was payback time. As a bonus, the board and staff at Springfield could save their hospital.

CHAPTER ELEVEN

He was like a cock who thought the sun had risen to hear him crow.
– George Eliot

REJECTION

Mind-fucking myself – it's my hobby, too hard to collect butterflies when you're on the road. I wanted to phone Pillar. Fear of rejection shot through my veins like news of a multinational takeover, and spun my corporeal Dow Jones into orbit. I made it to the toilet just in time to throw up. The hotel-room decor, Jewish Rococo, didn't help. Vitamised salmon-mornay pink semi-gloss walls, floral cafe curtains that folded forever and a lost soul's four-poster bed. It was vacant, despite my presence. I checked the back of the front door for the fire-escape route. The arrow on the map would indicate my exact location in the building. YOU ARE HERE! I like that.

On my knees, cheek pressed against the cool doorknob, I could hear another guest leaving a tray outside their room. And further on the map, the echo of a professional couple smiling at each other through cosmetic dentalwork. Slowly, I crawled to the bed and lifted my upper body enough to sink down on the edge of the quilted pavlova. From Pillar to post, head in hands, I consulted my inner voices. They were more pissed than I was. At the airport, I loathed him and his cross-trainers. At lunch he was so green and wet I imagined hydroponically growing tomatoes behind his ears. But somewhere between the sake and the main course, I'd bitten that apple.

I've been taught for years about being independent, but never about being vulnerable. Unquestionably, I'm shit sure that a responsive, confident man is an impostor, and I automatically feel vulnerable. If he's not lying, then he's stupid. If he's not stupid, then I'm not vulnerable, I'm confused. I don't pop my whistle for the Tom Cruises or Bonos or even Richard Geres or Mel Gibsons. I'm terminally attracted to losers, the second-raters, the wannabees, the schlepps. At school, receptive to religious instruction, I fell in love with Goliath. He was my man. I imagined him like a John Steinbeck character, big and dumb and tender. 'Ah'll go tend dem rebbits.' I pushed for Goliath to belt the shit out of that sucky harp-player.

The room unravelled around me like a trashed bouquet. I couldn't be sure which camp Pillar belonged to, dick-biscuit or hopeless flunky. The day had gone too long, I was over it.

I was keen to leave Canberra. By the time Christopher arrived to drive me to the airport, I'd showered, packed and lacked any pretence of enthusiasm.

'It's pretty crisp in the morning, colder than I imagined.'

'Yep, gets pretty cold here in the winter. We're in a valley. Sometimes it mists up real bad, you can't see the car in front.'

'Talking of sightlines, we'd better have another conversation sometime before the gig about the stage and where the sound system should go. If the sound dies, there's no show.'

'It'll be taken care of.' He was absorbed with the road, hypnotised by the white line like a chicken.

'What's up, did the sleep-fairy goof off last night?'

He didn't blink. 'I'd really love it if you could stay one more night. We're just beginning to get comfortable with each other.'

'Who writes your material? Not even the producers of 'Home and Away' would pay for that sort of drivel.'

His hands gripped the steering wheel at nine and three o'clock. At the airport, in the warm toxic haze of aeroplane fuel, I stifled an apology and suggested we have a coffee.

'Christopher, do you think you're attracted to me because you feel you know me through my work?'

'I'm not a star fucker,' he said without any hesitation. 'Your problem is that you're so bandaged up from scabs way back when you won't take a risk. Get off your high horse, roll around in the grass. Why don't you shut up for three minutes and listen to someone else – you might learn somethin. Except you like the sound of your own voice too much.'

'You want skinny milk or full cream?'

'Full cream. You're still on stage. Problem is, I never bought a ticket.'

I sank my teeth into my cheeks and bit back tears. My breathing was shallow, oxygen roadblocked in my chest. Crows' feet clawed around my squinting eyes to stop a salty overflow. 'You're cranky because I'm not impressed with your somersaults.'

The more he spoke, the less I was convinced. 'Have you ever taken a look at how you plan ahead? You're never present. Your body's here but your head's permanently over the page. Stop. Feel somethin for a day, half a day, two fuckin hours. It won't kill you, I promise.'

My body reminded me I wasn't getting enough oxygen. A hiccup attack. 'I know I must seem very rigid *ee-up* but let's *ee-up* cut the crap. You want a bonk *eep* and like I said, I don't sleep with *ee-up* work associates.'

He grabbed the back of my head with one hand and covered my mouth with the other. 'Quit talkin for a minute and hold your breath.'

The action was fluid, his control masterful, my neck fell into his palm. My lips stopped moving, my breath counted out the beats led by his baton. I could've stayed another night, but who wants to be another shrunken head hanging alongside his pager?

The more he tried to persuade me, the harder I clung to my snowy crag, vulture-like, picking at my own bones. We were sitting on white plastic chairs, the living art of airport coffee lounges. They're always far more animated than the people who work behind the counter. Christopher leant forward into me, elbows on his knees, so that I had to look down into his face. He spoke in a slow simmer.

'I don't blame you for thinkin I'm just another player, but if you can stay another night . . . I know we could . . . it's rare to meet another person and feel this comfortable. We've had a connection since the first phone call, that's what brought you to Canberra. You didn't have to see the venue.'

'Bullshit. I needed background material.'

'I could've mailed the brochures to you.'

'It's not the same.'

'Will you at least cushion the blow by thinkin about it for thirty seconds? *Then*, shove me aside like a slobbering puppy that can't stop humpin your leg.'

I was spinning into that hideous giddy destination, the corner of Walk and Don't Walk. I sat, back straight, and swallowed hard, willing something sensible to come out of my mouth. More hiccups.

'Will you promise me to at least think about what I've said?'

I nodded. He carried my bag and wrapped himself around my body like filo pastry to prevent the contents squirting.

'I'll ring you in a couple of weeks, once I've sorted through the brochures.'

I paid homage to Lot's wife and looked back at him as I boarded the plane out of Sodom. His eyes fixed on mine, seeking to drop anchor. Still more hiccups.

Thoughts at take-off: could I choose to be turned into a more sensuous condiment? Cinnamon or nutmeg? How did Eve feel after she'd convinced Adam to taste the apple? Was he more of a groover with knowledge or without?

Or was she the first woman with regrets? 'Adam, I'm sorry, I had no idea it would go this far. The apple was just a come-on.'

Inside the great winged blow-dryer, teasing through a bouffant of clouds, the altitude and change in air pressure replayed the last twenty-four hours to me with different orchestration. I enjoyed the new tune.

I learn by trial and error – numerous trials and frequent errors. I search for clues like a dog scratching at the ground, running ahead, running back, snapping at the air to sniff the scent of a trail I should follow. High above ground, intoxicated with the heady odour of aeroplane food, I scrabbled to find this scent. I felt suspicious of Christopher.

Back at home, stretched out on my own bed, safe and fully coordinated by my possessions, I tried again for an absolute answer, but there were no clues. Nothing out of place, everything was in its place: white walls, wooden floors, my low-to-the-ground red-lacquer Japanese table, a clear glass vase empty of flowers.

It was time for chaos. I rang him. 'Hi Christopher, it's Lola. How are things?'

Silence. I held in an involuntary groan of disappointment.

'Christopher, look, I know you probably didn't expect to hear from me so soon but I've been thinking about all that stuff you said and maybe you're right.'

Bigger silence. Loud enough to shatter my hopes.

'In hindsight, I probably should have stayed, but relaxation is not really my area. Anyway, I was thinking maybe I could come back to Canberra, soon-ish, before March.'

This was not something I'd ever done before. I was struggling, every word squeezed through rigid lips.

'Christopher, I've paid thousands of dollars in therapy not to feel dismembered when I expose myself. This conversation is feeling like a backward step that could take light years to retrace. Tell me you weren't bullshitting.'

He didn't get the joke.

I pressed the phone right against my ear and willed myself to stop shaking. We all bear scars from past humiliations and failures. I'm Jewish, according to 'Crimestoppers' we killed Jesus and he came back in three days. Fear of failure is in my genetic make-up.

'He-llo, earth to Christopher, communicate?'

A saliva bubble grew out of the right side of my mouth. I heard him wheeze. 'I'm thrilled that you thought about *all that stuff*, I hope it makes a significant difference. If I can get to Melbourne before the March show, sure, let's have us some fun.'

I remembered reading that a woman was knocked unconscious by a lightning strike while talking on the phone during an electrical storm. Later Telstra issued a press release alerting the public to a warning printed on the front of the directory. I checked, and, sure enough, there it was: WARNING – THUNDERSTORMS. *You can get a shock from your telephone (and other electrical equipment) during a thunderstorm.* It went on to give specific instructions. Don't use the phone during a storm unless it's urgent. Don't stand in bare feet on uncovered concrete floors. I make calls during thunderstorms if I really have to, but I protect myself with rubber gloves and flippers. At this moment, I stood dripping wet with fear, a walking target for renegade lightning bolts. I'd removed all protective gear and the fireball hit me like a million volts. I felt hollow: thoughts, feelings, sentences blasted away to dust.

'Christopher, stop me if I'm hallucinating. But two days ago, a criminal who must have stolen your name, your clothes and your face asked me to stay in Canberra so that he and I could get to know each other. This outlaw indicated what I understood to be a romantic interest. Quote: it's rare that you meet another person and feel this comfortable, unquote. Excuse me if I'm bitching, but you're talking to me like I'm the nurse who helped perform your circumcision.'

'Lola, ya got a great arse, ma'am, but ya oughta try gettin your head out of it sometime. Nothins changed, I still think you're sensational, I'd love to see ya, but ya know, I kinda like to put everythin in its own little box. If you're in town, fantastic, we can party. If not, then ya go into a little box till next time. I think ya sorta misunderstood my affection. I'm a very affectionate guy, knowhatahmean?'

'Oh pah-lease, stop being so enabling. Don't erase what little respect I would have had left for you. I don't get it, because clearly you're making this up as you go. I'm sorry, but I'm not into being bottled, packaged, bundled up into storage. I'll call you two weeks before the gig in March.'

'Lola, don't get crazy on me, ya thought I was talkin relationship –'

'But you were talking shagfest, right? I know that, I'm not a complete shmock.'

'Not totally –'

'What?'

'You're not totally right –'

'How could I be?'

'I am lookin for a compatible relationship, but not right now.'

'What kind of compatible, Christopher? Emotional, physical or IBM?'

He chuckled, on night rate. 'The word is shmuck, not shmock!'

I was on peak time.

'*Excuuuse* me, it's shmock, Yiddish for penis. Shmuck is the Anglo version. It sounds more flaccid, it's meant to. I'll call you to confirm final arrangements. Goodbye.'

CHAPTER TWELVE

If love is the answer, would you mind rephrasing the question?
– Lily Tomlin

WOBBLY

My nipples spiked like thorns with rage. I spent two minutes doing some heavy thinking, stomped into the kitchen, grabbed the hospital-grade disinfectant – guaranteed to kill *Salmonella* and *E. coli* – and sprayed the mouthpiece of the phone. En route, I dipped a clawed hand into the cupboard and grabbed three chocolate biscuits. I jabbed two into my mouth and slid one behind my ear for post-traumatic rage. Roller-coaster time, fun at the freaked-out fair. I didn't call anyone.

The next day I rang Amanda. We've known each other for eight years. She was the coolest chick behind the bar at the comedy venue where I did my first horrific try-out gigs. Amanda is uncontrollably flirtatious, she sleep-flirts. Amanda would flirt with mud.

Each week I'd drag myself in like something that even the cat had sniffed and rejected. Amanda curled around the tables like smoke, collecting empty glasses and giving me a thumbs-up whenever I raised the occasional laugh. Through beetroot-red lips and hennaed bird's-nest hair, she offered gentle, encouraging post-mortems. And afterwards, I'd listen to yet another cataclysmic outcome with whatever singer, musician, actor, wood termite with a press release she'd dated that week. A few days would pass, Amanda would phone and tell me about the best club to be at on a Wednesday night, the latest suicidal lead singer and her ersatz relationship-free life. She had a PhD in Anthropology but shit-for-brains when it came to selecting boyfriends.

I missed her when she left for London with a juggler and fire-eater; one person, two skills. He believed that washing your body too often 'diminished one's power to get in touch with the muse'. On his chest, just above his well-defined pectoral muscle, he had a Native American totem tattoo. Apparently, of an eagle. To me, it looked like a bunch of felt pens had leaked through his shirt pocket. Their relationship was shortlived, despite his combined skills. Amanda stayed in London and currently writes for all the must-have glossy magazines. She's having her bathroom redecorated and her tastebuds nipped to encourage a more conservative style. But she's still the very same Amanda who elevated blow-jobs into a new professional status.

Whenever I work in London we seize upon each other. It's a carefully planned mission. We bring in trolleyloads of carbohydrates, wear loose clothing and descend into the girlfriend bunker, embracing every extra pound and deeper wrinkle on the body of our friendship.

We blabber for days. About our workload, about dick size. We agree, again, that romance and knowing your bone density is bullshit, but checking for lumps is not. We approve and accept that we're swamped by our work. We like that. We have time for sex, but not for romance. Finally we confide to each other that we do want romance. And we do need good bone density so we can continue having good sex.

Now, when I needed to blame, to point the finger, to kick and scream like a banshee, I dialled Amanda's number. She answered.

I didn't say hello. 'I'm such a fuckwit. You're not going to believe this. I just bought a first-class ticket on the bullshit ride.'

'I'd love to empathise but this review was meant to be in an hour ago –'

'Yeah, but . . . '

'Bad timing, babe. I'm hormonal, over my deadline and out of cigarettes.'

'I need to –'

'It's a new version of *King Lear* without prepositions. I can't believe the shite I have to review. OK, headlines – just give me the headlines. What's up? Do we pray or buy weapons?'

I told her.

'It's so *King Lear* . . . passive-aggressive, misogynous shit.'

'What is?'

'His behaviour. He's into power games. A conquest junkie, one of those guys who make women fall for them, just to see if they can do it. Hang in there, I'll call you back when I've emailed this out of my life.'

She didn't call for three days.

'What happened to you?'

'I fucked up bigtime with the deadline. By the time I finally got the monster in I was so relieved, I went to the pub, ordered a half-pint, left it with Sarah and Tony while I went to the loo. I get into the stall, slip on the wet floor, hit my head, concussion, knocked out, sprained ankle. Can you fucking believe it? Hadn't even put the glass to my lips. Fuck this place. The weather's crap, the food's crap, I think I need to come home for a while.'

'We could go down the coast.'

'I wasn't reliable. Sorry, Lola. I feel wretched about it, I know how much you hate asking for help.'

'Shit happens.'

'Has he called back?'

'No. I'm over it, anyway. For about a day I was in unchartered waters without travelling expenses or a credit card. But it's useless trying to second-guess his behaviour. He's American . . . they're not like us.'

Lawrence dropped in unexpectedly at the end of the week. 'Hi darl, looking gorgeous, *hot for you.*'

He had all the answers.

'He's gay, darl, or he's way out of his depth. You're too strong for him. You know what you want and . . . and . . . you don't put up with soggy risotto.'

'It's such a cliché. I doubt you're right. I'm last week's bacon, he's seasoning this week's roast. End of story.'

Lawrence snorted, sprang forward full blown and squeezed me into his chest. Three condoms wriggled out of his vest pocket and fell on my face. He caught them before they hit the ground. 'Excuse me, haven't been home yet, last night was very-very.' He waved his arms in the air as if he were drowning.

'Deep, deep, deep, darl and,' he lowered his voice, 'deeply meaningful.'

I stayed glued to his chest. 'Where were you? Leaning on a bar somewhere, surveying the crowd for your prince in black leather?'

He lifted his head skyward. 'I'm not guilty of casting one's hook for shrimp on this occasion, princess. There was a meeting at the AIDS Council, followed by pizza, followed by me going to –'

'What's happened to Springfield?'

He took a deep breath and managed the key change. 'Not good news, darl, only more bad news. I met Adonis last night –'

'What about Nobb? Save Adonis for later.'

'She's guaranteed Joshua that the HIV community would ultimately make the decision as to where HIV/AIDS services would be located. Not *if* they would be. Sounds fait accompli to me. Boom-boom.'

Joshua Newbroom, the bushy-tailed but hard-boiled president of the AIDS Council, had tried to explain the new health funding system to me two years before when it was first introduced. I never did properly grasp the details. He'd called me romantic because I thought hospitals were venues offering care and compassion. Now I was trying to make sense of it with Lawrence, who referred to Joshua as 'that prick'.

'I understand it costs money to run a hospital.'

'Yeah, that's correct, missus, but this system's septic. Patients have been misdiagnosed, others discharged too early, all because of budget cuts. There are rewards for the speedy turnover of patients, it's just Casemix in action, no carcass being dipped in formaldehyde here.'

I must have looked like someone had drilled a hole between my eyes.

'Casemix, darl! It's a funding system that calculates hospital grants by setting a fixed rate for particular procedures. If a hospital manages the procedure for less then the fixed rate, it keeps the change. If a hospital spends more than that fixed rate, it has to either make up the difference, cut costs or stop offering the service.'

He fingered his nipple ring through his vest. 'I don't think making hospitals efficient is a bad thing, as long as it doesn't compromise patient care. At Springfield they've had to juggle budgets all along to save cuts to HIV/AIDS services. They can't keep doing it.

'Are you with me, darl? Springfield's closure is about economic problems, not health problems. Under Casemix the amounts set for HIV/AIDS are very low; in fact, deliberately incorrect, sweetie.'

I could taste the blood from where I'd bitten my tongue.

'So this discourages hospitals from providing services to HIV/AIDS patients because they know they won't get their money back, right?'

'Bingo! Springfield has had to pay for a whole lot of provisions for patients not covered by Casemix. And they've taken on a busload of AIDS patients from other hospitals because those hospitals wouldn't wear the associated costs.'

'Wouldn't it make more sense for the health department to make some special dispensation for funding Springfield rather than shut it down? Whichever hospital takes over, they're going to have to spend more on re-establishing special services anyway.'

Lawrence had his hand under his T-shirt. His compulsive fondling was irritating me.

'*What* are you doing?' I lifted his T-shirt.

'Stop it, those nails could scratch a man's eyes out. Ouch! I bet you can see *them* from outer space. Your hands are freezing, piss off.'

I pressed the back of my hand against Lawrence's breast. His nipple throbbed with inflammation.

'Shut up, I'm checking to see if it's hot. I think it's infected. Where did you have this done?'

He covered his eyes. 'I see a small shopfront in Fitzroy, no, maybe Richmond, no, hang on, it was in the city. I can't remember exactly. I was a bit under the weather at the time.'

I stood back, head pushed forward in persecution mode. 'I cannot believe you went to some slimy piercing place so off your noodle that you don't remember where it is or if they used clean needles.'

He stood towering over me. 'I was with Paul.'

'Well, *that* makes all the difference. Is he on painkillers yet for his neck or is he still doing the milkshake blend of soymilk, protein powder and amphetamines?'

'How do you know about that?'

I went to the bathroom for tea-tree oil and shouted. 'He tried to convince me to gulp down one of these shakes before weight training. He said it would give me great definition.'

'So does rigor mortis.' He put both hands over his breast. 'No, Mr de Mille, I cannot allow you to exploit my body in this way. I am not ready for my close-up . . . '

'Will you forgodsake move? Let me put some tea-tree oil on this nipple. It's disinfectant.'

'Will it sting?'

'Just tickle for a second.' I dabbed the swollen redness with a cotton-ball soaked in the oil and covered my ears.

'You lied. My nipple's frying . . . I can smell flesh burning. You put too much on!'

I mock-stroked his brow. 'I'd back off if I was you. Thank god you don't have to wax your bikini line. So the AIDS Council has more or less accepted that Springfield will close, without a fight, without protest?'

Lawrence crawled to the fridge. 'Have you got vodka?' He found the vodka, the tonic and went sniffing for a lemon.

'I'll do it. Relax, tell me what the AIDS Council is doing.'

'No, they're not *just* accepting the closure. But if Springfield can't provide the care that's required, they have to be realistic and think about relocating.'

'But how come *all of a sudden* Springfield can't provide the same care?'

'For starters, the laboratory services are going to be moved. And it's important that all the services like outpatients, day care and laboratories be together, all on one site. There's also the last report by the Metropolitan Hospitals Planning Board. It claims that Springfield is not financially viable and that another hospital should take over the HIV/AIDS services currently provided there.'

'A report by a government-established body has decided that the hospital is no longer financially practical, according to their calculations, based on their own figures? And they're already reducing services before it's been established which hospital will take over. Have I got it right?'

Lawrence did baby-claps. 'Bravo. Now, can I have my drink? My nipple's dehydrating.'

I handed over the glass and let go before he'd had a chance to take hold of it. Acting quickly, I darted forward to grab it, slipped and landed with my nails sunk into his chest. I was wearing a ring with an adjustable band. It caught on Lawrence's new nipple ring.

'Don't move, bitch!' I looked up to view a ghostly Lawrence, all the colour blanched from his face. He spoke slowly through cheese-paring lips.

'Stand up and try – really, really try – not to move your hand.'

I slinked worm-like off my knees and onto my wedges. Without breathing, as if diffusing a live bomb, I disentangled my faux cabochon from Lawrence's nipple.

'I'm sorry.'

'Hand me the frigging vodka.'

'I'll get another glass and the tonic.'

He shrieked. 'JUST GIVE ME VODKA, THE BOTTLE, FUCK THE TONIC . . . DO YOU UNDERSTAND?'

'You can't drink it neat.'

He snatched the bottle out of my hand. 'Watch me!'

'Is there anything I can do?' He slumped into the couch, modestly screening his chest and the bottle with a silk cushion.

'Have you got any anti-psychotic tranquillisers?'

'You don't need any medication.'

'*You* bloody do.'

CHAPTER THIRTEEN

Go, and never darken my towels again.
– Groucho Marx

SIDEWAYS

'Black, black, black . . . extra strong . . . extra black . . . loads-o-sugar.' Lawrence sagged into the couch.

'Mug or cup?'

'Bucket, darl! I didn't finish telling you about last night, your mouth opened and there was no shutting it till you shredded my bosom.'

I shouted from the kitchen. 'Go on, then.'

'I need your full attention.'

'I'm here already.'

He took the mug out of my hand. 'Sit down, darl. You're not going to believe this. Are you here, are you present, strapped in?'

I nodded with a blunt frown.

'After the meeting last night at the AIDS Council I went to the Sweat Room for anonymous sex.' He turned away from me impulsively. 'Don't give me your Siggy Freud eyebrow, it's my *preferred* way of enjoying intimacy.'

'Whatever.'

'As part of my new health regime I had a joint made from red clover and peppermint tea, no tobacco, darl, so I was a bit sideways when I arrived. Not *too* sideways to notice Mr Muscular, but not stocky, *signor-rr-r-ino-oh-oh this means trouble* leaning on the bar. I parked myself at his bumper and made it clear that misbehaviour was at the forefront of my intentions.'

I did my Pollyanna face. 'How?'

'*You* know . . . '

'No?'

He inhaled through boom-gate nostrils.

'Don't be like that, I'm making a scientific inquiry.'

He continued, 'I switched my weight onto one hip, transferred to the other, made sure I was standing right in the glow of the red spotlight . . . very flattering. Then shook my tail feather till there wasn't a speck of dust left in the place.'

'Did he notice?'

'Is the Archbishop gay? We were upstairs quicker than you can say fact-finding mission.'

'Don't go there . . . I don't need to know the rest.'

'Oh shut up, I'm not telling the sizzling gourmet meaty-bites. What happened after is what's really juicy. We were dressing – he'd left his boots and socks on – so adorable!'

'What's his name?'

'God, you're so wilful . . . *Geraldo*! Now, *list-en.* He said he worked at the Premier's department. I jumped right in and asked if he'd heard anything about Springfield.'

'He works for Dupleix? Why would he tell *you* anything? And why would you believe him?'

'Not all Germans were Nazis, darl. But you're not doing a bad job of Eva Braun at question time yourself.'

'Go on.'

'He says he's seen correspondence between the State Government and an American company that runs private prisons. Dupleix is negotiating to sell Springfield, site and building, to this crew.'

'What for?'

'They wanna send American prisoners to Australia. It's an experiment to try to reduce overcrowding in their prisons. It's *progress*, according to Dupleix. They need some place to send their prisoners, we need the moolah.'

'That's completely fucking bizarre.'

Lawrence shook his head vigorously. 'Can I finish? Geraldo wanted to leak this information to the press, but was smart enough to realise that he'd probably end up dealing with some B-grade journalist who'd do a beat-up job that wouldn't go anywhere.'

'It still doesn't make sense why he'd tell you. How does he know he can trust you? And what makes him think you'd believe information delivered casually after a hypersexual encounter?'

Lawrence groaned. 'I know a lot of people. A lot of people know me. I've done a lot of work in the field.'

'Yeah, right! So you think he's been stalking you to pass on this information?'

'Well –'

'And just happened to discover that he wanted to see you in a harness?'

'There was no harness!'

'I suppose any loser could figure out which venue you'd be at on any given night of the week.'

'He's working in the department, nobody knows he's gay or that he's a Springfield outpatient.'

'He's positive?'

'Right again, Miss Pesky. Pardon me for breathing, but is that sour grape juice oozing out of your mouth? You'd better get yourself some lovin real soon, missus or you'll marinate.'

Lawrence was right. I was still plucking Pillar splinters out of my ego. That didn't stop me from raining on Lawrence's parade. 'The minute you tell anyone, Dupleix will deny it all. They'll work out where the leak is, Geraldo will lose his job, confidentiality about his HIV status and you'll get fried for slander.'

'Who said anything about speaking to journalists? *You* work it into your material, get people laughing at Dupleix. It's a wacky idea, selling off a hospital to a bunch of corporate thugs so they can export their Village People lookalikes!'

'It's not easy making this shit funny. What's really incredible is that he thinks he can get away with it. Like no-one's gonna notice.'

'He'll just spring it on us. Clever dicks. They believe they can get away with it and they might, but let's make them sweat under their designer frocks.'

'They've done a dodgy deal, for sure. They'll just write the script to fit. We couldn't prove a thing. Remember they're protected from Freedom of Information obligations. Dupleix will spew up some new shonky legislation that'll conceal the truth. All we'll get is bullshit about a *government project won for the state by an obscure private company* blah-blah-fucking-blah.'

'I'm confused. Who's the fucker, who's the fuckee?'

'The worst part of it is that, if the prison opens we have no access to what's happening inside. It's all commercial in confidence.'

'C words forever, darl . . . '

'Two women died at the Wonthaggi private prison in the last month. The official statement is that the day-to-day running of the prison is commercial in confidence.'

'What the fuck does it mean?'

'The day-to-day details of running the prison can't be released to the public because it's business, it's confidential information. They're not obliged to explain a thing.'

'I couldn't do confidential. That's why I've never applied for a job with Madonna.' He squeezed his forehead.

'This system is totally barbaric. We'll never find out how these women died. What condition they were in, how they were treated. If they got medical attention. And because Parliament can't access the information it can't do its job and scrutinise.'

'I read about this guy who suffered Attention Deficit Disorder. Small-time crim. They sent him to that new private prison out in Woop-woop and he hung himself from the shower bar with the cord from his prison-issue electric kettle. Apparently, they were warned by the Parole Board, the Human Rights and Equal Opportunity Commission before the prison opened about design flaws that allowed people to hang themselves. The turds ignored them.'

The phone gave out a screechy peal.

I hesitated, Lawrence lunged. 'Private Penis Pty Ltd, can I help you?'

He recoiled as if he'd been hit. 'It's for you.'

'Who is it?'

He looked away. I knew immediately. The voice was like a blow-torch at my ear.

'Vy didn't you call?' My mother, Bella Finkelstein, the Jewish Cyclops. 'Too beesy to gib your musser a call?' I knew the script.

'Mum, it's not a good time, I'll call you back.'

She didn't listen. 'Vy should I belief anysink you say? Last veek you promise to reeng me next veek and today is already tree days efter dat and vot do I get from you *is not a good time*.'

'I'll ring you back today.'

She was on a roll. 'Zo, tell me plees, Mrs *very emportent persen*, ven ees a goot time? Ven I'm dead mebbe? Den you be ringing and I be dead, and still you seying, *I ring back, I got cuppla days before da reega-morris set in*.'

I bit through my lower lip. 'Rigor mortis!'

'Dats vot I said.'

I raised my voice. 'There's *someone* here right now. Please hang up. I'm not saying another word.'

She thumped the handset so violently I heard it crash to the floor. Spite prevented her from picking it up. Lawrence squinted at the unpleasant sting in the air.

'I'm uncontactable until she replaces the receiver. This woman carried me for nine months but I can't speak to her for five minutes.'

We were interrupted by a loud knock at the door. Lawrence drained the remainder of his coffee and turned to open it. He blew me a kiss. 'Don't fret, it's not she of the plastic-covered furniture. Not even Satan can appear that quickly. I asked a couple of friends to drop in. I hope you don't mind? They're working on the auction with me.'

The door flung open, my olfactory system retreated in toxic shock. The fumes coming off whomever stood at the door grabbed me by the throat like an evangelist heralding the coming of God. Hairspray, foundation, eyelash and nail glue and a man-made lake of Joy perfume announced the arrival of Smokey Topaz, goddess of drag goddesses, and her soulmate, the dashing Syrian hunk, Freddy. Smokey towered to Olympian heights. Red patent stilettos and strawberry blonde *big* hair nearly provoked a thermonuclear reaction in the stratosphere. She spoke like thunder, each word crashing off the walls.

'Miss Lola Finkelstein, pleasure to finally meet you. I'm Smokey Topaz and this is my *in-am-orato*, Freddy Farkqou.'

The phone clicked with affliction before I had a chance to respond. It was back on deck.

Not even a two-second delay and it was howling again. I snatched it up like a sumo wrestler, lifting the whole thing to my mouth.

I didn't wait for her to speak. 'What is your problem? *I said* I'll ring you back as soon as I can.'

Silence.

Then, 'Lola, I'm in Melbourne for the day. Perhaps we could have dinner or whatever or whoever you eat for lunch nowadays?' The come-hither, not so high-fidelity sound of William Lisbon.

Smokey slapped both hands on her hips and pointed toward me with her perfumed chin.

Lawrence played interpreter. 'She's a tad vexed with her mother.'

She shot me a look that in every cynical twitch and flutter of her eyelashes indicated she understood.

'Mothers! No logical explanation,' she spat harshly. All three escaped to the kitchen. I was stuck listening to the flicking of William's split-ribbon tongue.

CHAPTER FOURTEEN

It's not what I do but how I do it.
It's not what I say but how I say it.
And how I look when I'm saying it and doing it.
– Mae West

DINNER and SHOW

I was the first to arrive. Sam and Umberto did like Italians, kissed both my cheeks and the hem of my skirt if I'd let them. Satisfied, Umberto examined my outfit, black patent calf-high boots, black opaque tights, body hugging, alibi-provoking, leopard-print sheath.

'*Ciao bella, bellezza al bagno.*'

These two thin, short, but perfectly formed Adonises work the floor. Silhouetted against the stark white walls, they slip discreetly between lovers, ex-wives and recently dumped or soon-to-be-exploited-again singles. The last of the triptych, Renato, the chef, makes elixir in the kitchen. I usually don't greet Renato when I arrive; I know he'll come over and find me when he's finished cooking for the night. We flirt. I ask him about his wife and family, he squirms and asks about the food.

'How's the fish? I did it specially with lotsa garlic; that way I know no-one's gonna kiss you and I don't get jealous.'

A primitive display of continental sleaze. We both know that if I responded, he'd run and hide in the coolroom with the cold meats.

Zitto was my suggestion for the venue. It translates as keep your mouth shut, as in, zip, say nothing. The room is white white. White tablecloths, white plates, curved white walls and crevices where you don't expect them. The mythological pathless path to Persephone's underworld, sensually female, receptive but not passive. The crew that serve wear wholesome, robust smiles and are unfashionably attentive.

I headed straight for the kitchen and Renato. He was like a man running for the train.

'*Bella*!' he roared.

'I'm meeting a friend. We need to be alone.'

'You gotta date!' Broken-hearted, he held a huge frying pan across his chest. 'I promise I won't disturb, but you gotta let me check him out for you. A man can tell about another man, understand what I'm saying?'

'Thanks. But I don't need to know what *you* reckon this man is thinking.'

He sliced carrots. 'I don't care what he's thinking either . . . but what he's thinking of doing, that's what's bothering me.' I peeked over his shoulder, a voyeur of vegetable thuggery. He spun around and gave me a hug, knife in one hand, carrot in the other.

'Promise me you'll stay in the kitchen.'

'Who am I, Cinderella?'

One of the other chefs busy cutting onions looked at Renato, all tears and abandonment. He let me go.

'Sure, sure, go sit down, I'll stay in the kitchen with the rats and cockroaches. Let me know if the slipper fits.'

William blustered through the frosted glass doors. Head first, shaved to a fashionable five-o'clock scalp shadow. Smart black investment trousers; simple but effective metallic grey silk shirt and, taking daytime into night, a mid-length sixties-style suede jacket.

This was not the man from the campaign launch two years before. He must have employed a stylist. Daphne couldn't possibly twitch her way through a rack of Paul Smith shirts or select today's right shade of tan Patrick Cox loafers. He slid a pie-crusty cheek across mine. A kiss. I copped a round-faced nose-full of Gucci spray-mist. His eyebrows nudged together, one smaller than the other, making a Nike flash above his eyes. It gave him the expression of a delinquent gibbon.

I didn't shag him that night. He ventured into the Straits of Shag during dinner. To be more precise, during dessert, passionfruit pudding, just after he'd finished telling me that he's 'spiritually monogamous'. I thought he was attempting satire, but realised by the expression in his contact lenses that he was earnest. 'So what you're saying is that in your *soul* you are monogamous, but your flesh – more specifically, your penis – penetrates whatever is handy?'

He relished the image. 'You make it sound so carnal. You don't quite comprehend what I mean. You see . . . ' His chin lifted the rest of his face up to god. 'I don't believe in guilt. It's a futile emotion, doesn't do anyone any good. Naturally, I don't like to hurt people.'

'But if you do, you don't feel guilty about it?'

He poured himself more wine, not offering me any, then lifted his glass to his cheek as if to warm the alcohol or cool his face. Whatever, he was settling into sly-fox mode. Conveniently, I'd donated my red riding hood to the last Brotherhood of St Laurence collection.

'Daphne and I have an arrangement. We've been married for long enough for her to understand that I'm a walking bag of testosterone. I regularly venture into aberrant behaviour.'

'Trafficking in white slaves, smuggling firearms, selling classified information, that sort of thing?'

He slipped a mouthful of dessert into his maw. 'Gosh, the pudding is tart, isn't it?'

'Doesn't Daphne get jealous?'

'Jealousy indicates insecurity. She's not insecure.'

'How can you be sure?'

'She trusts me. I would never intentionally hurt her.'

His martyrdom peaked. He scratched behind his ear with the butt of his dessert fork. 'So will you sleep with me tonight?'

'I'll think about it over dessert.'

'I'm asking you to sleep with me. I do mean *sleep*. I don't want to fuck you.'

He was an almost impossible combination of awkwardness and arrogance, intellect and dork.

I considered my options. 'With or without jarmies?'

His cheek twitched. 'Without, if that's all right with you?'

It wasn't, for a million reasons. Three that irritated my tongue and made me windy, for starters. Daphne had the smell of a woman who could appear from behind the clothes-drier and stab you with a coat-hanger. Courtesy of Pillar, I was still gun-shy. And I was bloated.

'Do you really believe that we'd be able to share the same bed and not *fiddle* about?' My guts were bootscooting.

'I'm sure of it. I'm forty-eight years old and I don't *have* to. More importantly, I don't think we should.'

'William, this is not a trick question, but what about *me*?'

'Precisely! I believe it would be an excellent way of taking us into the next level of intimacy. In one of our brief telephone conversations you revealed that you're very shy. Well, so am I, and therefore I believe this way we could be more intimate, without that pressure of having to perform. I want you to feel comfortable.'

'The answer's no. But I'm fortified by your sensitivity.'

He looked down at the remnants of the dessert we'd been sharing.

'I'm a lawyer, advocacy is my thing.'

I hoped I'd offended him. Thankfully, my brain took over from my manicure and the wake-up-you-idiot bureau registered that he had less feeling than sawdust.

Question: How many politicians does it take to screw in a light bulb?

Answer: How many can you afford?

This was the laziest seduction attempt since Gabriel did the job on Mary, soon-to-be-mother of Jesus. Call me high maintenance, but I like to feel more than a receptacle for some guy's sperm. And I was uneasy with the 'Daphne and I have an arrangement' script. Productively, William used his lack of connection to others as an advantage. He came in on cue. 'Can I ask why you've decided against tonight?'

I relished the opportunity. He'd spoken about the pressures of being a politician, continually having to work late. How he'd be away for the important things like his son's birthday. Daphne couldn't grasp that politics was all-consuming. Blah, bullshit, blah.

'I've got an important gig tomorrow night and I don't want to be distracted. Footballers don't play up the night before a big match.'

Dupleix was expected to be in the audience tomorrow, why unleash adrenalin before the gig?

He laughed, and skidded into an ugly cough.

'Should I slap your back?'

He raised a hand to indicate he wasn't choking. 'I need to stop smoking. It's not true about footballers. Surely staying with me tonight won't interfere with your performance tomorrow? I'm at a gorgeous hotel – there's a spa. You can revel in all the five-star luxuries.'

I handed him a glass of water. 'I'd be day-dreaming about you in your boxers. Plus, sleeping together doesn't follow on as the next level of intimacy from having dinner. Call me coquettish, but even a *minor* display of amorous pursuit could be helpful. Remember kissing? Heavy petting? Putting your arms around each other, that sort of rubbish? Then the rumpy-pumpy follows. Finally, when you really trust that the other person is not going to steal your dreams in the middle of the night, you sleep together.'

His eyes closed as he nodded with recognition. 'I understand. You want me to do more lobbying.'

'I'd like to be sure you don't confuse your J curve with my G spot.'

I hadn't noticed Renato trot out of the kitchen. 'Whatsammatta Bella, not enough passion in the pudding?' He squeezed my shoulder, dragged a chair over from another table and sat down.

'William Lisbon, meet Renato Bertini, the chef and one of the owners of the restaurant.'

William stood to shake Renato's hand.

I was pissed off; he'd promised to stay in the kitchen. 'Pleasure William, siddown, relax. A Sambucca to finish off your meal?'

William nodded. 'Wonderful idea, thank you.'

'And you Bella, Frangelico?' He stayed in his chair, shouting to one of the goddesses behind the bar to fix the drinks. He sniffed William all over. I was sure he'd piss on his leg. I interrupted Renato's property search.

'The meal was delicious, Ren, but don't feel like you have to hang out to be polite. I know how busy the kitchen is.'

He slapped a garlic hand on the back of William's chair and leant into his face conspiratorially. The veins on William's temples bulged and gnarled, worms trying to exit his brain. He was frozen, the proximity terrified him. He registered Renato as an intruder.

'She's cheesed off because I told her I'd stay in the kitchen. You gotta be important man, because she never asked me to keep away before. I'm only doing my job as an Italian male of the species – someone's gotta keep an eye out after her, you get what I mean?'

William's sense of triumph burned into my cheeks. 'I certainly do. But you needn't worry, it's a business meeting. Ms Finkelstein wants to be discreet about the discussions.'

We were at a round table. Renato was to my left, looking straight at William, who was directly opposite me. Without shifting my painted smile, I carefully slid my left leg out in search of Renato's other foot, the one not in his mouth. I know he likes to wear soft Chinese slippers. Bingo. I dug my heel into the tender part of his arch. William's face remained telefriendly but I heard his abdominal muscles tighten. He lunged forward. Renato grabbed the table with both hands, stopping it from toppling over. This was live dumbo-tainment. The *high-lifers* in the room who recognised William stretched in their chairs to get a better view.

Someone – it had to be William – had a tight grip on my ankle. I slid down low enough to be able to see that Renato's feet were neatly tucked in under his chair. I'd missed him, but managed to simultaneously shoe-stab William and lose the entire glass of Frangelico into my lap. Renato stood up, leaning towards my side of the table. He hadn't seen William grab my foot. I winked at him with gusto, pretending I had both feet on the ground. William, with one hand above the table, used the other to wrench my ankle between his knees. Renato swerved towards the kitchen, arms stuck out in front like a sleep-walker, yelling back at us both.

'I gotta get this wax off my hand, the candle tipped over. What happened? Bella, you need a new napkin? William?'

'I'm fine, thanks, Renato.' He needed a cold shower.

'I think Ms Finkelstein would appreciate another napkin and,' bending his baldness toward me, 'another drink.'

I opened my mouth but he jumped in before I had a chance to speak. 'Touching *is* the next level of intimacy. I'm much more comfortable right now, aren't you?'

'Shut your mouth, William, or I'll have to get you a muzzle.'

CHAPTER FIFTEEN

Some Californian people with a lot of money came to me and said they'd support me if I ran for politics. I said if I could play six weeks in Vegas and do two pictures a year, I'd do it.

– Shirley MacLaine

MIMI does DUPLEIX

Dupleix observed Lola and the audience through hooded eyelids like an astigmatic snake looking for prey. It gave him a craving for a McFeast and large fries. It was parliamentary folklore that Dupleix bypassed the City Council's building regulations to allow a McDonald's franchise right across the road from Parliament House. He ached for their apple pie like Eros ached for Psyche. The new patron saints of the Bogey, Ronald McDonald and the Hamburglar, would cast their shadows across the oldest and grandest cathedral in Melbourne. Despite the numerous pleas and petitions from Catholics, Christians and gourmet town-planners, the crucifixion went ahead. Death by sesame-seed bun. And so it came to pass that the mingled scent of percolated coffee, fillet-o-fish and unclean spirit permanently hung like loo-freshener from Dupleix's body.

The audience were polite during his speech. They sat like automatons, hearing but not listening to his rattle. When it was over they didn't applaud. He left the stage, cheeks flushed, his minders slapping him on the back, like they were beating ants out of a blanket. He signalled his driver, met William at the smoky-glazed entrance to the building and they departed, followed by a plague of Dupleix's locusts. Bridgitte, unrivalled in her talent for running in high heels, disappeared into the kitchen. In faraway suburbs she could be heard screeching at the banquet manager. All was not well in Camelot. Lola was bringing down the drawbridge and hadn't noticed that she was up to her arse in alligators.

Ignoring William, Dupleix leant over to his driver while simultaneously punching numbers on his mobile. He was seething. 'Greg, listen mate, as soon as it's safe, be a good lad, do a U-turn and find us a Maccas. Go for one with a drive-through.'

He put the phone to his ear, picking imaginary lint from his trousers again. 'Dupleix here . . . I'm not great! That bloody scruffy tart, whatsherbloody face . . . that Jewish bitch, the comedian.'

William pretended he wasn't listening but stumbled. 'Lola Finkelstein.'

Dupleix snapped at him without moving the phone from his mouth. 'Don't distract me, no, not you. Yes, Lola Finkelstein. Will you shut up and listen! Hang on a minute . . . Greg, can you put your foot down, I'm busting for a piss and a feed. Yer there? It was a fucking disaster, shut up woman, listen. Explain to me why you can't just fucking close that bloody hospital and get those arseholes into some other bloody joint?'

He rested for thirty seconds. 'Quit whingeing. OK, give them better facilities. Put a McDonald's in there, promise them whatever they want. Do you understand? I don't want delays because the AIDS Council or any other group, Parents of Poofters or Lesbians for Labradors, think that they won't get the same quality of care or facilities elsewhere. We have to resolve this *debacle,* pronto. Be in my office by eight.'

He made a fist with his jaw and punched at her response. 'I don't give a rat's arse, make sure you're there.'

He switched off the phone and loosened his tie. 'Stupid, sour-faced slag. She should get a bloody nose job, looks like she walked into the cat-flap. She'd have to give good head, no other explanation for getting that Health portfolio. Next time, she's gotta go.'

William perched on the armrest, feathers ruffled by the boorish language. Being a Libran, he hated confrontation. Dupleix removed his tie and, to William's disgust, slipped off his shoes. It wasn't the discarding of footwear that made William's skin crawl but Dupleix's socks, red with blue Indy cars. William maintained a dignified composure.

Dupleix belched at the driver. 'Oi, Greg, you idiot, you drove straight past a big yellow M. Wake up, willya?'

'Yes, sir, but you wanted a drive-through.'

'Stop the car, fuck the drive-through. You get out!'

Greg stepped out, a bundle of squints and twitches. Dupleix threw money at him and got in behind the wheel. 'Get me two Big Macs, two large fries, large Coke and a cheeseburger.' He spun around to William, 'Anything for you, Minister?'

William stared, bug-eyed and straight-backed like a whiplashed rabbit struck on the road. He didn't reply.

'I'll take that for a negative. Go, Greg . . . I'll drive around the block and pick you up same place.' Dupleix turned left at the next corner, stopped the car and asked William to get in the front with him.

'Did you screw her?' Dupleix asked in his dog-kennel voice. 'It's a pretty straightforward bloody question, do I have to do the hand actions? Did you screw Lola Finkelstein?'

William wound down the window and inhaled polluted air. 'You're utterly contemptible.'

'Don't come at me with that moral high ground shit. We all join the safari for different reasons. Some for the travel, others to view exotic wildlife and some who pay extra to pull the trigger and watch the beast fall. We need each other right now. Let's just say I've been keeping an eye on my investment. I'd really appreciate it, William, if you could maybe steer Lola Finkelstein away from the subject of Springfield Hospital.'

Dupleix opened the car door slightly and spat on the ground with self-satisfaction. 'Right now, no-one's asking questions except the AIDS Council, the patients if they're still talking, their relatives and the medical staff. The general public aren't interested in any of this shit and if we guarantee better facilities elsewhere, throw in a bit of extra subsidy, they'll shut up. But if she keeps stirring the pot and some journalist starts on a treasure hunt, stumbles against the right rock and lifts it, I'll make sure your name is all over it, Billy boy, not mine.'

William drew air through his nostrils, letting it out begrudgingly. 'I've known Ms Finkelstein for a couple of years. We had dinner yesterday for the first time. We did not spend the night together. I may see her again. What I can tell you is that if I make any suggestion at all with regard to this topic, it will seem more appealing and quicken her curiosity.'

William knew that Dupleix had a great desert between brains and feeling, a McNugget in place of his heart. Dupleix saw this as an advantage. He bragged about his ability to use a hired gun while he dealt out the arsenal behind the scenes. He had enough ammunition on William to inflict a decent surface wound to his political career, but pretended he had more.

'Bill . . . you and I both know you'd fuck a hole in the ground if it smiled at you. Maybe if you distracted the funny bitch for a bit until the contract is signed and delivered, she'd stop mouthing off about Springfield. Yer with me, Bill? I'm suggesting a little hanky-panky with a twist. You fancy her anyway, it's not as though I'm asking you to fuck a bloke.'

'I've got the picture.' Against the night sky William's face paled considerably.

Dupleix threw his head back, yawning like an overfed rottweiler.

William stretched for the door handle, Dupleix pressed the master lock. 'Grow up, Lisbon. Pick up your dummy and get back in yer seat. It's all part of life's rich tapestry.'

He placed a socked foot on the accelerator. 'Better get that Maccas into me.' He jumped out, leaving the engine running, stood behind a shrub across the road and relieved himself. Sprinting back, he stumbled on a pebble. 'Blimey, nothing like a hard-earned piss when you've been hanging on.' He sped around the block, and ordered Greg to get in the back. Greg knew not to ask any questions.

'Gregmeister, I'm driving to my next appointment. You deliver the Minister to his hotel or wherever he wants to go. Pick me up usual time tomorrow morning.'

He steered the car south down St Kilda Road, cruised past the Arts Centre, the floral clock and the Great Pyramids of Advertising. Tramlines and tree shadows scurried past along the boulevard like sleazy peddlers in a Middle-Eastern market. William wasn't familiar enough with the city to know where it was they were headed. It was obvious that Dupleix's winding in and out of back-streets was a ploy to obscure the route.

He came to a jerky halt, slid out of the car holding his shoes against his chest with one hand and grabbed the food from Greg with the other. Square shoulders and meat with preservatives striding into the night.

William checked for a street sign. 'What suburb are we in?'

'No idea. Where would you like me to drop you off?' Dupleix ran a tight-lipped ship.

'I'm staying at the Grand Hyatt.' He was in the front seat, bubbling in his own steam, host to several thousand fidgety parasites. 'The Premier and I had a bit of a chat while we were waiting for you at McDonald's, that's why I'm in the front.'

Silence.

Greg paid no attention; he, the steering wheel and the pedal were tethered in a threesome of accelerator sex. William rubbed his forehead and temple, trying to straighten his thinking. Without warning, he felt feverishly hot, slightly nauseated. His heart began to cha-cha. Practising cognitive behaviour therapy techniques, he took deep slow breaths, reminding himself that he was in control and avoided the Panic Express.

He'd always believed Dupleix was a fool, a soufflé commissar. Now it was clear the man was disturbed. He'd never witnessed such cupidity. The sooner Springfield was sold, the sooner he'd no longer be present in the madman's life. And if Lola Finkelstein was going to delay that process by creating unnecessary media attention, he'd have to set her on another course.

Romance. He'd cast a spell on her.

Eyes glistening, Dupleix scurried up the back stairs of the 40s-style flats. Each balcony, fully enclosed, masterfully gave the illusion that it held an individual universe. The smell of cat's piss and omelette collected between steps. He groaned as he made his way up. On the back door of flat 6, he impatiently tapped out his signature knock. Tap, wait a beat, tap-tap-thump.

Mimi recognised the pattern and took her time getting to the kitchen. Why did he always arrive as she was about to go to bed? Why couldn't he ring first? 'Vait, vait, I'm rushing now, I be there, just a moment.'

This was no ordinary woman but an Ottoman she-bear. A powerfully rugged beefy goddess, a jungle of dark-brown hair and Balkan breasts. Bosnian-born in a small village north-west of Sarajevo to a peasant family, she'd survived a knife-wielding, misdiagnosed schizophrenic Greek father, an almost always absent Macedonian sailor husband, the Communists, and Slobodan Milosevic. For her, J. C. Dupleix was a day at the hairdresser's. All that effort only to fall flat with the first puff. She couldn't pronounce Dupleix; she called him Doopa, Polish for arsehole. It was her private joke. She didn't have many.

'Come, come in, Doopa, vy you come so late always?'

Dupleix clumsily put his arm around her chunky shoulders. 'Don't give me a hard time.'

She could disembowel him with the lift of an eyebrow.

'I want you to read to me.' They were walking into the tiny loungeroom, Dupleix feverishly unzipping his trousers.

'You relaxing here for moment till Mimi return . . . just a minute.' Murmuring to herself, she took the five steps to the linen cupboard in the hallway and extracted the whip and the book of fairytales from a yellowing damask pillowcase.

In the bedroom she threw off the towelling bathrobe, slipped on a pair of stay-up stockings and G-string. She looked over at Tito's cage, camouflaged by the tartan rug she'd only bought him that day. Thankfully he wasn't awake to greet Dupleix with his usual screeching and chirring. Tito was jealous of anyone who came near her. His displays around Dupleix were maniacal.

In the bathroom, she made the sign of the cross. Meticulously applying lipliner and flame-red lipstick, she fashioned a bigger, fuller, pitbull mouth. She lit a cigarette, resting it on the single narrow glass shelf under the bathroom cabinet. The smoke made her squint. She knew it would soon be over and he'd be on his way home to his wife. The money would help get her brother out to Australia and Dupleix's contacts guaranteed no immigration problems. Stifling a belch, she snapped the plastic pig-nose into place in the middle of her face. She'd stopped trying to find logic in the sexual proclivities of politicians.

Sourly, she growled across the narrow corridor. 'Doopa! You must to be good boy.' She took one last drag on the cigarette, pushed the butt down the sink, adjusted her nasal prosthesis and sashayed unblushingly into the loungeroom.

'Tree Leetle Pigs, Doopa, or Jack and Beanstalk?' she cracked the whip inches from his face.

CHAPTER SIXTEEN

I did not sleep. I never do when I am over-happy,
over-unhappy, or in bed with a strange man.
– Edna O'Brien

RE-ENTRY to the DAY of the FIASCO

'Why didn't you wake me up?' I leant over the kitchen bench. Sinatra crooned 'My Funny Valentine'. Christopher had his back to the door and hadn't heard me come in. He spun around, a tea-towel frisbeed from his shoulder across the floor. He was panting. Panting and glaring at me like a wounded rabbit transfixed by a second pair of oncoming headlights. 'I didn't hear ya come in. How long ya been standing there?'

I slid off and away from the bench. 'I've only got socks on, they don't make much noise.'

He sneezed, covering his face with a paper napkin.

'Thank you.'

'What for?' He stood opposite me ready to crush garlic.

'Leaving the jumper and socks out for me. They're perfect, in an oversized kinda way. It's very thoughtful.'

He wasn't relaxed, maybe even gloomy. 'Ya told me you didn't have any leisurewear with ya, remember? Maybe not? Bumped your head pretty hard.'

He stepped out from behind the bench, came around and handed me a tall glass.

'What is it?'

'A migraine.'

I felt a throbbing pressure on the right side of my skull.

'Vodka and tonic, right?'

I rubbed the egg-shaped lump on my forehead. This switched on the ache in my lower back and elbow. Until that moment I hadn't been aware of any damage.

'Thanks for embracing my jerkdom, I'd nearly forgotten.'

I plunged into the vodka. He tapped my shoulder. Like an obedient diver I came up for air. He dropped in a slice of lemon and kissed my forehead. 'Poor baby.'

'Excuse me, what is that?'

'It's a slice of lemon.'

'I mean that lapse in your credibility.'

He humbled himself before the refrigerator, beseeching the god Thaw for hidden bounty. 'This refrigerator's part of the David Copperfield whitegoods range – ya put food in and it damn disappears. Sorry, I can't find the mustard, it's startin to . . . piss . . . me . . . off. What d'ya ask me?'

He went into head-in-fridge gibberish. What's with men and refrigerators? The thing they want can be screaming at them, but they don't see it. The mustard was tucked into the middle shelf of the door, between mayonnaise and milk. I handed it to him. He never responded to my question about his phony affection. He was preoccupied, but not with the cooking. I left it alone, this was a night off, not a Mars probe.

Showtime. Sinatra belted out 'You Make Me Feel So Young', warbled through the 'Shadow of Your Smile', 'I've Got a Crush on You', 'All of Me' and joined Count Basie for 'Makin' Whoopee'. By interval I was bloated – too much pasta, never too much Sinatra. We sat on the floor, backs on pillows against the couch. I hadn't bothered to take a good look around. The whole night had a familiar, comfortable smell. Like the jumper he'd left out for me to wear. Hand-knitted, with a gaping unravelled armpit. In spite of Christopher's initial frightened response, I unwound enough to abandon my usual search, hunt and poke-around-in-every-hole pattern.

Until I smoked the joint. Then, on cue, I set off to navigate the bottleneck of paranoia. First obstacle. I was certain Christopher had put into action the stray-dog strategy. Wait till it comes to you, then lead it home. Put out a basket with some old clothes, secure the animal with familiar sounds and enticing aromas and it will lick your hand obediently forever. I turned on him like a rabid mongrel.

'How did you know I adore Frank Sinatra and pesto and oversized hand-knitted jumpers with unravelled armpits?'

His arm shot out, grabbed the ribbed collar of the jumper and pulled my neck in towards his face like a hand-mirror. I wasn't too stoned to know that I should keep my mouth shut. His nostrils flared. Close-up, his skin needed professional extractions. My radar wasn't transmitting, I had no idea what lay ahead.

He spoke quietly but with force. 'Listen Lola, I'm knocked out that ya wanted to stay with me. But did I say anythin about sleepin together?'

'Not directly,' I mumbled.

'Not at all ma'am, your bed is in the spare room. If I wanted sex why would I put myself through this shit? Grow up. There's a truckload of women I can phone. In fact, without fluffin my own feathers, they usually call me. We get together, have fun, that's it. They're happy, I'm happy. I'd recommend a lobotomy to any guy who wants to have a sexual encounter with *you* and thinks he can walk away without his self-esteem totally demolished. Call me a hopeless invalid, but I value my sensibilities more than gettin my dick wet. *Comprendez-vous*?'

'I didn't know you spoke French.'

He released his grip. I put forward my hand to gesture a handshake. 'I never mentioned sex.'

How had he known what I was thinking? Obstacle two: was I that transparent?

He rolled onto his stomach, gesturing for an arm wrestle. 'C'mon, fight like an Amazon.'

'Please don't patronise me. Do you have a chocolate stash?'

His display of anger was reassuring. He was human and it was this hole in the wall of protocol that I fell through, finally landing on a small patch of intimacy. It was all too cosy. I began to feel anxious. I worked vigorously to suspend judgement and not to vomit. He ceased being a kvetch and laughed so hard, he cramped.

At 12.30 a.m. his sister arrived from the coast where she lives and grows hydroponic lettuce. She generally phones ahead when she wants to sleep over but this time she'd forgotten. 'I had it on my to-do list on the fridge but I *sorta* didn't check the list before I left, sorry. I'm giving a talk to the Canberra Fruit of the Month Club tomorrow so I'm *sorta* . . . distracted.'

Christopher and I stayed with vodka. Jean had a peppermint tea and went to bed. 'Great meeting you, Lola. I won't see you in the morning, I leave pretty early, so . . . uh . . . have fun, OK? Nighty-nigh, big bro.' She was younger, less brain-fagged, a female feral version of him. And she was in the spare room in my bed.

Christopher disappeared and returned triumphant with a packet of scorched almonds for me and a Scotch and Coke for himself. 'I'll sleep on the couch, you jump in my bed.'

'That's too stupid. You're frazzled, I'm overtired, there'll be tears if either one of us has to make a decision. I propose that I go back to the hotel.'

He persisted with wanting to sleep on the couch. 'Don't even think about it. The last thing ya need right now is to move to another location. The couch will work.'

'You're six feet four, this is a cosy-ish three-seater. By morning you'll need a back brace.' I stood right up against him. 'I'm shorter. Even you can see that makes more sense?'

The squabbling continued till 3 a.m.. When neither of us could figure out what to say any more we sprawled out on the floor like overfed hounds among the flotsam and jetsam of plates, cutlery, glasses and our inhibitions.

Outgunned, I suggested the obvious. 'We're adults, we're tired, this is absurd – let's sleep in the same bed,' I heard myself say and felt nothing except a breathless longing to shut my eyes and drift off.

He was cautious, hands folded behind his head, eyes closed. 'Well, I'm not sure about that. There's no guarantee you ain't gonna wake up in the morning and accuse me of orchestratin this whole episode.'

I responded with the tone you adopt when confronted with a toddler buttering bread for the first time. 'Relax, Max, I'm about as arousable as cold porridge.'

We consummated the deal with my promise that I would ignore all thoughts of his having predetermined this event and his promise to wear pyjamas. I undressed in the en-suite bathroom, re-entering in one of his T-shirts, the woolly socks and a G-string. I don't do panties.

The bedroom was as cold as a stepmother's kiss and only half-lit by the lamp on my side of the bed. I slid like noodles under the doona, not wanting to rouse him. He was making small animal-like wheezing sounds. I let my head and body fall all the way down, stretching my index finger to switch off the lamp. Rolling over onto my stomach, simultaneously slipping my hands under the front of my thighs, I faintly remembered how nervous I'd been centuries ago this morning and floated off without a life-jacket. Woman overboard.

'Lola wake-up, Lo-la.' I stirred, but didn't open my eyes. 'Lo-la . . . hey Lola, the show's over, everyone's gone home . . . the mike's off.'

Someone was prodding me. I opened my eyes. His Adam's apple

was in the middle of my face. I wrapped one arm around his neck and pulled the doona over both our heads with the other.

I went full speed astern, steering his body via primordial navigation. With no celestial guidance I skimmed his neck, glided against his chest, put the rudder hard right at his hips, slid out from underneath him and downed his flannel sails. I was hauling up, sailing close to the wind, when I felt Christopher put his arm around my waist and drag me back up towards him.

He spoke with restraint in mega-bass. 'There's something about me you should know.'

CHAPTER SEVENTEEN

I don't make jokes. I just watch the government and report the facts.
– Will Rogers

RUBBER

'Latex sensitivity?'

I felt like an exploded egg in a microwave. 'What the fuck does that mean?'

'I can't use condoms.'

'What happens if you do?'

'Headache, rash. If it's real bad, maybe asthma attack.'

I covered my mouth with both hands to speak through turquoise jewellery. 'This is so not funny.'

'I'm not joking.'

I stuck my nose in the air and inhaled to regain my poise. 'Do you own any juggling balls?'

'No.'

'Juggling compensates for sexual frustration.'

'How about golfballs?'

'Great. Talk to me about golf, that'll really explode my libido.'

Neither of us had had much sleep. Christopher leapt out of bed paramilitary style. He pulled on shredded navy-blue track pants and a faded black skivvy. 'Toast or cereal?'

I waved my hand in the air in response. 'Caffeine.'

He walked out of the room, burst back in and threw himself on top of me. He was heavy human freight.

'I can't breathe.'

He put a hand over my mouth. 'Every time ya speak, money is being transferred via a secret voice-activated PIN from your account to mine.' His other hand looked for mine under the doona.

'Ya did say coffee?'

He lifted himself off with a push-up and sat on the edge of the bed.

'Don't fuck with me, Christopher.'

'I want to be able to make this happen, but . . . '

'I don't get it!'

'What's to understand? I've got an allergy to latex. If I'd known ya were crazy horny, I'd have slept on the couch.'

'Excuuuuse me, I wasn't the one to start sniffing around the warm damp tufted parts of *your* body and I'm not *that* horny.' I'm expert at digging myself into bigger holes. 'It's not like I'm sitting on your face throwing a frisbee and yelling ride-'em pony!'

He slithered towards me, more than a worm, but less than a viper. 'Damn. I don't have a frisbee.'

I hit him across the head with a pillow. He fell to the floor and played dead.

'You're an idiot.'

'Willya please listen?'

Ordinarily, I'd have required a non-speaking, cooling-off period, but I knew our time was not negotiable. 'No-one's getting laid here, go forth and make coffee . . . my bladder's aching for it.'

He'd been gearing up for another skirmish. 'Ya aren't gonna put a rusty blade in my razor?'

'What sort of fresh hell are you living in?'

Still unbearably caught up in the mood of the moment I thought about masturbating while Christopher brewed coffee. He was back in less time than it took for me to find my genitals. Sliding a tray with two mugs and a plunger professionally on to a safe corner of the bed, he took the words out of my mouth. 'Why are you staring at me?'

'I was asleep.'

'Your eyes were open.'

'I was awake asleep. Asleep, but my eyes hadn't closed yet.'

He poured the coffee and handed it over. I didn't respond. He raised his voice, 'Any customers?'

I lifted the coffee from his grip. 'I think I'll need a couple of these.'

Sitting not quite upright, backs snug up against several pillows, it looked like a lacklustre domestic breakfast. But in my waters, I knew an alien was about to burst through the sewer. 'So, Mr Tall, Dark and Tongue-tied, speak to me.'

He spoke slowly. 'I know why Dupleix's closing Springfield. I've got details that'll encourage people to ask the right questions. The deal is, ya never ask where I get my information or what my interest is. And, ya don't ever tell anyone – and I mean *anyone*, and I mean *ever* – where ya got this information.'

'So is ASIO using low-level electromagnetic radiation to make me forget to do things like pick up my dry-cleaning?'

He was silent.

'OK, I'll keep shtoom. Why *is* Dupleix closing the hospital?'

'The State is in mega-debt. He's sold off whatever he could to bring in the cash. In the process, by installing buddies in clever positions, he's also managed to drain some bucks off for himself. He stands to make a shitload of dollars.'

A sinister chill floated out with his words. 'By eliminating the Auditor-General's department, shafting the Director of Public Prosecutions and reorganising the Equal Opportunity Commission, there's no-one left to ask questions. He doesn't expect to get busted, so he's outta control.'

I put a pillow over my stomach. 'The Health Minister's office keeps putting out releases saying Springfield is losing money and not reaching the required targets. Nobb reckons it's not viable to have a separate infectious diseases hospital. That HIV/AIDS patients would be better off getting treatment in a larger hospital with more facilities and easier access. Where does Dupleix come in? Why doesn't the Federal Government just override his decision?'

He shut his eyes and tugged at the tip of his nose.

I felt my body tighten. 'What sort of body language is that? Are you getting the shits?'

He stood rigid, expressionless, only his eyeballs tilted. 'Listen and it'll begin to make sense.'

I was up and pacing by now. I indicated for him to continue.

'Dupleix is ready to sell the hospital, land and buildings to an American private prison organisation so they can set up an experimental prison.'

My cramp clenched like a bull terrier's jaw. I deliberately held onto my head, remembering what Lawrence had said.

'What kind of experiments and for what prisoners?'

'Americans. This private company wants to ship them out of the US, bring them over here as a trial solution to their problem of over-crowded prisons. They figure that if the prisoners are in another country with no family and no contacts they won't attempt to escape.'

My blood turned saline. 'What sort of dangerous loonies are they transporting? Investment advisors to the President?'

Christopher blinked. 'Road-rage offenders.'

'WHAT?'

'Ya heard right the first time. The US Department of Corrections is delivering a jumbo-jet load of road-rage felons.'

'OK, give me the bad news. Who will the prison officers be?'

'Prison guards, Americans, specially trained. Mostly to keep their mouths shut and to supervise counselling, retraining, delegating workloads.'

I was on the floor face down, bodysurfing the pillow. 'Why not send them to Siberia . . . there's a few disused gulags just begging to be redecorated? Bold primary colours painted straight onto floorboards, designer-shredded blankets, the single-noose mobile hanging from the ceiling to create motion – it could be breathtaking!'

'They researched the former Soviet bloc, but the mileage and transport routes were a problem.'

He knelt down, face to face with me. 'Ya want Alka-Seltzer?'

'It's not anything I've eaten. Lack of sleep, maybe. Heady mix, politics and hormones.' I pushed him away. 'How does Dupleix reckon he can get away with it and why are you telling *me* this?' I clung on to hope and the pillow.

He sat cross-legged, looking at his hands. 'Dupleix's being looked after by someone higher up. I'm not sure who it is yet, but I'll find out. Dupleix's Cabinet don't know about the plan for the hospital. Dita Nobb believes it's running at a loss. Besides, she's benign. Ya have to love a woman who wears hand-knitted sweaters.'

'Are you saying that it's not?'

'The hospital is losing money, but millions of dollars could be saved if the number of beds were reduced and some kind of link established with a larger nearby hospital.'

'Like the Austin?'

'Ya got it! The two hospitals could link services. Let's say, like intensive care and infectious diseases. Maybe money could be saved from catering or gardening and those savings could be used to create more AIDS-dedicated beds in another hospital across town. As long as Springfield retains its research facilities, specialists from the newer hospitals can continue learning from hands-on, on-site experience.'

'But where does the money come from to revamp the old wards?'

'The dumb bastards have got the cash. It would cost roughly two to three million dollars. The new casino opening is being budgeted at around sixty million.'

It was raining. The light in the room was dull. The Canberra chill snuck in while Christopher spoke. I affected a power surge. 'No-one can stop me from saying anything as long as it's funny, right?'

'Wrong! Dupleix's got an eye on you.'

I sat up, propelled by righteous indignation. 'How do you know?'

'Remember the deal? No questions.' He stepped into the other room and returned clutching a fax.

'Recognise this conversation?'

I scanned the page. It was a transcript of the telephone conversation I'd had with Lawrence at the hotel in Canberra when he'd first told me that Springfield was closing.

'Shit. They've blacked out Lawrence slagging off Dita Nobb . . . all the swear words, Frank Dixon's name.' I was standing but not looking up yet. 'Where did you get this?'

'Trust me when I tell ya that Dupleix's not shy about using any available resources to stop this leaking to the press. Once the deal's signed, his arse is clean whatever happens.'

'I don't get how?'

'Exactly like all the other shit-heel deals he's been in on. His buddies are the signatories. No-one can prove a thing. In this case the US government is helping to cover his tracks because they'd rather the President not be associated with this right now. He's got enough crap happening with sexual harassment allegations and questions about funding for his last campaign.'

I managed to crack a quarter-smile. He turned away from me, rearrranging the roll-neck of his skivvy.

The room was in semi-darkness. I pushed a switch. His shadow leapt halfway across the floor and up the wall, the part of him that wanted to escape. My digestive microphone started to feedback.

I disappeared behind the bathroom door. 'Could you leave the room please?'

'What was that?'

'Get away from the door.'

Silence. A note slipped through the crack of light between the floor and the door.

I'm in the kitchen. Can't guarantee Dupleix hasn't had the S-bend wired. But if he has, you can bet it'll be digitally recorded – any hissing, blurping, woomping, squeals and static will be removed. Enjoy.

CHAPTER EIGHTEEN

Hydra: A monster with many heads slain by Hercules: whence any multiplicity of evils is termed a hydra.
– Samuel Johnson's *Dictionary*

the FICKLE FAX

I arrived at my flat grimy with cobwebs of lust, dialled Lawrence's number and babbled into the answering machine.

'It's me, I've been filthy with the man in Canberra, ring me.'

My stomach was still in sick bay, fluctuating from greasy-spoon cramping to five-star gourmet flatulence. But my appetite knows no shame. I ventured out for a maternal chicken soup at the Klutz and Kishkes, a cafe as famous for its cabbage soup and table-top sized schnitzels as its smorgasbord of waitresses.

The cafe buzzed with the friction of polyester against nylon gussets. An Amazon swaggered over. 'Goot eefening, madam, vot you vont to eat tooday?'

I looked up into the face of a swamp goddess, hypnotic blue eyes like cavities in her head tugging at my curiosity. 'Chicken soup, please.'

She shoved the pen between her teeth, the order book under her armpit, and grabbed a clump of vagrant frizz about to leap from her topknot. 'Joost a meenit, excoose me, seez hair shoot be chopped, vood be making me less nairvoos. OK, OK, now repeet me pleeze, joost chicken zupa?'

'Yes, that's right.'

She grabbed my chin with a hand the size of Poland. 'You don't look goot, missus. If is tummy problem you shootn't hev nothing fatty, if it's man, also you shootn't hev nothing fatty and you shoot forget him. I breeng zupa, but I don't bring bread, you don't need bread.'

That's why I come here. For an hour someone else takes control. Decisions are made; I shut up and wear it. It's a humbling experience being bullied by a Slavic sorceress with foreign hair and over-enthusiastic breasts. She returned with a glass of water and cutlery. Squeezed into a hip-hugging pencil skirt stretched agonisingly over her belly and broad-jump thighs, she set the table. Her legs were protected by tan pantyhose over which she wore socks with white plastic Cuban-heeled mules. Wild combo.

It was an ergonomically cool look, practical, but *à la mode* at the same time. I couldn't wait to try it myself. To look into her face I had to squint past the glare of her chaos. The left-turn smirk she handed over was worth it. I wanted to know her.

'I'm Lola.' I held out my hand, she leant over and grabbed a fistful of my cheek.

'Mimi.'

'It suits you.'

She frowned in a nanosecond of deep thought. 'Is better than Fatima. I breeng your zupa.'

She smelt of chicken fat, onions and despair, an olfactory sensation I was familiar with. What was her story? Where did she get her mules?

Lawrence should be here by now. I phoned to check my messages. 'Howdy, Princess, I'm fresh out of the frying pan. What man in Canberra? Too many loose ends, call me.'

I rang before the soup arrived.

'Go ahead, I'm listening.'

'It's me, get your arse to the Klutz cafe in Acland Street. It's the one next to your favourite cake brothel. You know the one?'

'Well, girlfriend, who's got a dose of the pushy virus? I'll be there as quickly as you can say, I'm a *top*!'

Mimi delivered juice of dead chicken. 'You must to eat dis before it's too cold, you understanding?'

I humoured her by smiling like a three-year-old, swivelled around and picked up a newspaper from one of the other tables. The elderly couple sitting there didn't hear me ask if I could read it. Both deaf, spluttering at each other with Holocaust accents to pass the butter. Both faces draped with translucent skin, both scalps littered with clumps of white hair. Both mouths talking, while both sets of dentures bumped and grinded through the food. Lambada for gums. Did they starve in the concentration camp? Does their deafness stifle the ancient but still clear howls of torture in the shadows? They survived; they deserve to make as much noise as possible.

IT'S OFFICIAL: SPRINGFIELD TO CLOSE. The headline hit me like a left jab. Confusion and pain. Unknowingly, I was poking the butter knife into my left breast while I read:

The Health Minister Dita Nobb announced today that Springfield Hospital will close by July of this year. This announcement follows the recently released Final Report of the Metropolitan Hospitals Planning Board which has made a series of recommendations about the future of Melbourne's hospital system. One recommendation was that the first State-wide service to go to competitive tender should be infectious diseases, including HIV/AIDS. These services are currently provided by Springfield Hospital. To tender infectious diseases is to close Springfield.

My hand turned into a fist supporting my head. I withdrew into the paper so totally that I didn't notice Mimi flip-flop towards me. Startled by the grizzly snarl as she snatched the newspaper, I leapt up quickly to move away from the table. My foot had gone to sleep without saying goodnight, and I went down awkwardly on my left side. Grabbing the tablecloth in a triple treat of chook soup, cutlery and embarrassment, I only barely missed drilling my eye out, because the plate, thanks to the laws of gravity, landed on my face before the knife did. The noodles trickled down my damp, steaming bosoms, a shipwreck of albino earthworms.

Mimi wiped them off me with a rancid-smelling tea-towel, which stung even more. She was crouching over me. 'Vy you been reading when you shoot be eating?'

I raised myself onto one knee. She reached out to give me her hand. I ignored the gesture. 'It's none of your business. I come here to eat, I pay, I do what I want.'

She gave me a blank look. Mr and Mrs pass-me-the-butter kept filling their mouths with bread. They were submerged in the diving bell of atrophy, they heard nothing.

Lawrence came bounding through the door wearing black and a pale young man. He tilted his head bull terrier-like but said nothing. I stood all the way up and gestured to Mimi.

'This is Fatima, she's the good-manners Gestapo.'

She stood like a giant date palm, hands on hips, eyes moist from the humidity. 'I not wanting to teach. I forgetting dis place is not my home, and not my country and I must to do like you people and be more minding my own business. Let me to clean up the mess, you go sit with your friends over there and I breeng again.'

She pushed all three of us onto another table, marching back briskly with menus and a fresh soup. She was too silent. I put my hand around her wrist as she replaced cutlery. 'I'm sorry I yelled.'

She parachuted in without missing a beat, loud and lashing. 'Exact-ly vy I'm taking the paper from the table! You get angry, your guts squeezing tight.'

Her face folded like a concertina. 'The food sits rotten in da bowels.'

Lawrence raised his eyebrows and did that expression of boneless lamb that always gets my attention. 'Lola, Geraldo – he works in the Premier's department.'

Mimi glanced at Geraldo, as if begging him to vanish. She winked at Lawrence. 'Cen I take your order pliss?'

'No pork on my fork. Veal schnitzel, thank you.'

Geraldo wanted dialogue with the cabbage soup. 'I like to glance at the menu until something talks to me.'

Was this the true state of affairs in the Premier's department? Is our public service supervised by experts in asparagus speak? Mimi scudded off to order from the shadows in the kitchen. Lawrence took over. 'I thought you two should meet.'

Geraldo spoke in a smooth, compact, filing-cabinet voice, never gesticulating with his hands, as if expecting to be slapped if he did. He sat straight-hipped, feet on the floor, hands folded on the table in front of him. His small, dark eyes, set too far back in a wide bull-dog face, made him look permanently rejected. He began by frowning.

'Lawrence has told you that I know why Dupleix is closing Springfield. You find this incredible?'

'Sure, it's incredible. Nobb woman says the hospital is running at a loss, based on some report. Dupleix's name hasn't come up once.'

He swallowed hard. 'He's orchestrated this deal so he's not implicated in any way. He's the master of satanic cunning.'

Lawrence shuddered. 'Darling, I wouldn't go there, Dupleix's not that smart . . . or that attractive. I've always believed that Satan is a New Romantic and looks like Adam Ant did in 1980, all frills and ruffles and tight leggings in high black leather boots . . . '

I had to stop him. 'Get a grip, we're talking about Dupleix.'

I nodded for Geraldo to continue.

'Dupleix's been approached by an American private prison contractor from Tennessee, inquiring about sites for a trial off-shore prison experiment. They've made no secret of the fact their penal system is in crisis. Overcrowding is a major problem. They need more space to house their prisoners at an affordable price.'

'How did you find this shit out?'

He unfolded his hands only to hide them under the table.

Mimi arrived with a tortured smile and the rest of the food. 'Excuse-me pliss, one cabbage zupa, schnitzel and Lola for you I order small-size chicken schnitzel . . . enjoy . . . compliments of Mimi.'

To anyone watching, it appeared we'd stopped breathing.

'Ees everysing OK?'

It was obvious she was curious to know what we were discussing. She'd gone weird when she'd heard that Geraldo worked in Dupleix's office. She glanced at Geraldo and out of the corner of her eye noticed that I was watching her.

'Thanks, that's great, chicken schnitzel . . . exactly what I wanted . . . matches the soup on my shirt.'

She cast her eyes on Geraldo. 'Be careful, deh plate ees very hot.'

She moved out of earshot, Lawrence and I went back to Quasimodo positions and Geraldo rang his bell. 'I was in the department about six months ago when a pile of faxes came through from the Premier's office. His people and our department are in the same building, different floors. I'm with the Ministerial Liaison Unit.'

He put his hand at his neck, clutching an imaginary string of pearls. 'I deliver letters to the policy officer in the unit; they draft replies to whatever correspondence is relevant to their area. What generally happens is that the Premier's private secretary sorts out the correspondence he needs to see and puts it in the IN tray. Dupleix then scans through it and it goes off to different departments for responses.

'Dupleix responded to the Americans' inquiries about sites for prisons and stupidly put the letter upside-down in the OUT tray. He then put another three letters on top of that one in the same tray and, on the last one, attached a sticky note asking his secretary to fax the pile to several different departments for responses. The secretary comes in the next morning, Dupleix is interstate, she picks up the stack, all A4 white paper. She removes the sticky note, shoves all the letters in the fax machine, punches in the numbers, sends them off and walks away. But, she leaves the keys to a filing cabinet on top of the fax machine, so she's back in three minutes and notices the letter stamped HIGHLY CONFIDENTIAL disappearing down the fax machine. Are you with me?'

We were both panting. Lawrence bit his nails. 'Don't stop, I'm right there, I *am* that secretary.'

'She stops the machine, but one set has already gone to the first number, which happens to be my department.'

My head dropped onto my chest. I felt the weight of the State on my shoulders.

It was Mimi's leviathan palm. 'Vy you not eating, cold schnitzel tastes like old stocking?'

'We haven't seen each other for a long time.'

I willed her to go and make pancakes from any garment she desired. Lawrence poked Geraldo in the shoulder. He had a teensy blobette of saliva in the corner of his mouth. I blotted it with the napkin. He began again.

'It's almost 9.30 a.m., I hear the fax machine, I walk over to pick up the paperwork. The phone rings. It's Melanie, Dupleix's secretary. She's speaking so fast she sounds like she's been body-snatched by aliens.'

He cleared his throat, pretending to be Melanie. '"Ger-al-do . . . this is Mel-an-ie spea-king, don't touch the faxes till I get there. Do you un-der-stand, Ger-al-do. Your life is worth less than an ant's if you dis-obey me."

'I didn't let on the faxes were in my worthless ant's hand and that I'd spotted the highly confidential stamp. In the four minutes and twenty seconds it took her to arrive at my office I shredded everything, except the reply to Tennessee Shackles, signed by the Premier and confirming that the site of Springfield Hospital would be vacated in the next six months and it may prove to be the ideal location for Operation Road Runner.'

I positioned a piece of old stocking in my mouth and spoke, not anticipating the breadcrumb shower effect. 'What happened when she got there?'

They closed their eyes to avoid schnitzel shrapnel.

'She clutched the originals in her hand, whiter than the A4 she was. Her eyes widened like huge mushrooms and seemed to spring in and out of their sockets like a wind-up toy. She pulled me towards her.

'"Geraldo, did you touch that correspondence?"'

He shrugged and smiled. 'I'm real good at playing obedient . . . I told her what I knew she wanted to hear. There were *no* faxes, sweetie. If you cancelled as they went through then you aborted the process. Please love, sit down, can I get you a cup of tea?'

CHICKEN SOUP

The great Jewish all-purpose-cleanser. Domestos for the insides, it cures everything from gut-ache to nasal-tinea, only currently it's not fashionable. Young urban Jews, wanting to dump their kosher stock have embraced a more gentile kitchen.

Sushi, laksa and Singapore noodles are the current feast displayed on designer dinnerware. As it happens, chicken soup has always been served with noodles, but they're not angel-hair pasta and the chicken is not free-range so it's not sufficiently socially integrated. Ergo, chicken soup with noodles is not hip enough, not cool enough, not sexy enough and, most shockingly, it's served in that least provocative of all utensils, a soup bowl.

Jewish guy gets stopped in the street and asked, 'Would you like to have super sex?'

'I'll just have the soup.'

CHAPTER NINETEEN

Don't be humble, you're not that great.
– Golda Meir

CLUB TONGUE

Two messages from Christopher on my machine: 'Howdy, ma'am, just makin sure that ya got home in one piece. Hope you've removed that bayonet from your stomach. Thursday 9.30 p.m., give me a call.'

Later: 'Hey, Lola, I just got a carton of milk outta the fridge and noticed your message. Thanks, call me, I'll be up late.'

Moments before we left for the airport, while Christopher manoeuvred his car out of the tiny garage, I arranged his alphabet fridge magnets diagonally across the freezer door to read WONDER-SHLONG. It was too late to call him now. My capacity for listening had been exhausted.

I attempted to collect and dispose of the day's lint from the cerebral dryer. The banjo theme from that 80s epic *Deliverance* repeated its chorus in my head. I imagined a posse of escaped hill-billies in Holden utes terrorising elderly women in white hats, three abreast in a powder-blue Volvo, on their way to play bowls.

A prison, chockful of American road-rage offenders, fifty minutes from the CBD? This had to be a joke. A TV producer's idea for an episode of 'TV Producers' Dumbest Ideas'.

Only sleep would make them all disappear. Maybe. I lay down across the width of the bed face-up, arms bent, palms crossed under my head. Eyes wide open, unfocused, portholes into a brackish unconscious. I tried to decipher the truth by writing notes in the dark with a lazy, sleep-deprived finger.

Bullet point one: Why is Christopher Pillar warning me about Dupleix? Why is he offering me this information and encouraging me to write it into my stand-up? The last time I appeared on television doing political material the producers edited my eight-minute spot down to three sentences. I came across like a dickhead, what I said didn't make sense and, more embarrassingly, it wasn't funny. They'd excised the funniest bits. I don't have solutions, I'm a comedian. It's part of my job description to look out for and expose the truth. If I don't tell the truth, I'm not funny and if I'm not funny, I don't eat. Truth helps me maintain correct body weight.

But is Pillar telling the truth? I pushed the tiny switch on the Japanese lamp and punched out the number I'd memorised.

Two rings later he answered. 'Pillar.'

I hadn't looked at the time. 'I can't sleep.'

He spoke in a whisper. 'I'm too far away to gib ya a back wub.'

'Oh my god, you've had a stroke in your sleep. It happens. I'll call triple 0 . . . they'll send an ambulance. Can you hear me? Can you move? Try wriggling your toes.'

He shrieked down the phone like a man about to split a brick with his bare hand. 'Lawh-la, thut-da-fuck up! I'm OK!'

I stayed silent. I'd read that out of fear and frustration the stroke victim, in an attempt to deny symptoms, can be very aggressive in the initial stages. I was shaking, simultaneously quivering with fear and the realisation that he would never be the same again and that I should have fucked him when I had my chance.

He inhaled so deeply I thought he'd suck the phone out of my hand. He spoke in a deep bronchial, exorcist tone. 'I habn't had a thoke. Da dop of da doofpaste tube was dight, I twied to skew id off wiff my teef.'

He paused, homesick for normal speech. 'I've bidden righd drew the dip of my tongue. Ids very bad right now bud id'll be fine in a couple of days.'

My informant bites through the tip of his tongue trying to open a tube of toothpaste with his teeth. Convince me there's no such thing as karma.

I hinted at being helpful. 'Have you been to a doctor?'

'Id only happened a couple of hours ago, afder I left ya dose messages.'

I heard the smile come across his face. 'I lubbed da fridge art.'

'I guess you're off the road for oral sex?'

'Dats why you're callin at doo a.m.?'

Interrogating him was futile, he could barely enunciate. 'Your message said to call you back.'

Silence for a few seconds till he unravelled the puzzle. 'Da AIDS Council, thpeak to the prethident aboud da dendering process.'

It was frustrating. 'Dendering?'

'Hospitals den-der-ing to get the thervices from Springfield. Da thervices they're goin to thplit up. D'ya underthand?'

I repeated the word, *dendering*, out loud. It clicked. 'You mean tendering, as in other hospitals tendering to take over the different services currently at Springfield?'

He tapped in triumph on the mouthpiece. 'Bingo.'

'Think of Helen Keller and consider yourself fuckin lucky.'

I was getting that swaying vibe that indicates the sleep tide is in. It was too depressing trying to get information out of Captain Club-tongue.

'OK, I'll call Joshua Newbroom in the morning. Thanks, good-night.'

I heard his offer of *thweet dreams* as I hung up to follow my own route to night-time tooth-grinding and interrupted breathing.

Seconds after, the phone rang, only a half-ring followed by a peculiar whirring sound. I put my ear right onto the thrumming matt-finish plastic and addressed the *hash* button sotto voce.

'Fuck you, whoever you are!'

Would Joshua be willing to talk? He'd only recently succeeded in being voted in as President of the Aids Council, in spite of a campaign of slander by opposing factions within the organisation. His sharp mind, caramel style and administrative skills gleaned as a political adviser scored him a victory on the day. He was a pro. But he hadn't anticipated the slithery antics of Barry Compostella and his conga-line of carnivorous toy poodles. This gang, fuelled by rage, in some cases, born of the uncertainty that is being HIV-positive, had succeeded in creating such havoc that the organisation was losing political credibility. Joshua knew that without credibility there would be no force or funding. His gig was to plaster the fractures, bind the splits and bring back some morale into the organisation.

I figured he probably didn't much trust anyone right now, but we have a history from his days with the AWU. He'd fax me useful information that he thought could be funny. Our friendship bypassed all the defensive bravado. Joshua is a living, breathing, political success kit: everyman height, everyman weight, schoolboy charm, backstreet cunning, old-lady blue eyes and a dentally diaphanous smile. Mix with water. Instant politician in a cup.

I woke myself up snoring. The phone really woke me but when my eyes opened, I was snoring. I moved my lips but no sound came out.

The voice on the end of the phone took control. 'Hello, is this Lola Finkelstein's number?'

I recognised the pointy bits on the end of his words. 'Morning William, *arhmn, arhmn*, my voice is AWOL this morning.'

I moved the phone away from my mouth, heaving to full capacity to flush out my throat, but careful not to blow out his sphincter.

'Did I wake you?'

'No, not at all, I always lie in my bed from around 11 p.m. till 8 the next morning.'

I noticed the time. 'Why are you calling me at 7? Are you in Queensland or some other weird time zone where it's 10 a.m. the day before, three years ago?'

'No, actually, I'm in Canberra.'

'Well, there you go, 10 a.m. June 1939.'

I heard his mobile ring. 'Excuse me, will you?'

I could barely hear him, he had his hand over the mouthpiece. I was sure I heard him say Springfield, but it was like listening through heavy traffic with earplugs on.

'Sorry about that, depressingly busy time, masses of activity with Medicare. Two staffers off sick. I'll be in Melbourne tomorrow. Could we have dinner?'

He had to know about the plans for Springfield's closure. It would be useful for Labor's credibility to butt in and save the hospital. The Opposition is popular in Victoria, and Dupleix's weakness has always been Health. If Labor wanted to connect with its people again saving Springfield would be a surefire winner.

'Can I call you tomorrow morning to confirm?'

He sounded flat. 'Certainly, you've got my mobile number. Call anytime, day or night.'

'Don't you sleep?'

'I'm sad to say I don't very much. I suffer from clinophobia.'

'Cleanaphobia? What is that, fear of vacuuming?'

'*Clinophobia*, it has to do with going to bed. Fear of the devil, darkness, ghosts, that sort of thing.'

'You have a phobia about going to bed?'

'Not precisely about going to bed, more a fear of dreaming, nightmares, encountering monsters.'

'Maybe you're confusing your dreamworld with your waking life?'

He ignored the free consultation. 'I have to be in a meeting shortly, I'll hear from you tomorrow?'

'Absolutely.'

He rushed off to play grown-ups with the other lads. I had my own moves to make and I needed to make them creatively.

But first, a high-protein kick. Breakfast was mock omelette: one yolk, four whites with ersatz cheese, 97 per cent fat free. It's yellow, does all the cute cheesy things like melting, but tastes like crayon.

'Joshua, Lola Finkelstein. Long time no speak?'

I'd found Joshua at his day job, Dallas, Topper and Silverberg, a law firm that specialised in work-related injuries. He was friendly, but couldn't discuss Springfield on the premises. We agreed to meet at one of those tucked away inner-city cafes where the tables are too close for the waiters to walk between. Predictably, they bump into the back of your head and with the neatest smile spill a little of each item down your neck.

Joshua Newbroom stepped in from the Melbourne drizzle in a margarine-tone mackintosh. The damp pinkish glow of his cheeks, raindrops on his face and eyelashes gave him a fresh-out-of-the-womb look. I checked his belly to be sure the cord was cut. I was seated at a coaster masquerading as a table and couldn't stand up to welcome him for fear of slashing the ear off the neighbouring diner.

I flew non-stop business class to my destination. 'Joshua, I want to write some stuff about the pending closure of Springfield. I don't understand the tendering process. How the Victorian government can justify its closure. I thought, who better to prod than the president?'

He gave me a wormy look before checking the menu. 'We'd better order first. I've got to be back at the office in an hour.'

He chose pumpkin soup, I flirted with the pesto, but was finally seduced by salad niçoise. We ordered.

He spoke unhurriedly, like a dentist gently inserting an anaesthetic needle. 'No-one wants Springfield to close. Based on an assessment by the Metropolitan Hospitals Planning Board, it was recommended that services across the entire hospital network should go to tender. And the first service to go to competitive tender should be Infectious

Diseases, including HIV/AIDS. Currently Springfield provides these services. The tendering process is therefore predicated on the closure of the hospital.'

I heard him but couldn't listen. 'Joshua, you've already accepted that the hospital will close – I don't get it?'

He lifted a spoon of steaming pumpkin mush to his lips, blowing on it first. 'There's no doubt that Springfield is an important institution.'

'So why is fungus-face insisting it close? Doesn't it match her cardigan?'

His smile gleamed like a blade. A bald Salvador Dali wannabe shunted away our plates and wiped my face with his moustache. I was way overstimulated and steering into the thin strip between fury-lite and full-strength fury. 'Do you really believe that putting it out to the bidder with the sexiest prospectus will ensure the same quality of service?'

Joshua grabbed the wheel. 'This isn't new. There's been ongoing uncertainty around Springfield's future for years, long before Dupleix. It's not feasible to have a hospital that specialises in only one area.'

'According to who? The duke of expediency and his gang of sniffer swine?' I took a sip of espresso and choked.

'Where did you learn that?' He'd used the Heimlich manoeuvre.

'Breathe in . . . stop talking.'

'OK. What guarantee do you have that the existing independent facilities on-site, like the laboratory and the research centre,' I faltered, my chest heaving, 'which everyone knows make for speedier *and* more accurate diagnoses, won't be spread across half the fucking State? Call me an idiot, but it's bullshit to say that it's uneconomical to have a specialised service with experienced experts in the field.'

Joshua jumped in. 'They've done all sorts of modelling to predict the best outcome.'

'For who? Nobody would ever suggest replacing the State's major renal or cardiac unit with general practitioners with no prior history in those areas, but that's exactly what this government's planning for HIV and AIDS.'

'Hold on just a minute . . . ' Joshua tried.

'Who's gonna wipe the blood off the tracks, Joshua, because you and I know there'll be heaps of corpses buried in the night?'

He looked down at his watch and back up at me. 'I believe that engaging with the government in the planning of the relocation *is* the only way to secure a beneficial outcome. We've got a series of minimum conditions that would have to be implemented.'

'Your conditions don't matter a flying fuck. Dupleix's already agreed to sell the hospital buildings and site to an American private prison organisation.'

He went the colour of clay.

I didn't hesitate. 'They're planning an experiment.'

With mock nonchalance, he crossed his knees. 'Who is?'

I pulled my head back in, shoulders down and made sure both feet were on the floor. 'Americans. The penal system in the US is fucked, they're chockers, run out of space. Judges have been forced to stay the sentences of convicted criminals for lack of space to incarcerate them. There's even a name for this procedure, "convicted without correctional space". As a creative solution, some constipated meat-head swallowed a sachet of laxatives and came up with the idea of exporting their criminals. Kinda like the way they export all their dodgy pharmaceutical drugs to Third World countries.'

Joshua gulped water.

'Foul taste in your mouth?'

'Go on.'

'The US Bureau of Prisons came up with the idea and an independent private prison organisation took over. As a preliminary exercise, they contacted the appropriate authorities in a handful of countries they thought might want to cooperate, Dupleix's office was one of them. Snap. They found their boy. He couldn't have wished for a better Christmas-stocking filler.'

He inhaled like a man about to ignore the truth. 'Lola, these are very dangerous allegations. Where did you get this information?'

'I can't tell you,' I said, a bit too sharply. 'I think I know where you're coming from. I understand that this is not what you need to hear when you're about to start concentrating on the process of tendering. But the hospital hasn't closed yet. Maybe there's a way to delay the process.'

I tried for a smile.

'I appreciate what you're trying to do, I know you're being encouraged by others who don't want to see the place close. But it's inappropriate for me to ask the Health Minister if she knows anything about Springfield being sold off to some private prison organisation.'

'Of course you can't do that. She probably doesn't even know herself, Dupleix is not really into sharing. And even if she does, she'll deny it.'

'How do you know your source is bona fide?'

'I could ask you the same question. Trust me, if an opportunity arises for you to publicly query her about the findings of the Metropolitan Hospitals Planning Board, the journos will take over. Let them ask the sticky questions, that's their gig. That way, your position on the evaluation committee isn't jeopardised. I'll be out there doing gigs, ACT UP will distribute leaflets and the gay press will continue with their own guerilla tactics. Collective butt-kicking.'

Joshua asked for another napkin to blow his nose. He held onto his nostrils, shuddered, jerked, spluttered, collapsed deep into his seat. 'You've got to understand that it is more than likely that Springfield will close. What's really crucial at this juncture is to try to ensure that a new location will provide the same standard of services. Engaging with the government in planning for this relocation is the most productive way to secure the outcome we want.'

'I'm not convinced that the government gives a shit. They agree to everything in principle, then they'll find some reason why the research laboratories have to go to one site and the resource centre to another.'

He smirked at the deserted cutlery.

I insisted. 'This could force them to agree to everything you want, like a site for HIV/AIDS services on both sides of the river.'

I was looking into the face of a man who was being buried alive. 'Maybe, but the other aspect to this indecision is the incredible stress it's causing patients who have a life-threatening disease. I know the hospital's closure will be devastating, but once we've grieved we can get on with relocating and re-establishing confidence. It's far worse not knowing what the future is at all.'

'But isn't that what HIV is all about?'

He got up to leave. 'Springfield's sense of community could never be reproduced. But if our conditions are met, and the government continues its commitment to services and research, we'll have the best of what Springfield had to offer – access to better facilities and an extra location. In the long term that can only be good.'

'Sure. Father Christmas lives in the North Pole and there's a pot of gold at the end of the rainbow. Problem is, Dupleix owns the road construction permit from the valley of dry bones to the rainbow municipality. Good luck!'

He stepped back out into the one-way traffic. My mobile barked. Lawrence, doing mock-French in a squeaky concertina voice. 'He-llo cherie, have I got a leetle somesing for yew.'

'Has someone got a hold of your balls?'

He cleared his throat. 'Miss Bossy made a comeback, has she?'

'I just had lunch with Joshua. He's resigned to the idea that Springfield's closing and there's not much we can do about it. He's convinced that Nobb is the best option. He's worn out, doesn't believe the prison stuff.'

'Poor love, he's being stoned from all sides. Goes with the territory. You know what they say – if you can't stand the heat, get out from under the dryer. Now, listen, list-en, I can't talk, can't explain, but I'm at the Aids Council. Get your arse down here pronto. Byeeeee.'

CHAPTER TWENTY

Q: What do snakes do after a fight?
A: Hiss and make up.
– Pundemonium

the LETTER

Lawrence can make ballyhoo over nothing, but in my waters, I knew it was more than his usual thirst for drama. I got in the car, switched the radio to the hurry station.

There was a 'Baby on Board' sign in the rear window of the Pajero in front of me. Call me a psychopath, but I see one of those signs, I want to drive straight into the back of the car. What am I supposed to do? Drive past cheerfully, make goo-goo eyes? Sing a lullaby?

I made the quick-tempered trip from the city to Prahran, where the Aids Council building is. Last quest, to negotiate a parking space among the skittish South Yarra soup ladles. I squeezed in between a Cherokee and a Range Rover, their intrepid owners having crossed all that rough terrain between Toorak and Prahran. My head was still in the carpark when I arrived at the building. It took a few minutes to register the gaggle of journalists standing around fidgeting, sucking on cigarettes, method-acting being journalists.

A double for Columbo tapped me on the shoulder. 'Lola Finkelstein, how do you feel about what happened here today? What prompted this violent action? What does it say about the Health Minister's pending decision to close Springfield Hospital?'

Lawrence hovered at the top of the front stairs. He spotted me, straddled several steps, lifting me up and over the small but frothy crowd. I was disoriented but impressed. 'Soooo butch!'

He raised his eyebrows in an I-don't-need-this-shit expression. As he pushed me through an office door, I saw blood all over the reception desk. I tugged full force on his leather vest and made him stumble.

'What the fuck happened here? Was there a shooting?'

My head started to float off, the aftermath of dark threatening forces. I imagined the worst. I was fifty steps ahead of myself, like an old washing machine gone feral, on overload, out of balance, agitating and rumbling my way out of the laundry onto the verandah, about to hurl over the edge. I screamed like a two-year-old, 'LAWRENCE . . . what happened?'

He grabbed one arm, tucked it behind my back police-enforcement style, covered my mouth with his other hand, and headed for a small windowless room. Dishevelled and muttering, he slammed the door shut behind him. His eyes were the size of large pizzas. I was trembling.

'Howthefuck can I tell you what's happened out there in the foyer, with photographers drooling over every detail?'

I had homoeopathic Rescue Remedy in my satchel. I passed it over to Lawrence. He inhaled it.

'You dickhead, it's Rescue Remedy.'

'So's amyl!' He threw it down his throat like a shot of vodka.

'It's not as bad as it looks. Two hours ago some scone came in, lost his noodle and threw red paint all over the receptionist and ran out before we had a chance to get a good look at him.'

'So no-one's been wounded?'

He sat on the floor, back against the wall. His head slid and dropped toward the door. 'We're all wounded, darl. This guy happened to explode today. Who knows what prompted him? Maybe he'd just lost a lover? Maybe diagnosed positive? Shit happens.

'I wanted you here because it'll make the news. Nobb woman and her trolls will twist this into a major negative and right now, we need all the time we can get.'

'Has somebody phoned Joshua?'

'He arrived the same time as you did, came in the back way. He's here somewhere . . . being poked and prodded. A small group of gnats is conspiring against him because they think their needs are being ignored and that he's being Mr Compliant. Submitting to the Minister in order to feather his own political nest. Till now, they've played childish passive–aggressive mind games. Now, they've progressed to aggressive–aggressive arsehole behaviour.'

'Like what?'

'Today someone put the word out pretty snappy – there were photographers on those steps in ten minutes. At lunchtime on a Friday, when most of them are at the pub, wrapping their lips around a beer bottle. Give me a break!'

'I don't recognise all the ingredients in this goulash, but the in-house politics seem so irrelevant right now.'

Lawrence checked outside and shut the door again. 'Settled down a bit. I asked Smokey and Freddy to meet us here. We need to organise a benefit to raise money for the volunteers working round the clock at the hospital.'

'I heard on the news that there's been a breakdown in the negotiations between health unions and the network that runs the hospital.'

'Exactly. Our people are being asked to do more work because of bans in place across the entire network.'

'*Another* benefit? Jee-sus, Lawrence! That means I'll have to get a new frock. I can't possibly wear anything those bitchy queens have seen before.'

'Ohmygod! You *are* a gay man trapped in a woman's body.

My ex-boyfriend Joseph used to say, "You're born naked and you die naked. Everything in-between is drag."'

A voice burst in, jumped off the walls and took possession of the room. 'Did someone say DRAAAAAG?' Smokey rode in on an imaginary horse with her invisible posse. She bootscooted over to me, craning to look down my cleavage. 'Not bad. Did you get those with Fly Buys?'

A hot pink cowboy hat sat perched on her bouffant like a bird in its cage. I tried to slap it off but it didn't move.

'They're originals, if you don't mind.'

She cocked her head and sneered in disbelief. Freddy swaggered in looking like he had just stepped out of the barber's chair. He swerved his head out to the foyer. 'What went down out there, it looks like a war zone?'

Lawrence was over it. 'It's just red paint, forget about it, darl . . . new hair, very sexy.'

Smokey sat on the end of a chair, wrestled her boots off and threw them out of the window. 'Leave them there, they're so *live* with streptococks they'd kick anyone who tried to pick 'em up.'

'It's streptococcus,' I said.

'Go tell someone who cares. I'm soooo hungover my feet have got a head on them. Has anyone got a Panadol?'

Lawrence reached into his satchel. 'There you go, darl. Go the forte option.'

'Thanks.' She threw them down her throat without any water and swallowed hard, then took Freddy's hand and looked into his eyes.

Freddy stroked her face. 'Let's talk about the benefit, Lawrence. I gotta get the lady home before she gets horizontal. It'll do my back in if I have to carry her.'

We formed a circle of chairs and huddled like a clutch of five-year-olds at playgroup. In my accepted style for these occasions, I was whining. 'It's impossible, there's not enough time . . . we'll end up with omelette on our face.'

'Look at me, you old bagel!' Smokey broke in, raising herself to full height. 'I'm the eldest of five boys, son of a dairy farmer on Phillip Island. I wore a beanie every day of my life till I was fourteen. Herringbone was a style of dairy, not tweedy textile, bella! Chicken shit was what made cabbages grow and a cow cocky wore leather as part of his day job, *not* as bodywear. I was diagnosed HIV-positive ten years ago. They told me I'd die in a year, maybe eighteen months. Fuckem, *nothing* is impossible.'

Freddy lit a cigarette. He spoke in a soft dark chocolate monotone, bitter-deep with a sweet aftertaste. 'We gotta get professionally organised, collect good people, reliable, youknowhatumsayin?'

Smokey laid a proprietorial hand on Freddy's shoulder. 'Farid must be related to Lawrence of Arabia.' She snapped her fingers. 'That knack for mustering up a crowd, he's there!'

'Should get him on board,' I said.

She glared at me, one raised eyebrow and menacing mouth. 'This *is* Farid!' poking Freddy on the side of his face. 'His name's *Farid,* it's Syrian. Freddy and his family landed in Melbourne in the Sixties, the termite brain at Immigration couldn't get his piss-swollen tongue around Farid, so he scribbled down *Freddy.*'

A faint knock at the door propelled Lawrence into orbit. He opened it, peeped around. Our necks turned like a row of clown heads at Luna Park, mouths open ready for the balls to be thrown in. He reached out, encouraging the visitor to enter.

'Gang, meet Deidre. She rang last night, offering to help. She's a whiz at aunty admin.'

Deidre was neatly filed. Commonsense short, blonde hair, organic, tucked behind elfish ears that bookended a moonish face. She sniffed a little, quite audibly. A tiny frame glued together in a pale-blue twin-set, brown wool skirt, opaque brown stockings and Nike joggers. She stood with feet apart, as if to secure her balance, both hands in front, holding a manilla folder. Deidre was the sort of woman who could sniff out the one mildewed strawberry in a punnet.

Freddy helped slip off her backpack. 'Siddown, Deeds, I'll get another chair, I been keeping this one on slow sizzle forya.'

She sat next to Smokey. Lawrence flung an arm around Freddy as he walked past him and turned him back into the room. 'Before you leave the room, let's introduce ourselves. Deidre, this is Freddy Farkqou.'

Freddy took a bow and backward stepped through the door. 'Smokey Topaz, Lola Finkelstein, introducing Deidre Graham.' We both shook Deidre's hand, Smokey unavoidably lifting her a solid cheesecake height above the seat.

'You weigh less than a G-string. You better come over to our house and Freddy'll cook up his kibbeh nayeh.' Smokey's face was motionless, but for gloss-enhanced lips. 'Very, very, ve-ry finely minced raw lamb with cracked wheat through it, served with onions and olive oil on pita bread, gourmet quality.' She drew a deep lascivious breath and blew me a kiss. 'Can you smell the cumin, honey?'

Deidre turned to Smokey as if to Mecca, and for the first time we heard her speak. 'Thanks, but I don't eat meat.'

'That's your problem, girl. Protein – more of it.'

'I don't eat anything with a face on it.'

Freddy walked back in carrying a chair above his head.

'Smokey, leave the woman alone. We can hearya three suburbs away.'

Smokey positioned herself with a thud even closer to Deidre. Tenderly, with just one oversized falsely nailed finger she slid a wisp of Deidre's fringe away from her lowered eyes. 'That's better, we can see more of you now.'

By happy hour we each had designated tasks.

Geraldo stumbled in as we were about to scatter. Enveloped in a cool mist, he spoke without energy. 'Sorry I'm so late, it was a battlefield today.' He quivered, closing his eyes. 'Dupleix is losing it, for sure.'

I took over. 'Geraldo, this is Smokey, Freddy, and . . . '

He blew a kiss to Smokey. 'They're almost family.'

He waved sluggishly at Deidre, as though she was behind glass. 'This is our details person, Deidre Graham.'

She waved back.

'What about Dupleix?'

In an exaggerated gallant gesture Lawrence stood up. 'Put it down, Ger, I'll get another chair. Who wants coffee while I've got my apron on?'

No reply. Lawrence controlled himself with effort. 'We really need something a bit stronger but no can do here. I'll be back.'

I prompted Geraldo. 'Are you OK talking in here? We can go across to the hotel.' Geraldo closed his eyes and opened them to connect with Lawrence's, who was back with the chair. He sat up straight to make an announcement, chewing on his upper lip.

'I've got the letter from Dupleix to Shackles-R-Us.'

I walked over and checked the door. He loosened his tie.

'I never had a hard copy because I shredded the original. After Dupleix's tantrum today I know my future there is pretty grim so I accessed Dupleix's computer with the password.'

I was impressed. 'How did you get hold of it?'

Geraldo grinned, finally. 'Dupleix is so paranoid, he changes his password regularly. But he forgets it and has to chase up his secretary to remind him.'

Five heads tuned in stereo to Geraldo. 'A few months back, Melanie, Dupleix's secretary, and I were leaving the building for lunch. Dupleix charges out of the lift like he's been busted whacking off in the stairwell, grabs Melanie, pulls her back a few steps in towards him and asks *What's my password again, Mel?* She's trying to be discreet . . . she mouths it. I'm a shit-hot lip-reader, so voilà! I was sure he'd changed it, but tried anyway and there it was. I printed one copy only.'

He passed it over to me. 'Are you OK?' He sucked his breath in.

'Hunky-dory.'

Something had changed.

Freddy stood behind his chair, bending onto his elbows. 'Did he crack it because someone chucked the paint?'

Geraldo paced. 'Yep, totally nutso. He went ballistic, storming around the office throwing stuff, yelling that *AIDS research was a waste of money, if those perverts keep fucking each other they deserve to die, screw AIDS, fuck political correctness . . . if one more person puts a red ribbon anywhere near me I'll shove it up their clacker.* I was up there collecting correspondence. Everyone scattered like ants. When he noticed me waiting he slammed his door a nose-job away from my face.'

I pointed to Geraldo. 'You'd better explain the letter, we said nothing.'

Lawrence did a quarter-turn, nodded to me. I stood holding the door ajar. 'I'm off to the ladies.'

The journos had left to scavenge elsewhere. I stepped over unrecognisable, crushed objects left lying like flotsam and jetsam across the floor in the foyer, an angry teenager's shattered landscape. The automatic doors sliced open. I bent over, legs apart, upper body hanging down, blood rushing to my brain, dustbusting scarifying demons. Good news, my head is still attached to my neck. Arching my back up, chin forward, head straight, I could see a man pretend-leaning on a car a short way down the street, not far, maybe ten cars. He had a huge head, no neck and broad shoulders. Shortish. Hard to know whether he was coming towards me or going away from me. A bodybuilder's physique. He spotted me staring and slid into the passenger seat.

This is a barren, no restaurants, no residential houses street, only rows of brown-brick offices and warehouses. Why would anyone be lurking here? A slimy photographer, maybe? I couldn't allow myself to get anxious – my naturopath was away for a month doing a women's empowerment workshop in Bali. I tried to focus on the numberplate; neons and night sky made it impossible. I couldn't identify the make or type of car either, maybe sedan, big-ish, family car-ish. I know more about Gloucestershire Old Spots pigs.

Back in the bunker Geraldo delivered answers on private prisons. 'We can't really know what goes on, particularly not in this case, because it's a trial run for the Americans. Once they have the site, if Dupleix's successful in pulling this off, like any privately owned business they can do what they like. Sorry to add to the universal gloom, but this is the paradox with private prisons. They get leases under the prospect of cost saving for the State, but at the same time their long-term goal is to make a profit. Progress.'

Deidre tugged so hard on the top button of her cardigan, it hung grievously by one thread. 'Who are these people accountable to? What if someone dies or someone's abused in this sort of prison? Who asks the questions, the State?'

Geraldo's face glowed. Red eyes blinking like a railway crossing. 'That's the point, it's easier to push a prickly pear through your . . . '

Lawrence winced. 'Geraldo, pah-lease!'

' . . . than trying to extract information from private prisons on conditions and practices. These businesses pay a high insurance premium to protect them against possible litigation and don't forget, they're contracted to the State. It therefore follows that, if they're sued for abuses, the State, the contractors and the insurance company will all be out there doing the Adolf Eichmann monologue, "I vas a soldier, I vas doing mein job!"'

Smokey exhaled a painful groan, shaking her head, her thoughts elsewhere.

I wanted to view the extent of the damage. 'Geraldo, I have to leave. You'd better give me the letter, if that's still what you want to do?'

He averted his eyes when I looked at him. 'Absolutely, put it somewhere safe.' He handed me an envelope with a State government crest on the back. It wasn't sealed. I unfolded the A4 sheet, sat on the floor in the centre of the circle of chairs and read it out loud. I rolled each syllable over my tongue. Every new sentence, hot in my throat, sparked another flame.

25 June 2000

Re: Victorian Prison Services

Dear Doc Bush
Thank you for your correspondence of 17 June 2000 and the subsequent opportunity to meet yourself and Mr Larks of Schwenk and Daggers . . .

I straightened up, nodding to Geraldo. 'Schwenk and Daggers, isn't that the largest lobbying company in the world?'
He puckered his lips. 'On the knocker!'

You would be aware that the decisions relating to contractual arrangements with respect to service delivery in this area, due to human impacts and sensitive factors, are taken at this political level.

Geraldo played queasy-faced interpreter. 'It's my gig; don't even think about talking to anybody else.'

My government's policy position vis-à-vis the redefinition of 'core business areas' for the conduct of government enterprises is well-known.

I was clear on this one. 'I'd privatise my dick if I could.'
Lawrence applauded.

The concerns with respect to efficiency, service delivery, and focus on cost-effective outcomes that underpinned your political contributions are well understood by my administration.

'He's scored a fucking deposit off them; no wonder he's making sure the hospital closes,' Geraldo said.

In fact, our shared interests regarding administrative efficiency dividends and mutual commitment to appropriate limitations on the scope of Government activity underpin my decision not to proceed to open tender on this project.

Smokey grabbed the baton. 'The gig's all yours, baby.'
We sat staring at each other. Speechless at the sewer that presently was our reality. I broke the silence.

The Office of the Minister for Corrective Services will contact your office in the near future to initiate discussion on appropriate contractual arrangements subsequent to the appropriate decision making processes of Cabinet.
Thank you for your attention.

Sincerely
James Cefn Dupleix

Smokey got down on all fours, straddled the chairs and us, stuck her head out the door and bellowed like a bull. 'NO FUCKING WAY, DUPLEIX! The man is a necrophiliac, only dead people would let themselves get fucked over like this.'
Lawrence lunged forward, dragging her back into the room. He was breathless. 'Listen up, gang, let's head across the road to the pub. We need to get sideways. You too, Deidre, it'll smarten you up.'

PART THREE

CHAPTER TWENTY-ONE

Come to where the flavour is, Marlboro Country.

– Press ad

DEADLY VIRUS

'Welcome to Melbourne, enjoy your stay and thank you for flying with us.'

The purser hid behind a fuck-you smile. The flight had been delayed for an hour while security gremlins climbed into the aircraft to retrieve an abandoned suitcase.

Christopher arrived late at Springfield, nerves raw from mining in Dupleix's shaft. His stomach groaned, empty, announcing that he'd forgotten to replenish his supply of medication. He zoomed into the counter, watching the young fragrance-free nurse dispensing and jiggling the toxic-bright buttons into plastic containers.

'Howdy.' He held up his laminated ID card between his thumb and forefinger like a white flag.

She nodded professionally, scribbling medical secrets onto a clipboard. 'Can I please have one of those plastic cups? Need to drop these right away.'

Still counting, she reached out and passed him the cup in slow motion.

'Thanks.'

'Sixteen, seventeen . . . not a problem.'

He'd missed one dose. If it happened again, the virus would regroup, do polls, get ratings and come up with another winner.

It's a high-maintenance relationship, virus and host.

Protease inhibitors were the new drugs. They worked like scavengers to reduce the amount of virus in the bloodstream. He'd responded well. After being treated for only a few weeks there were no detectable levels in his blood. He was lucky; results weren't guaranteed. He wouldn't forget the clinic in Sydney. The doctor, hygienic in mid-length white coat, slim-fitting and shiny black leather pants, delivered a passionless fluoride smile.

'The virus can't reproduce by itself. It invades a cell, evicts the native DNA and inserts its own, turning that cell into a viral reproduction factory. Do you understand?'

'How does it reproduce?'

'By chopping itself up into smaller pieces. This enzyme, protease, acts as the blade.'

'I get it. The protease inhibitor blunts the blade.'

'Kind of. More precisely, it seals it. Take these three times a day, at eight-hour intervals, always on an empty stomach.'

At first the triple dose of nausea, diarrhoea and fatigue had been overwhelming. Having no other option, he'd held on shakily and managed to ride it out. The nausea remained, swirling sluggishly in a vortex of other minor afflictions and constant anxiety.

'It's not a cure, you understand, but it might give you some long-term control.' The doctor spoke while systematically rolling up his sleeves. Christopher had absorbed the knowledge that he would die, but he nevertheless continued to live as though he wouldn't. The doctor had been clumsy.

'Christopher, these may not make any difference.'

'We're all dyin doc, I got lucky and scored preview tickets.'

A shirt button near his waist was undone. He hadn't noticed. He felt the metal sink, frigid, against his bare stomach. He slid the capsules onto the back of his tongue and swallowed. The cold winched him back into his body. He felt safe in the hospital toilets.

Looking at his image in the mirror, he thought of David. After all this time, he asked himself, would they recognise each other if they accidentally met in the street? What would David say? *Back off.* 'What else can I do?' he spoke out loud to the mirror. 'My methods are no worse than theirs. How do you judge my actions against their ideals?'

The memory of David's death lived with him. It was always there. He felt guilt at being alive, but he was HIV-positive, so it wasn't like he'd escaped unharmed. His reason for living had been to disarm, even momentarily, the powers that destroyed David.

Initially, he had little time. But the new drugs had delivered him to another destination. He was going to live. For so long, screened by the blinds of time, distance and urgency, he'd protected himself and his secrets from outside and from within. Now he remembered who he was and felt crushingly isolated. For a split second, he even felt deprived of the virus he was successfully eliminating from his body.

He despised himself for being possessed by these moods. He kept going, accepting the changes in his body. Defying death, as far as he could tell, was a pyrrhic victory. He still had to iron shirts, floss after meals and service his debts.

The man in the mirror looked back sneeringly. Lola's laugh rustled in his ears. His tongue and presently the throbbing lump at the tip of it could summon up the taste of her. The swelling and slipperiness of her lips, the arc of her breast, the raisin-stickiness of her nipples. He tried, unsuccessfully, to secure the slimy flesh with his thumb and forefinger to check for more damage. Only days before, this tongue had circumnavigated Lola's body without going afoul. Like a water-diviner it found places of moisture way below the surface. This organ of taste and master of sounds flapped and turned and swam inside her mouth like a salmon en route to spawn.

He pressed the redial button on his mobile.

'The good news is, you've reached the right number. The bad news is, I'm not here to take your call. Leave a message.'

'Hey Lola, my tongue's no longer impersonatin a crumbed veal cutlet. Call me pronto.'

Years ago he'd dabbled into the notion of psychic pain provoking physical symptoms. This idea had crossed his mind more than once in the last twenty-four hours.

On his first return to Nicaragua after David's death, and not long out of hospital, he came down with a violent bout of laryngitis. Vigilant about making contact only with those he was sure he could trust, he visited an ageing medicine-woman who lived in the hills around Bocay. Her skin and flesh were so thin she appeared fossilised. Up close, her face resembled a miniature Jackson Pollock masterpiece. Capillaries splattered, sun spots and ruby eczema blotches spread formlessly from ear to ear. Her smile was the colour of nutmeg, revealing toothless shrivelled gums that scraped together when she spoke.

She had one foot in the grave and probably, he thought at regular intervals, she stuck her head in to check her options. She'd shoved a small bag of herbs in his palm and closed his hand around it. Five frail, chilly fingers not quite surrounded his fist as a gesture of this being the medicine. She gave instructions. He was to cook the leaves with a single chicken leg in a pint of water on the full moon, she held up two fingers, two days from then. When the stock had boiled down to half a pint, he was to let it cool, then drink it, eat the chicken leg, but not the leaves.

She wouldn't accept his money but demanded cigarettes. He gave her the packet with his lighter. Lighting up, she inhaled deeper than the Marlboro man. She tugged on his sleeve to pull him down to her mouth. Scraping her gums furiously, she gave her prognosis. 'For a short time the demon of deception will be your ally. These herbs protect you from losing your soul . . . your voice . . . to him. But turn your back on the truth, completely, for too long . . . '

She snapped her mouth shut, grabbing a fistful of air. A shriek mellowed into a choked gurgle. 'He'll steal your tongue and rip out your teeth.'

He laughed off the sinister prediction. His voice returned the day after the full moon.

He strutted from the toilets along the corridor, into the lift and down to the main reception area. The side exit doors opened and closed with confident certainty. Hesitatingly, he hailed a taxi. 'The Sheraton, please.'

The driver didn't speak until Christopher tried to wind down a window. 'You're in the twilight zone, mate.' He sat up straight, news-announcer style. 'Do not adjust your set. We control the vertical and the horizontal. How low d'ya wanna go?'

'All the way down.'

'Let's limbo then.'

Christopher withdrew. The driver didn't. 'Rex is what they call me. It's none of my business. Visiting a loved one, areya?'

Rex spluttered out of a plastic, navy-blue air-force jacket that spat and gurgled with every hooligan turn of the steering wheel. He had deep furrows around his mouth from years of small talk. He kept both eyes on Christopher and a third one on the road. 'Like the fresh air, mate? Don't get claustrophobic, do ya?'

'Yeah. Sure do. Sometimes I feel like I'm bein buried alive. My heart's racin . . . '

'The head's gotta go out that window mate, she'll be right.' He sped up, weaving in and out of brain-slowed drivers. Cars like conversation bubbles floated across a cartoon city-scape.

Christopher breathed easier, comfortable in the familiar fascist glare of headlights.

'My boy gets car sick. Spews every time I take him in the cab.'

'Have his ears checked.' Christopher didn't want conversation. The words fell out by themselves.

Rex rescued them. 'Did that.' He slammed on the brakes. They exchanged a panicky glance.

'Bloomin idiot. We checked every bloody thing. One fella, child-head-doctor type fella, he says the kid's angry with me but can't express it. What's all that about, I ask him? I can't answer that, he says. That's his bloody expert opinion then, *I can't answer that.*'

'My brother did things to piss my father off. Mostly I tried to keep out of his way,' Christopher leaned back and rubbed his temples.

'Express your anger, didya?'

'Let's quit this conversation, Rex, it's squeezin my brain.'

Rex drove through shadows of buildings and entered a neon game of snakes and ladders. 'I'm avoiding the footy crowd . . . chockers around the main oval exits. Follow the footy?'

He hovered for a response. Christopher cleared his throat but said nothing.

'Mate, I reckon *you* need to get out more . . . get pissed . . . wake up the next morning shitfaced, have some fun, mate –'

'The fun's about to begin.'

Rex stopped the car at the top of the ramp, right outside the hotel foyer. Pillar handed over a fifty-dollar note and stepped out of the car. Pushing the door closed, he spoke through the gap of the window. 'Keep the change.'

He seeped into the night's complexion like moisturiser.

CHAPTER TWENTY-TWO

The breakfast of champions is not cereal, it's the opposition.
– Nick Seitz

GERALDO CASTRO

'WHAT'S YOUR FUCKING PROBLEM, PILLAR?' Fillet bullied down the phone. 'Did the Hamburglar turn your fucking brains into fucking mincemeat? Speak to me, cowboy, and it better fucking make sense.'

Christopher had almost forgotten about his tender tongue until he picked up the phone to hear Fillet's abuse half an arm's length from his ear. He went to speak but not one feature of his face felt like it was in the right place.

He waited for a pause. He spoke confidently, in slow motion. 'Howdy, Fillet, what kinda load you dumpin tonight?'

Fillet snorted, swallowed and lowered the volume. 'I'm getting grief from Dupleix's people. They're developing an allergy to this Finkelstein bitch, asking me how come I don't know what's happening next. We've got to be a step ahead. From where I'm standing, I reckon you're so busy getting your dick wet you're forgetting what your brief is. I need information, Pillar, and I need you to convince her to piss off out of the way of Nobb's office doing their job.'

'I understand,' Christopher sympathised, 'but she's not an activist. As far as I can tell she's a comedian.'

'Then tell me, Popeye, what was she doing at the AIDS Council yesterday?' Christopher could hear Fillet's stomach growl. 'She arrived an hour after some fuckstick threw a paint bomb at the receptionist and stayed till bloody teatime!'

'I've got no idea. I'd say she's workin with them on a fundraiser. She's done one for them every year for seven years now . . . no weird shit goin on there. What I wanna know is why Dupleix is goin after her. Why is she a target? Because frankly, Fillet, I'm not sure what I'm supposed to be lookin for here.'

'I don't give a rat's arse *why* they want what they want. My job is to give it to them. There was a guy in that building last night, Geraldo Castro, he works at the department, he's AIDS-positive.'

'HIV-positive.'

'Pillar, don't fuck me round with politically correct crap. That hairy Mary's got the virus and he bloody deserves what he gets. You go sticking yer dick where god didn't intend it to be, you pay the price. Listen to me, I saw a bumper sticker when I was in *your* country last year. *The miracle of AIDS turns fruits into vegetables* – my sentiments exactly.'

Christopher unclenched his teeth, tenuously mindful not to spark Fillet's suspicion or penetrate his tongue. 'Since when are you on god's team, Fillet? Since you learnt to spell the word hypocrisy? What's your problem, you freaked someone's gonna find out your son's gay? I know Frank Dixon is your boy, Fillet. He told one of the guys he'd changed his name to his mother's maiden name so no-one would make the connection. Ashamed of your own son, Fillet?'

Christopher knew he'd said enough, Fillet was back in his box. He chuckled at the novelty marketing potential of Bigot-In-A-Box, running the commercial in his head: *A toy that everyone can play with. Just push the right button and out it comes, your choice of racist, misogynist, homophobic or the multi-dogmatist Bigot-In-A-Strait-Jacket.* He swung back to Fillet, hoping he'd steer back with him, not make a U-turn.

'This guy Geraldo?' Fillet had spotted the signpost.

'We need to know what he's up to. He's in Correspondence. Got direct access to the department's mail. He could be a leak.'

Christopher was treading on ice so thin he could make out crushed tinnies on the bottom of the lake. 'What information should I be makin enquiries about?'

'Potential damage to the State's security.'

'This is makin less sense than Aussie Rules.'

'Pull back, Pillar! Pull real hard on that fucking handbrake. I don't have to listen to this crap from a bloody septic. You ring that sheila Finkelstein, find out what you can about Geraldo woosieface.'

Pillar tried again. 'But is there evidence to suggest this Geraldo character is plotting to disrupt the government by leaking information or any other means? And that Lola Finkelstein is involved?'

Fillet threw the phone at a hard surface, probably his head. Christopher hung on patiently, grinning. 'Pillar, I'm just the orange-boy, you're the fuckin clever dick with the verbal diarrhoea. You go play boy scout then tell me whathefuck is going down!'

Christopher lay on the bed, planning his next move. The music from the room next door trampled like a despot's footsteps all over his thoughts.

He phoned Ed Laurie in Canberra. 'Any background on a Geraldo Castro?'

Ed was about as close as Christopher came to trusting someone at Operations. A regular married guy, kids, back garden and the illusion of security.

'I'm in Melbourne sniffing for Fillet. How's the kid's baseball?'

'He's not the best at bluffing his opponent.'

'Tell him not to show any fear.'

'Ya not wrong.'

In darkness, the information on the screen of his computer reflected on his face. He needed to feed Lola with substantial background material, orchestrate the subject matter in such a way that it pointed to where she could dig for bones. But in the end, she was mistress of her own excavation. He cross-checked security files, copies of letters and documents extracted from the Premier's office. He couldn't believe how vulnerable these files were to electronic attack. Nothing had been done to protect them from hackers. That alone placed the State's security information at risk.

Dupleix had been keeping tabs on Castro for two years, but Christopher couldn't make a link. Dates, locations and intercept details had been scrupulously recorded. Over eight months Geraldo met regularly with someone called Jackass. Meetings were at a range of locations: Boy Precinct, The Works, The Tub and Club Male. Frank Dixon's name burst onto the screen. He'd made a call to Jackass around the time of the last election to confirm Lola's presence at a Labor fundraiser and followed it up with a call to Geraldo.

The obvious question ascended into his inquiring gaze like an escalator. Why was it that whoever kept this record logged the full names of Geraldo, Lola and Frank Dixon but not Jackass?

Frank Dixon.

Christopher knew where to find him. At any night of the week between six and seven Frank would be shedding body fluid on the treadmill at Colt's Gym in Prahran. A talented but arrogant little shit, an expert juggler with a live act of important individuals' testicles in his hands.

Christopher pointed the remote control in the right direction and a female voice penetrated through the half-light. 'We're working and living in a political climate that places unrealistic demands and financial pressures on our health-care system.' Footage of the paint-bomb attack at the AIDS Council the day before.

The camera found Lola. Christopher recognised the man

immediately behind her. Norbert, Fillet's favourite flunkey. He pushed the off button with one hand, pulling on the track pants he normally slept in with the other. Fishing out a musty singlet from the bottom torn corner of his overnight bag, he sniffed the thing, gently easing it over his head. The day had flown by like a seagull that shits on your head and squawks with *joie de vivre*. The perfect frequency in which to punch Frank Dixon's lights out.

Lola woke up late from the night's entertainment schedule of one Hitchcockian tangled nightmare after another. Her head, stuffed with wadding and filler, had metamorphosed into an armchair. Her crumpled face begged the daddy-bear question, Who's been sitting on my head? Her first thought beyond vanity was to call William and change the dinner date to lunch.

It was a cold, grey Melbourne bathroom she entered. She'd never switched onto the colour scheme. Eggplant (read black) tiles on the floor, Ambiguous (read grey) tiles on the walls and Angel (read white) vanity, bath and toilet. Lowering her body for the first piss of the day, she imagined an entire plague of marketing locusts getting paid blisteringly obscene wages to invent kooky colour classifications. Bonus. It loosened her bowels.

Shampoo kickstarted her memory. She'd check with her old friend Lance before meeting William. Lance always knew who did what . . . and to whom.

Nine o'clock, however, was not the best time to locate a school teacher. Her first encounter was with the receptionist. 'This is not a very convenient time for any of our staff, Mrs Finkelstein.'

'I'm not *Mrs* Finkelstein, that's my mother. A woman phoning a school doesn't have to be a parent. And if I am, I may choose not to be married. I'd suggest you refrain from using this title, it's very offensive.'

'It may be offensive to you Mm . . . Miss . . . Ms Finklestein, but some of us are very proud and happy to be married.'

'Go tell someone who cares but first, could you please put me through to the staffroom?'

Lance's voice was at the other end. 'Good morning.'

'I think I over-reacted with Medusa at reception. Where did they get her from, Temps from Hell?'

He giggled like a bad boy. 'That's Joan of Arc. She makes a bonfire for herself every day and we let her burn in it. She means well.'

'That Catholic education did its job. Someone could bash you over the head, steal your car and, more importantly, your 70s disco collection and you'd still manage to find something noble about them. My roots stipulate suspicion of anyone or anything that breathes until I have it in writing.'

'Stop it, I've got class. What can I do for you, girlfriend?

'I need dirt on William Lisbon.'

He was cautious. 'Rightee-o. What sort of dirt? You want to throw some in his face or bury him with it?'

'Neither. I want to talk to him about Springfield. I don't have a clue how much he knows or even cares. Street goss in Canberra is that he's on your team. I reckon you'd know.'

She heard Lance pull the staffroom door closed. 'I'd have his pants down in a minute. As far as I know he's happily married, that's the press release. I've never stumbled over him.'

'As ex-president of the AIDS Council what are your thoughts about my bringing up Springfield with him?'

'Have you run it past Joshua?'

'No, he's got enough on his plate. It's not like an official thing, William wants to have lunch with me.'

'You lucky thing! He must be straight.'

'Who knows and who cares? He's Federal Health Minister – maybe he can stop the Nobb.'

'Slow down, Lola. Dupleix doesn't give a shit about his own people. Why would he listen to the other team's Health Minister?'

'The kids in Canberra know Dupleix is Mr Popularity in Victoria at the minute. But the one area he's really vulnerable in is health. Wouldn't this be a great opportunity for political point-scoring?'

'Sexy idea.'

'A step ahead, baby. We have to outfuck the fuckers.'

CHAPTER TWENTY-THREE

For three days after death hair and fingernails continue to grow
but phone calls taper off.
– Johnny Carson

CLOSE SHAVE

'Lisbon's phone.' The high-pitched busy voice of Wendy, William's adviser. She came from a farming family and spoke with the economy of words typical of rural folk.

'Wendy, Lola Finkelstein. How are you?'

'Who's this?

'Lola –'

'Right, sorry mate. I'm with ya. How ya goin?'

'I'm fine. Could you get William to phone me right away?'

'I'll give him the message, can't guarantee anything. He's a psycho beast today, every man and his bloody dog wants him.'

'I understand.'

'Excellent. Seeya!'

He phoned back in ten minutes, swallowing a yawn as I answered.

'Did I wake you?'

'I'm not being stood up, I hope? I don't know when I'll be in Melbourne again.'

'No, but is it possible to meet for lunch? It's late notice, I know, but I've just been asked to MC at an awards ceremony tonight.

The person they'd booked broke his leg. It's a favour for a friend.'

He cleared his throat. 'I'll call you back.'

His desire to meet with me was baffling. But who am I to try to decipher the labyrinthine thought processes of a Federal Minister? I'm confused by alphabet soup.

'I've rescheduled my next appointment. Can you be at La Luna at the top of Collins Street? It's close to my 2.30 meeting.' He ran out of breath before he'd finished the sentence.

'Are you coming down with something?'

'Can't sleep lately. I'm totally wiped. We've been on and off planes for the last couple of months, takes its toll. But forget all that, I'm longing to see you. Midday, La Luna. Ciao!'

I had just over an hour to be there. My head felt like a bank robber's, squished under pantyhose. I threw myself at the fridge, grabbed the jar of ground coffee, making tiny panting noises as I nursed it snugly between my breasts. I snapped the lid open, permitting its full aroma to massage my nasal passages. I heard the phone ring, but caffeine demanded all my attention. I overfilled the plunger, spilling coffee between my toes. I poured, seizing the mug and with any luck, the day.

The answering machine parted the sea of coffee, blinked and grabbed my attention. Three messages: Christopher, Lawrence and Sylvia Birner, a friend of my mother's. I phoned Sylvia first. Maybe my mother had fallen over and learnt to love again.

'Hal-lo, Sylvia spiks here.'

She had an almost-impossible-to-understand Hungarian accent. 'Sylvia, Lola. I can't talk for long, I'm late for a meeting. Did something happen to my mother?'

Her sigh created enough chaos to snap the wings off butterflies thousands of miles away. 'Meeting, shmeeting. Shveetie, listen to me. Your mudder is awright for now, but I want to spik with you because I dinking she's getting demsha and she shood be go to the doctor.'

Her sentences were like a fur ball in my head.

'You mean dementia?'

She cursed in Hungarian. 'Dats vot I sed. Got help me pliss, it's running in da femily. Looks like you gotit too.'

'I'll call you later, I can't talk now, OK?'

'Sure, go. Hurry hurry, don't miss de plane.'

I felt sick at the thought of Bella suffering from dementia and driving a car. Until now, I'd only joked about how she'd survived thus far, without mutilating more lives than she had.

After an episode when I'd exposed my deepest fears to her, we'd fought. Her mouth opened like a blazing furnace in the middle of her face. I escaped, luckily with only minor burns, but the umbilical cord melted into a stump.

William sat squashed into a corner table. Black wool suit jacket, indigo-blue cotton shirt, same colour silk tie. His trousers, mostly concealed by the table, were held up by an unobscured black leather Gucci belt. His expression was that of a man who'd been looking for a toilet for a week. He stood immediately, pulling the table toward him to make room for me to sit. There was ample space, he was putting on a show. He gave me a pre-selection hug, each hand gingerly placed at arm's length, regulation proximity, around my biceps.

'How delicious finally seeing you again. Certainly worth rearranging my day,' he spoke in flirt tense. Eyes dark and intense, sticky-hand gestures. His choice of words, pauses and honeyed tone were apparatus for seduction.

'I've been overwhelmingly busy . . . I haven't phoned. After our dinner I couldn't stop thinking about you. I didn't push it because you're special – different.' His eyes gazed at me, two orbs of broken promises and ruptured capillaries.

I laughed. 'Excuse me?'

He stuck to his script. 'I'd guess we've both been waiting for a long time to be able to have a grown-up relationship. When you meet that person, it's frighteningly awesome.'

He was passionless, the sort of man who wasn't into oral sex but enthusiastic about oral hygiene. He probably flossed before each encounter.

I bit the bullet. 'William, I want to understand why you guys in Canberra haven't responded to Dupleix's planned closure of Springfield Hospital. It doesn't make sense, carving up the facilities, setting up . . . '

He pounced, lifting his pincers up in the air. 'The battle to save Springfield is over.'

He'd begun digesting his prey. 'Dita Nobb moved on the advice of the Hospitals Planning Board. Springfield has been losing money for years. A newly appointed committee will evaluate tenders for HIV/AIDS services from other sites. I'm confident they'll seriously consider the needs of the community and that wherever the services will be relocated to, the facilities will be far more comfortable and up-to-date. Tragically, Springfield is a dump. It should've been condemned years ago.'

During the thirty-second grab, the temperature dropped on William's side of the table. His face became elongated and penetrating, the chin stretching so taut it almost tore away from the rest of his head. Horrifyingly, his shoulders rose and his back arched. A suffocating, overripe putrid stench scraped at my nostrils with each exhalation.

'I know the hospital needs renovating and more equipment, but that's still a cheaper option than setting up new wards at other locations. You could pass legislation to stall the closure, siphon through federal funding to make the changes and you'd win a shitload of votes. Not one voter understands the National Health Policy anyway. Can't you force the State Government to keep the hospital open?'

'Really, Lola, that's an indescribably naïve view of how things work.'

'People are going to die. Once the Springfield team splits up, not only will all the expertise go down the gurgler but symptoms could be misdiagnosed by staff at the new locations who haven't had the hands-on experience.'

He turned his body away from me. 'Why such little faith in the health system?'

'Because it's not about the health system. It's about economic reform and creatures who attach themselves like parasites to a larger host and go into a feeding frenzy.'

He playfully put his hand over my mouth. 'Remember whom you're with.'

I moved his hand back on to the table, feeling the chill of his frozen compromises. 'Don't patronise me, William.' I wanted to bite, but wasn't up-to-date with my tetanus shot. 'You have to admit the argument to keep Springfield is compelling. The dedication of the staff, the fact that a patient's relative or lover can stay the night. The AIDS garden where the ashes of many of the dead are spread. The flowers, the breeze, the sky – these are all vital when your world has shrunk to a hospital room.'

He was breathing rapidly. 'St Patrick's is one of the locations being considered. It's an excellent facility.'

'Yeah, right. It's a Catholic facility run by the Catholic church. Their god isn't kosher on homosexuality or euthanasia.'

He turned back toward me, his face dark with bad blood like a giant haemorrhoid. 'We're never going to agree on this issue, so let's enjoy lunch.'

'I can't eat right now.' I excused myself to find the ladies and phoned Christopher on the mobile.

He didn't let me speak. 'Where the fuck have you been? I've called you at home, I left messages there and on your voicemail. Why have the fuckin technology if you don't use it?'

Why is it that some days are diamonds and other days are just shitty John Denver replays?

'Back off, Dracula. What happened, someone spike your blood supply?'

'Things are movin quickly, in a new *and* different direction. Don't mention Springfield – there's a lot of shit goin down, more people involved than I originally thought. I'll fax you tonight with the details.'

'Get some multivitamins.' His laugh messed up my hair. 'I'm serious. A vitamin deficiency can provoke paranoia.'

'Check your fax when you get home. Where are you now?'

Footwear entered the room, invited itself to stand in the cubicle one down from me. 'I'm in the toilet of a restaurant. I'm having lunch with William Lisbon.'

'Whaaaat?'

'Hold on!'

His balls took over. 'WHY ARE YOU WHISPERING?'

'Because I'm in a stall. Someone's next door.'

'Where's Lisbon?'

'He's ordering lunch.'

His balls handed the microphone back to him. 'Listen up and listen good. Get the fuck outta there. Go home. I'll explain later.'

No goodbye, seeya later, have a nice day, you're the only woman I've ever loved, ciao baby. Jackshit from Jack Shit himself.

A waiter stopped me en route to the table and handed me a note. 'The minister had to leave.'

Apologies, I couldn't wait, there's someone expecting me at 2.30. Please call me later this afternoon, I plan to stay another night. William

The afternoon transported events into cryptic crossword territory. My answering machine delivered three progressively more spooky messages from Christopher, but no fax. A message from Lawrence to meet at 8 p.m. at the AIDS Council and, for the finale, a freaked-out cut-off call from Geraldo. I replayed it several times trying to unscramble its meaning.

'Hey Lola, it's Geraldo. I'm bailing out. Ciao, good luck with the gig. Don't jive with the Jack . . .'

We all need conflict in our lives. Without conflict there's no drama, without drama there's no chicken soup. The Universe provided conflict and drama, Mimi would deliver the chicken soup. I picked up a glossy magazine to inhale and claimed my dung heap at the Klutz and Kishkes.

I'm certain that Condé Nast or whoever publishes glossy magazines spikes the paper stock with some kind of psychotropic drug that temporarily turns our brains into marshmallow. I examine fashion shots of a woman twenty feet taller than me with long shiny, straight hair and squeaky-clean, unblemished skin modelling a vinyl pencil case masquerading as a skirt. And I think, yep, I could wear that. I check the stockist on the back page and enthusiastically copy the details into my diary. I put the magazine away. Later I'll go through painful withdrawal, seek help and be forced to engage with an enabler type in a twelve-step program to get off the glossies.

Mimi delivered the steamy bowl of soup, the bread and butter, the cutlery and a pamphlet from STTARS, Survivors of Torture and Trauma Assistance and Rehabilitation Service. A note was scrawled in the margin. *Please meet me here tomorrow at 1 o'clock, is emportant. I know Dupleix.*

She returned to clear the table. I tried to hand back the pamphlet, but she slapped my hand with the knife.

'Ouch. What are you doing? Last time you almost broke my neck, now you want to smash my hand?'

She bent over my shoulder as if to clean the table and whispered to the bread. 'Don't make noise, please not to show paper I gib you. I see you tomorrow. Please – is very emportant.'

What was going on?

Was I the only actor who didn't get their script this morning? I ordered blintzes with ice-cream to expel the nauseated, hollow feeling. A wrinkled, sad little man sat alone two tables down towards the back, deep in a book on the cross-pollination of orchids. As Mimi approached with the blintzes, a mist seemed to thicken and close in around her. When the mist cleared, he was gone.

CHAPTER TWENTY-FOUR

A little hush money can do a lot of talking.
– Mae West

WARD 4

Frank Dixon had the kind of face just begging to be slapped. He projected a bull-bar breed of arrogance that would pulverise any animal in a collision. Physically he was plankton-man, a creepy, floating little weed. He spotted Christopher manoeuvring uncomfortably towards him. He shot more gum into his mouth, strutting double-time on the treadmill toward an imagined destination.

'Frankie, my man, gym workin for you?'

Christopher's pupils were so dilated Frank could see his own puffy reflection. 'Haven't seen you around here before, sweetie. Preparing for an active sex life again, are we? I guess you'll be needing my services. Isn't that why you're here, looking for *moi*?' He chuckled at his own cheap joke.

Pillar checked for witnesses. His arm whipped forward in a flash, grabbed the hood of Frank's soaking designer-grey sweatshirt and pulled his head over the panel of the treadmill. He thumped down hard, up and down again. He shoved the other hand down the back of Frank's trackpants, tugging at the pants and the band of his athletic support to stop him from slumping down onto the machine.

'Calvin Klein G-string, Frankie? All the boys are wearin Tommy Hilfiger this season.'

Christopher dragged his prey to the men's showers, shoved him face first into the tiles and held him there with one hand round his neck. Frank tried to lift his head back round to catch his breath.

'Pillar, you just made the biggest mistake of your life, sweetie.'

'Who ya gonna call *sweetie*? Daddy? He'd bust your arse even harder than I'm going to. He's mighty disappointed, Frank. You represent failure, the failure of his manhood, the failure of his marriage, the failure of his whole fuckin life.'

'Let's move past the family therapy, Pillar. To what do I owe this display of your un-dee-vi-ded affection?'

Pillar swung Frank around, digging his fingers into his throat. 'It's not that I don't like you, Frank, but I got a cake bakin in the oven, so I don't have much time. The quicker you give me the right answers, the less nasty I get. *Comprendez-vous*?' His eyes glistened with menace. 'Who or what is Jackass?'

Frank's defiant back-of-the-bus cackle pushed Christopher further into brutality mode. Only the rubbery squeak of cross-trainers on lino bounding through the door stopped Christopher from beating Frank's brains into pavlova.

'Frank, the department doesn't pay for cosmetic surgery. If I were you, I'd be thinkin about how much damage I can afford. Today's word starts with the letter J.'

He punched savagely into his groin. Frank dropped to his knees in a cloud of duty-free cologne.

Christopher turned a tap on to rinse muck off the walls. Frank was losing blood but not his defiance. 'It's just like the shower scene from *Psycho*.'

Pillar dragged him closer, directly beneath the shower head, held him there and slowly increased the flow of hot water.

It took less than thirty seconds.

Frank appealed, 'OOOOOUCH, enough . . . stop . . . turn it off. I couldn't wear those flesh-coloured post-burns body stockings, they're hiiiid-eous.'

Christopher shook his head.

'Talk to me, Frank.'

'I snuck in some sherry, darl. Siddown for a mo, we're not here for long. A smooth medium-dry before we leave?'

Lawrence was stage-managing, I had no idea what was happening.

'You scheduled the meeting for 8 p.m. here. We can't go anywhere, the others will turn up.'

'Wrong. They'll turn up where they're supposed to turn up and we won't be there, get it?'

I stared into the glass, three-quarters full and sticky with fingerprints. I drank in every detail around me but not the sherry. My life was an empty sizzling platter; only the fat remained, no meat. I nodded at Lawrence, raising my hand for silence.

I addressed myself. 'Finkelstein, you're such an idiot, you can't even tell you're an idiot. The smartest thing to do would be to find someone with the courage to tell you you're an idiot. Then you'd be certain that at least one thing you heard today is correct.'

Lawrence leant sideways into his leather satchel. He held his glass out to the other side for balance. With a single hand he poked around the fossils of his life.

I continued my monologue. 'How fucking arrogant! To think that I have control over my life? I barely have control over my oestrogen levels. Tell me, there's a bigger plan and head office forgot to send me a copy. Can someone give me the clues?'

He thrust a shabby child's toy in my lap. 'Drink your sherry, darl, and cuddle the small furry creature. I found it very soothing between rehab and Prozac.'

'What is it?'

'I'm not sure. I bought it at the Wilderness Society Shop. It's a mammalian scavenger, probably extinct. That's why you don't recognise it.'

'It doesn't have a head.'

'Precisely, that's why it's extinct, survival of the fittest . . . blah, blah, blah . . . can't survive without a head!'

The headless toy rode roughshod over my bewildered state and jolted me into the present. 'Jesus, I almost forgot. Geraldo left a message on my machine. Have you spoken to him?'

Lawrence sat tentatively on the edge of a chair with a history of fickleness. 'He rang me too, sounded spooked. Maybe he got busted using Dupleix's password. The letter? Where did you stash it?'

I pulled a copy from my bag. 'I made a copy for you. The original is in my safety deposit box. What do you think will happen to him?'

He stared at the floor. 'My hunch is he split back to Manila. Shame.' He gave me a droopy look. 'Forget it, no time to explain. We must away.'

'D'ya reckon Dupleix's people know we've got the letter?'

'Probably.'

I drove.

'Where are we heading?'

Lawrence wound down his window to fully enjoy the exhaust fumes. 'Springfield. Smokey and Freddy are meeting us there. Deidre had a seizure late last night. They admitted her this morning.'

'Why didn't she say anything?'

'Why would she? When she told her dentist she was positive he charged her double.'

He pointed to a queue of cars moving through a McDonald's drive-through. 'Everybody wants Barbie doll instructions, darls – Heat 'n' Serve, Tear on the Dotted Line, Pay Here, Eat Here or Takeaway.'

Impatient with the snail's pace of the Volvo in front, I swerved into the right lane without indicating.

'You're saying because she doesn't present like a junkie, because she's not a gay male or a sex worker, because she smells like she bathes with Lux soap and brushes her teeth after every meal . . . '

He poked my thigh. 'And, and, *and* . . . she's a heterosexual woman in a stable long-term relationship.'

'Too scary right? Poses too many questions. It's not consistent with what they wanna believe.'

Lawrence was distracted by the car behind us. 'You betcha. Positive women deal with a shitload of stigmas that the guys can't even imagine.'

'Eve came from Adam's ribcage and the cage still haunts her.'

The blue light flashed in my rear-view mirror. 'What the fuck do *they* want?' I pulled over and prepared to speak in monosyllables.

'Good evening, officers. What's the problem?'

The man–child with the grown-up hat and prematurely-ejaculated smirk asked for my licence. I handed it over, he walked away and played Tonka-trucks with his buddy. Lawrence said nothing and tapped his watch-face. Plodmeister returned, magically making sentences with verbs and nouns. His little button eyes glued on me.

'You changed lanes back there but failed to indicate. You do realise that could cause a nasty accident, Ms Finkelstein. Any explanation for this negligence?'

Lawrence dropped his head in his hands, I sucked in air. 'We're in a hurry to visit a friend who's just been admitted to hospital. I guess I'm not really concentrating?'

He leant on the side panel. 'Which hospital is your friend at?'

I squinted at Lawrence. Here we go, I thought. I'll say Springfield, Plod will display the empathy of a homophobic wild boar and hit me with a bazooka of a fine.

Lawrence replied with the salinity of a pickled cucumber. 'Springfield, darl. You're looking gorgeous tonight.'

'Phyllis?'

Whodunit-boy bent down on one knee so that his face was level with mine. He gave Lawrence a broad, lubricating grin. 'It *is* you!

What's shakin, you slack tart?'

Lawrence slithered down his seat to take a professional look. 'Hi darl, looking extra gorgeous, sooo hot for you!'

'Lola, meet Steve. Steve, Lola. You can shake hands now.'

We did.

'You'd better keep moving. Make sure you concentrate.'

He tapped the bonnet, saluted me and blew Lawrence a kiss.

'Where do we know Steve from?'

Lawrence wrung his hands like a plastic surgeon spying a woman with exceptionally small breasts. 'I purchased Steve at a slave auction.'

'Would you mind repeating that?'

'You go to an auction, you buy slave dollars, like buying chips at a casino. One dollar might be equivalent to one hundred slave dollars. You bid for the slave you want, sometimes you pool your resources and form a consortium and purchase an individual between you. Get it?'

'Does anyone get hurt?'

'Only if they fall in love.'

'Where do these slaves come from?'

'Forgodsake, they volunteer! You're still so stuck on that Christians and lions thing. Get over it! We do it for charity. You volunteer to be a slave and try to raise as much money as possible. The last auction, where I bid for Steve,' he snorted, 'was to raise money for PAWS.'

He was rolling a joint on his lap, using a magazine he'd pulled out of his bag for a flat surface.

'Where did you get that magazine, Lawrence? Off a toilet floor? It's disgusting.'

'Why?'

'Every page is shredded. The truth, Lawrence. You're into closet découpage?'

'I collect toilet rolls and old magazines.'

'You know I hate people smoking in my car.'

He didn't look away from the mull. 'I'm *not* smoking in the car. I'm not going to smoke it at all, it's for Deidre and a couple of the guys in Ward 4. Shut up, will you?'

I dreaded asking. 'What's PAWS?'

'Pets Are Wonderful Support. It's an organisation that looks after patients' pets if they go into hospital or respite care or if they can't look after their own pets. You take them for walks, feed them, visit le salon de pooch, whatever.'

'And who's Phyllis?'

He threw back his head, nearly unbalancing the mix on his lap.

'Shit, I nearly dropped the lot!'

'Keep your knees together, that'll help.'

He twisted around to face me, but only from the waist up. 'It's my *girlie* name, *Phyllus-in*.'

Ward 4 is the AIDS ward. There's a communal area at the end of the hallway where I could hear the laughter of nurses dealing tenderly with exacerbated patients. The stain of humanity doesn't always rinse out with bleach and disinfectant. We followed the trail of Smokey's hair products and found Deidre. Freddy was sprawled across Deidre's feet at the end of the bed. Smokey was busy unwrapping an oversized pair of pearl earrings to replace Deidre's sedate studs.

'They're clip-ons. Put them on, you'll feel a million bucks.'

She'd restyled Deidre's hair. 'A dab of Vaseline on those parched lips?'

Turning to me, she used her middle finger to Vaseline my eyebrows. 'Luscious Lola, what's happening? Who's gonna appear on our show? And where's my man Ger-al-do?'

Freddy gurgled like a hungry producer.

Lawrence took over. 'Geraldo's disappeared. Don't know what happened. Lola and I each got a call saying, well, who the fuck knows what he was saying. He was pretty hyped.'

Smokey deftly ran her fingers through Deidre's hair, creating more bouffant. 'Well, we've lost one of the team, shit happens.' She kissed Deidre gently on each cheek, three times, the French way. 'You'll be home in a couple of days?'

Deidre held up both hands with her fingers crossed. Freddy looked over at me, screwing up his face as a gesture of affection. 'She didn't touch her food.'

Smokey slapped him across the back of the head. 'Put a sock in it, Freddy! When she's got her appetite she'll eat. You sound like your crazy mother.'

She steered the boat toward a different shore – the benefit. 'The date's locked in and management are happy for us to have the full ticket price as long as they can keep the bar take.'

Freddy showed us artwork that a printer friend had mocked up for a poster and press ad.

'Cool ad, Freddy, but who pays for the printing and the advertising space?'

'Syrian dudes. They owe me . . . they're sponsoring the advertising.'

It was my turn to report. 'The AIDS Council is providing volunteers for front-of-house duties and I got an affirmative from every performer on our wish list.'

Deidre gave me a wink. Painfully thin arms folded around a giant heart-shaped pink satin pillow that Smokey had brought for her. 'You want a glass of water, love?'

She shook her head. 'No, thanks. Lawrence, did you bring a joint?'

He gave me one of his I-told-you-so sneers. 'Sure, darls, all done.' He slipped the joint between her lips and lit it. I shut the door. Smokey stared at my hand around the doorknob.

She smiled, turning a corner with her mouth. 'Baby, without that manicure, I'd swear that was a man's hand.'

'I got my father's hands . . . chunky.'

Lawrence grabbed my hand, smoothing it over his genitals. 'Not big enough, sorry!'

He disappeared to distribute bags of mixed lollies and to slide joints into willing mouths. Smokey and Freddy followed with hair and make-up. I was alone with Deidre.

'I'm sorry you found out this way.'

'I was expecting a press release.'

Her breathing was laborious. Her heart beat overtime to supply blood and tear away the triple-stranded wire and vicious hooks that held it together.

'I'm learning to trust people again. For a long time that seemed impossible. Three years ago I was pregnant. I went along to have all the regular blood tests. My doctor asked for an HIV test. When I went back to get my results he said, "I've got good news and bad news. The good news is the pregnancy is going fine. The bad news is you're HIV-positive." I went home and told my partner. The following week he was tested, and was negative.

'Within days I was losing fluid. I knew there was something wrong with the baby. I needed to go into hospital. But my doctor wouldn't allow me to be admitted to the local hospital because *I might infect others*. My baby died, induced by another doctor because my doctor wouldn't return my calls.

'Within two weeks, I'd been told I was terminally ill, given birth to a dead baby, been abused and left by my partner of six years and treated like garbage by hospital staff. I was never promiscuous, I wasn't an intravenous drug user, I'd had a monogamous relationship with someone ten years ago whom I've since found out has died of AIDS and that's how I became infected.

'If I had cancer I'd have been treated with compassion.'

Lawrence skidded back into the room. 'Let's blow this dive . . . go find some other bar.'

CHAPTER TWENTY-FIVE

Girls got balls. They're just a little higher up, that's all.
– Joan Jett

MIMI

I stepped through my front door a safety catch away from midnight. I'd reached that point of hyper-anxiety that doesn't register fatigue. The drive back from Lawrence's was uneventful, aside from the dark stranger masturbating on the corner of Kooyong and Alma roads in Caulfield. Following road-safety guidelines, I came to a halt at the red light. No other car at the intersection. As my vehicle paused obediently, I became aware of a flash of movement to my right. I turned my head only; it was late and I was through with expending unnecessary energy. And there, right in front of me, stood a man, naked aside from his balaclava, masturbating. He didn't offer to clean my windscreen. I swung around checking for camera crews to see if this was being filmed for the 'World's Dumbest Criminals'. Television is so much more validating than reality.

Maybe nude-man had intended to rob a bank, changed his mind, and thought, *Bugger it, I'd rather jerk off in public today, I can rob a bank some other time*, and forgot to remove his balaclava. He stopped about three metres from the car, that is, he stopped moving toward me, but not thrashing his salami. Amber turned to green, but my eyes were peeled for any identifying features. The balaclava guaranteed anonymity. Annoyingly, there wasn't enough light to distinguish if he was Jewish. But his thighs, more precisely his quadriceps, writhing, contorting and bulging, telegraphed a complex inner life spent mostly on a push bike or squatting. It presented as a spooky tableau. Against the moonless night sky, the illusion was that of a headless naked male using his body as a percussion instrument.

I accelerated, foot as flat as a Cuban heel would allow. Proceeding with my journey, I rang the local police station on my mobile to report the incident. A recorded voice lamely listed the opening hours of the station and offered an emergency number. I rang the emergency number to be put on hold, and hold and hold.

In another life an officer answered. 'Detective Sergeant Wayne Straitman, St Kilda Police. What can we do for you?'

'There's a naked man – not exactly naked, he's wearing a balaclava – masturbating on the intersection of Kooyong and Alma roads in Caulfield.'

'Your name, madam?'

'Who cares?'

'Official procedure dictates the procedure I'm obliged to follow, madam. An officer must record every detail for the report vital for apprehending the alleged offender and check for spelling mistakes and punctuation. Thus we speedily proceed with the job of enforcing the law.'

'Forget it, he came an hour ago!'

At home. Messages from my mother, William Lisbon and a one-page fax from Christopher. I was crazy for a bath. I needed to soak the stains out of my head and gently peel away the soiled bandages from the pit of my stomach. My hand spun the taps, poured in the Epsom salts and ylang ylang, rose geranium and jasmine oils. My feet followed the scent and hoochie-coochied slowly down into the steamy bathos.

Wrapped in a dishcloth bathrobe, I read the fax while stirring chocolate powder and milk.

Howdy ma'am, I don't want to appear alarmist but you're in deep shit. Unable to deliver details at the present time. Tomorrow 6 p.m., drive to Prahran Market carpark. On level two, look for an old Bedford van. VASILIS WHOLESALE FISH SUPPLY signage on the side. Ask the driver if he's seen an RACV service car in the area. Tell him your car broke down and you've been waiting for thirty minutes. You had to go find a public phone to call them again. You thought maybe the RACV drove past while you were gone. He'll ask if you drive a metallic blue Toyota RAV. You say No, a white Suzuki Vitara. Let him take care of the rest. Pillar

The bath was wasted. In less time than it takes to say Diazepam, I was sweating feverishly. My breath was a gluggy vapour of hot chocolate and adrenalin. The unplugged vents of my brain were once more percolating with paranoid thoughts.

I dialled Christopher's number. No answer. I went to bed, but not to sleep. Instead I lay with my arms by my side, legs straight, practising to be a corpse. I intimidated myself with a fantasy in which I lay flat on my back, trapped under the gigantic leather jackboot of a hippopotamic wart-faced evil despot, who misunderstands my tongue poking at him as a sign of sexual attraction.

I woke before the alarm, all my pulses throbbing.

I rang Christopher. No answer again.

Next best option for ruining my day, I rang my mother. 'I never knew you such an ehlee raiser?'

I'd begun bringing her a cup of coffee in bed when I was only seven. I've always been the first one up in the family. 'Bella, have you noticed that you've been forgetful lately? Do you walk into a room then forget what you went in for?'

Bella cackled wickedly. 'If you traying to convince me dat I'm getting a bit demsha so to be put in a home, forgetaboutit. I always bin a leetle bit fargetful, mebbe alotta rubbish I wanna farget, like vot happened to da rest of mein family in Poland. You remember when I used to be smoking, I hev a cigarette burning in ashtray in every room in the house. Remember? Howcome you didn't ask me zen if I'm fargetting?'

'Someone's gotta keep an eye on you!'

'Don't vorry about me, you keep an eye fer yourself. I don't need your eye. I need a pee. I gotta pee twice as often dis days. Who knows why. So, quickly, tell me, vot are you ringing me at seben in da morning?'

'You left a message on my machine?'

Fudgy silence.

'Are you sure it vas me?'

I tested her. 'Remember you taught me when I was very little that when you break a promise you break a person's heart?'

'Offcourse I remember, how could I farget?'

She stalled, then continued tenderly. 'Lola, you're mein daughter, how could I forget? Excuse me, do you mind? I gotta pee.' She pummelled the phone into its slot.

Emptying my bag of yesterday's global junk, I found Mimi's note. I'd forgotten the promise to meet her at the STTARS office. It seemed incredible that she knew Dupleix, but I recognised the swallowed-something-bitter squint in her eye and felt obliged to go.

The STTARS office was a small shopfront in Elsternwick, divided into cubicles by slim partitions. Conversations infused like solvent through these screens, leaving only the thinnest of skeletons floating in and out with the reverse-cycle air-conditioner.

I scanned the room for Mimi. Not there. Bending carefully, bum first, into one of the waiting-area armchairs, I picked up a brochure. *This organisation treats and cares for people in the belief that everyone should be able to live a life without being consumed by events of the past.* A woman sings softly in an unrecognisable language down the back beyond the cubicles. A man with one arm walks past me, a vacant sleeve tucked neatly into the waist of his jeans.

'Sorry, Lola, I bin rushing. Rushing, rushing all morning like crazy woman. You bin waiting long time?'

I put my arm around her. 'Relax, I only just got here. It gave me a chance to find out about the place. Is this where you come for help?'

She slid her arm through mine like a best girlfriend from the old country. 'I come here for my English. Sometimes to interpret, to help newcomers joost arriving like me not so long ago from Bosnia.'

We walked the couple of blocks to Mimi's flat. Not along the main shopping area but through the back lanes behind the shops. 'Is habit. Too many years escaping snipers. I never walking in main street in daylight.'

Her flat was tiny, exquisitely neat and functional. Refugee Bauhaus. Every article perfect in its place, folded or stacked, ready for a speedy exit. I didn't need to ask Mimi questions about her past, it leaked into my own cavities from the minute she opened the door.

'You want coffee?'

I nodded enthusiastically.

She disappeared down the doll's house corridor made even smaller by her buxom succulence. I heard a clattering noise, followed by the smash of a plate. Mimi screamed, then went the Slavic blitzkrieg at someone in the kitchen. I looked for somewhere to hide, but yelled out to her just the same.

'What's happening?'

'Coming here, you see.'

My back against the wall, I checked left, right, stuck out my chest and stepped into the kitchen.

As soon as my face came through the door, a small savage shape charged at my nose. A truckload of deodorant in aerosol cans exploded in my head. I came to on Mimi's couch with a lump on my head the size of a ram's testicle.

'What hit me?'

Her eyes fixed on mine, with embarrassment.

'Nothing, you fall backwards and heet your head exactly on the corner of de shelf.'

'Something hit me in the face.'

She brought her hand around in front of me and there perched on her forefinger was the bastard blue budgerigar, a ferocious handful of toe-clippings covered in feathers introduced to me as Tito.

'He's very bad boy, but I bring him with me from my country and he is all my family now.'

'How did you get him through Customs?'

'I give sleeping tablet, knock heem out and keep heem for whole trip in my bra. He speaks English, listen please, *Tito what you like now*?'

The leprechaun beast hopped onto my chest, relieved himself and screeched in Yugoslav English exactly like Mimi's.

'Tito vont beeskveet, Tito vont beeskveet, chir chir babble babble.'

She disappeared quickly and returned alone with a sponge to remove his show of affection. 'Sorry again for deesgusting deesplay, but he is trying to protect.'

We spent the afternoon recovering. She was pyrogenic with the full-bodied flavour of life and I relished the warmth. We covered a lot of ground. Mostly I asked the questions.

'Didn't you say you'd been married?'

She made a blank expression. 'I vos young, he vos brilliant mathematician. I love him, but never it could work. He sit at desk for hours, like man in trance, meditating the concept of zero.'

Eventually, I brought up Dupleix. Sitting well back into her chair, she winced and drew one knee up to her chin. 'Pliss, not to judge me, OK. I read about you in newspaper, that you disagreeing with closing of Springfield Hospital, correct?'

I raised a thumb in confirmation.

'I also read that you think Dupleix is closing hospital for some other reason than he is telling, correct?'

I blinked in affirmation.

She continued. 'Dupleix, he comes here to my place, meybe once a week, meybe once a month. He geebs money for me to read to him special stories to help him to forget his pressures. Do you understanding?'

I sat up and held my head with both hands, fearing it might snap off and roll away. I was confused with Mimi's diplomatic interpretation of events and asked for more detail.

'You sit here be staying comfortable and I explain.' Ten minutes later she strutted into the room wearing stay-up stockings, stilettos, leather bra and G-string. Horse whip in one hand, a book of fairytales in the other.

She paced the floor. 'I removing his clothes off, tie heem up with silk scarves, leetle bit tight, not serious. I begin to reading him fairy story and every few moments I flogging him with whip and swear at heem in my language. He has no idea vot I am saying. Many times I am repeating shopping list for next day, but I make with terrible nasty voice.'

She pulled a bully face and spoke in a stern staccato. 'Butt-er, sug-ar, bis-keets, two kilo ripe tomato, lo-cal limonade . . . he is loving dis.'

I'm not a smug purist but I had to ask. 'Do you have sex with him?'

She spat on the floor. 'Pliss, dis I would never do! The game begin when I was live-in housekeeper for him and his wife in Heidelberg. One night he sneak into my bedroom when I am undressing. He not knocking, like pig he break in and he beg me to read to him from book of fairytales. Next day, I find peckage on my bed, inside is money and whip. So we begin. He never ask for sex and I would not do. This money I save to bring my brother from Bosnia. Plane ticket is expensive, but also I must give money to bribe officials.'

'Why are you telling *me* this?'

She threw on a bathrobe. 'One time he is here, he make call to America from my phone for safety. I hear him speaking about hospital and he is making deal for big money from dis sale. I know him. I know this evil before in Bosnia. Bad meat smell bad anywhere.'

I could tell Mimi made goulash into a pastime.

'I can't make jokes about this. He'll deny it, charge me with slander and send you back to Bosnia.'

'No, not never you speaking about this. But now you know his veakness, you can use it to destroy him.'

I couldn't wait to see Lawrence's face explode with the news of Dupleix's whip fetish.

Outside the sky was school-uniform grey. The sun lay limp like a used cotton ball behind a bin of clouds. It was late afternoon. I had to meet the fish wholesaler at six.

'Thanks for the information and the afternoon.'

'Hospital must not to close.'

I was tongue-tied. She hugged me so enthusiastically my eyeballs popped out of my head and I had to balance them gently in my hand.

CHAPTER TWENTY-SIX

Every great mistake has a halfway moment, a split second when it can be recalled and perhaps remedied.
– Pearl S. Buck

RENDEZVOUS

I obsessively scratched the tiny mole on my wrist each time I looked at my watch. Should get it checked. At 4 p.m., it appeared benign. The pending rain with her dance-team of dark clouds made it seem later. I decided to leave my car across the road from the STTARS office. It would be harder for someone to follow me on public transport. For starters, my arrival could never be guaranteed. I walked to Glenhuntly Road and waited for a tram in the doorway of a pizza parlour, a handful of dough away from opening up for evening trade. I fought back the gnawing urge to order a small napolitana, no anchovies.

I'm blushing, and must admit that I'm perversely excited by the whole insecurity-of-life spy schtick. Give me the tight-waisted snappy trenchcoat, the satellite-dish-size dark sunglasses, worn at all times, especially when showering. And, most importantly, the Dionysian, square-jawed, tall, massively-shouldered arch-rival and I'll volunteer to provoke any counter-revolution. I squinted into the headlines coming towards me. A tallish, darkish, massively-shouldered trenchcoat stepped under the tram-stop shelter reading a tabloid. His face was hidden by the arsenic print. The number 67 hung above his head, the tram rattling towards us. We lifted ourselves into the incredible hulk, me and he who must be observed. I stood behind him. His cologne hinted at smoked salmon; my lips moved closer, quivering for a bagel with cream cheese.

Unprovoked and without sugar, I felt unusually apprehensive. I practised my positive self-talk. *Either you take this seriously or abandon your fission . . . fuck . . . mission, now. Should you decide to continue then play it cool, be that secret agent you've always wanted to be, believe it, know it, own it.*

I felt a sharp prod in my side. I hesitated before turning, not wanting to observe the wide-eyed narcotic face of the fiend poking a gun into my ribcage. I stood feet apart for balance, pulled back slowly and rotated, all in one movement. Pity I never took up figure-skating. It wasn't a knife, but it could be. A serious insect-like student of drama had unintentionally and without future permission from his agent jabbed me with his hardcover copy of *An Actor Prepares*. Next time Pillar sends me instructions, the first thing I'll buy is a three-month supply of Vitamin B forte and a tub of lipgloss. In the arid territory of undercover work, chapped lips were the real high risk.

The tram made its way stealthily along Glenhuntly Road, turned right into Brighton Road, eventually appearing solo on that grand-stage boulevard, St Kilda Road. The city looked gorgeous, fresh out of the shower, getting ready for an evening's performance. Avoiding eye contact with Dionysus, I swerved to view the floral clock. I took comfort in the knowledge that it hadn't been replanted in a digital display. At forty minutes past sweet alyssum, almost the hour of the snapdragons, he got off the tram at Flinders Street Station. I watched him walk up the steps to stand under the Frankston-line clock. As he reached into his pocket, turning his head side-on, I understood why he had every reason to cover his face.

Jumping off the No. 67 in Bourke Street, I slid onto a No. 86 light rail stammering in a northerly direction toward Fitzroy, the opposite direction from where I was expected. I was creating a geographical cryptic crossword, each number concealing a possible clue. If anyone wanted to keep on my trail, they'd have to pickle their cucumbers very tartly. At Brunswick Street I stopped for a coffee at the Black Cat Cafe and pretended to read the paper. I waved to the Fitzroyalty parading past, Imogene, Randall and Caitlin, whoever they were, then left to purchase the latest in personal development trash at the bookstore a block down.

I lingered for five minutes, checking a flock of hats in a milliner's shop window, walked backwards down a laneway towards Johnston Street and without any prior intention jumped onto a bus going back into the city. The driver got out at a McDonald's and bought a thick shake. I abandoned the bus with him, scraping and chipping against the city traffic, moving with and against it. The sky was the colour of toothache. I hailed a cab and because I'd dressed for comfort, not sure what the day would deliver, I asked to be dropped off at Colt's Gym, opposite Prahran Market. Unable to escape the plaque-forming image of a naked Dupleix being mock-flogged by Mimi, I jogged for twenty minutes on the treadmill.

I don't believe in itself the sexual dramatisation of *Cinderella* or the *Three Little Pigs* is evil. But what else does it tell us about the man so menacingly motivated by the desire to advance his career? I decided he must have had a harsh education in cleanliness in those early formative years of his life. You know there are masturbators who specialise in looking up dirty words in works of fiction? Imagine providing your reader with such cheap erotic pleasure. I mudwrestled my way to the female change-room, brushed my teeth and spearminted on to rendezvous with the fishmonger.

Bingo. The old Bedford van, Vasilis Wholesale Fish Supply painted on the side. The stagnant smell of fish floated around me like dead carp. An ankle wearing a white gumboot held the driver's door open.

'Excuse me –'

'Yeah, I'm heya . . . it's awlright, mate.'

White gumboots leading to white overalls smeared in fishy graffiti unfurled like sails to present a head. The smile gleamed like sunlight on water. I was forced to squint. The voice smouldered around my nostrils.

'WhatcanIdoforya?'

It was Dionysus.

'Have you seen an RACV service car go by in the last few minutes? My car broke down. I've been waiting for them for ages. I went off to find a public phone to ring again and the service centre said they were in the area. I'm checking if you've seen them go by?'

He puffed out his chest, threading his slashed, thick fish fingers through the black outcrop protruding from the top of his overalls. He yanked open another stud. 'Izat your car over there, mate, the blue Toyota RAV?'

'No, the white Suzuki Vitara.'

'Ya betta jump in the van.'

He drove out of the carpark, turning in a northerly direction up Chapel Street toward Richmond.

'Scared, areya? I might jump ya, izat what youse reckon? Long, loose and fulla juice . . . all that crap they tellya about Greek guys, right? I gotta MA in ancient Greek Literature, mate. I might look like a thug, but ifya don't mind me sayin so, itsartin to give me the shits. Yaknowhatamsayin?'

'I've never seen a nose like that before, it's . . . '

'Humungous, mate . . . '

'In an ancient Greek god sort of way.'

We stopped at red lights. For one lecherous, itchy moment I wanted to sit on it.

'It's fucked, excuse my English awlright. Wot happened, izat to begin with, it was an early Ionic nose, then I dived into the bottom of a pool, broke it in two places and it healed sorta lumpy.'

He grabbed at my hand, positioning my thumb and forefinger. 'Youse can feel it cantya? It's officially a Doric nose. Last yee-ar I got busted up on a job by some gorilla, didn't bother with a surgeon. It's a work in progress now.'

'Can I take my hand away?'

He made a fist, and thumped the side of my leg. 'Na mate, youse gotta hold on for the ride.'

He fumbled at my wrist, returning my hand onto the dashboard. I stuck it right out again. 'I'm Lola and your name is? One of those mythical Greek names like Dionysus, I bet?'

He laughed so hard another stud burst open. I had to look away.

'Shtoopid name, Dionysus. My name's Eros, mate, now yasee – that's a proper Greek man's name.' We shook on it.

He turned the van masterfully into a thin, black, licorice strap of a street, stopped, but left the engine running. We were outside a tall, cylindrically-shaped building with balconies jutting out of it like a multi-tiered ocean liner.

'What is this?'

'A silo redeveloped into apartments, mate. Greek guy was the architect mate, it's in the blood . . . Partheneon . . . Acropolis. You press the buzzer for number 5 at that big gate there, infrontya, see it?'

'Yeah, next to a streetlight. But there's no lights on in the building. It doesn't look built yet. Are you sure this is it?'

'Certain for sure, one hundred per cent mate. I'll wait hereya till ya through the gates.'

I slid from the seat, feet onto the footpath and away from a once-in-a-lifetime opportunity. Eros drove into the hands of fate at around twenty kilometres an hour.

A light drizzle shimmered in the flood of light from the streetlamp. An illuminated lone snail, shy of the spotlight, retreated conspicuously into its shell. Mindful not to tread into its slick path, I pressed the buzzer for apartment 5.

'Lola?'

'Pillar?'

'The gate'll open and close behind you automatically. Once you're in the courtyard go to the front door, press the black button on your right and that door will open. Step in and stand by the lift. Did you get all that?'

'Sure. Next time I'll do the drive-through.'

I approached the black button. In seconds I was inside the foyer. In the half-light still radiating from the streetlight, but more from my desire for Eros, I became part of the builder's showbag. Glass sheets, bags of concrete, planks of wood, bubble-wrapped plastic surprises. Add water and mix to create a lifestyle.

The lift arrived, the doors slid open, a dog – more precisely, a bull terrier – gave me the superficial nod of a local. I got down on all fours and waited for a sign that it was OK to cross his boundary. He sniffed my face, gave me that *giz a kiss* curled lip and growled politely. I stepped in. He stood on his hind legs, pressed the button with his podgy paw and suggested we have a cocktail in his basket around midnight.

The doors opened again. Christopher on his hind legs pressing the button. The contents of the room flickered in candlelight. He pulled me toward him and engulfed my whole body. It was a novel experience, not worth getting used to. I'm too selfish to be co-dependent.

'Who's your friend?'

The dog was mixing a martini in the kitchen.

'Clifford? He belongs to the guy who lives here. I wanted to come stay, he took the opportunity to go to Sydney for a couple of days without worryin about the dog. We're old buddies from high school.'

I stepped further in, striking a voyeuristic pose. 'He's got great taste, urban high life meets too-busy-to-care chic. Especially the dog, he's perfect.'

I made sure Clifford could hear me.

'Charming, protective and such a powerful jaw, I'm captivated. Is he single?'

Clifford groaned from his basket, Christopher groaned from his stomach.

'You look crap.' He had the look of a man who's just found half a worm in his apple. I put my hand on his forehead.

'Hooley dooley, Pillar, there's a meal defrosting in there.'

He shook his head. 'I'm fine. Slight allergy to dog hair, that's all.'

Clifford yawned with considerable hauteur.

'I beg your pardon. So! Why am *I* in deep shit and what have you found out about Dupleix? By the way, I, too, have lifted a plank on that termite.'

He pointed to the couch, handing me a glass of wine. 'Dupleix and Lisbon –'

I choked, coughing wine in his direction. 'Lucky you're not wearing a white shirt.'

'I am.'

'Too dark to see, perfect.'

He soldiered on. 'Lisbon's into some kinda bizarre sexual proclivity.'

'Give me a clue?'

'Can't work it out myself. This guy Geraldo Castro knows but he's disappeared off the radar. Lisbon held parties for young offenders under the guise of coalface community involvement. One of the kids talked . . . '

'He's a paedophile? Is that what I'm hearing?'

'Can't say one hundred per cent, I didn't chase details. But where it fits with Dupleix is that with the right kind of lobbying, the Federal Health Minister could intervene through legislation to keep Springfield open.'

'Exactly, that's exactly what I said to him and he replied in his nauseating child molester voice, *It's not that simple, Lola.*'

'Did he seem rattled?'

'Yep, like a caged baboon. He didn't want to know about Springfield. He looked like he'd been embalmed, only they forgot the bandages.'

'He's correct. It ain't that simple, not for him, not ever again. He was set up with the help of Geraldo Castro and Frank Dixon. Both of them separately and, on occasions, together procured whatever cast of players Lisbon wanted. All of it orchestrated in triplicate by Dupleix. He's selling off Springfield to Shackles Inc. By exploiting every avenue to have his mates tendering to supply services, he stands to make a shitload of money. He wasn't taking any chances having it screwed up, so he sniffed around everybody's slop bucket for a while until he found the biggest turd.'

'Lisbon's freaking that Dupleix will drop the can and worms will crawl all over him if I keep prodding, is that correct?'

I stood motionless in what must have looked like a weird interpretive dance pose.

'*He-llo*?' Pillar displayed all the control of a bench scientist. I tilted my head with deliberate slowness.

'Information's blending on high speed in my head. Can I have a minute to think?'

He looked for order in my chaos. I ignored him. 'I never sniffed Frank as a stooge for Dupleix. The fact that he was and still is doesn't really surprise me. But that I never even got a hint of it . . . I should be wearing a terry-towelling hat and driving a Volvo. Why? What's in it for him?'

He scratched his right eyebrow. 'Who cares? Probably chip on his shoulder about his father.'

'What?'

'His father, Bruce Price. The lunatic, homophobic head guy at ASIO. Frank lived with his mother for eighteen years, tried to come out to his father, probably felt rejected. Who knows, who cares? He had access to security files, he knew the tricks, the weaknesses, areas of vulnerability and he had Geraldo. Together they had carte blanche on all fronts straight down the line from Dupleix.'

'He'll have a sex change.'

'Is that supposed to mean somethin?'

'He wants to be Linda Evangelista.'

Christopher slid forward to stand but collapsed back into the couch, grabbing my shoulder. He tried to suck on his puffer as he fell. I helped him down gently. 'I don't think so –'

'I'm fine, caught a cold in this stoopid weather.'

'The voodoo expression tells me this is not the work of a suburban cold germ. You want a bucket?'

He shook his head, letting it drop and squeezed my shoulder harder. Submitting to his fate, he coughed up a thunderstorm for several minutes. I took his spare hand between both of mine. It fell into my lap like a dead fish, cold and slippery. He moved it to cover his mouth. His eyes were skittish, one eyelid twitched. 'Fever, no sleep, bad combo.'

'You think your friend would have a thermometer?'

His head jolted upright. 'Not up my –'

'Don't go there! Under your tongue is my preferred destination.'

He leant forward enough for his hand to slide nearly around my waist. I curled one arm up and around his neck, drawing his head down. A kiss. A hand slid up between my thighs and around my buttocks.

'You're only *just* breathing.'

He sank further into the feather down of the couch. Both hands finally around my waist, raising then lowering my body, pressing me onto the lump in his groin.

I released the buttons of his shirt, the palms of my hands like sensors against his chest, fondling, recording and transmitting information throughout my arousal network. I could feel his laboured breath against my neck. I hesitated kissing him on the mouth in case he'd suffocate. I massaged his forehead and around his eyes, hoping to shift his congestion. His head tilted back, yielding to the gentle kneading. His fingers continued to squirm and flap about like a shoal of fish between my legs.

'I can't handle another elevator ride to nowhere, it gives me skin eruptions.'

His laugh switched to a hacking cough. Within seconds he was wheezing, reaching for his puffer. 'Sorry . . . ' His voice sank into heavy breathing. He tried lifting his head. His lips moved but the words stayed indoors.

I straightened his body out on the couch, limb by limb, put a pillow under his head and draped a blanket over him. In the kitchen, I sorted out which abstract Alessi shape was the kettle and made a cup of tea. By the time I came back around the buffed stainless-steel corner, he was sleeping. Sitting on the floor next to the couch, I wiped saliva oozing from the tiny cracks in the corners of his lips. His breathing was slow and uneven, raspy on the inhale, smothered on the exhale. His glands, the size of large olives, bulged like a bag of naphthalene balls down the side of his neck.

Clifford splayed on his belly next to me at Christopher's side. Now, when he sensed I was leaving, he stretched to come with me. I scratched the soft, fleshy, vulnerable spot right under his jaw. His eyes rolled back into his head.

'Forget it, you stay with him. Wake me up if he stops breathing.'

He dutifully padded over to the CD collection, selected an Erik Satie compilation and hunkered down for the night on a hand-woven red-and-gold meditation cushion directly opposite the couch.

Christopher woke up feeling no pain. He had a sense of being cherished, protected, maybe even loved. He'd forgotten momentarily who he was. The dog's yawn flew him back economy class to that nauseated terminal that was his life. He turned to face the dog. The room was in pre-dawn semi-darkness, but the blemish of light on the blinds was enough to make out Clifford's silhouette.

'Hey Clifford, *buenas dias, donde querida*?'

The dog groaned and farted, letting Christopher know unquestionably that it was exceptionally boring to be bilingual so early in the day.

He watched Christopher sheepishly raise his upper body just enough to get a grip on the top of the couch, pause, then lift himself into a sitting position. His lungs felt like a week's worth of garbage tightly crammed into two thin plastic bags. About to sneeze, he grabbed a pillow to cover his face. When the shuddering was over he pulled the pillow away. It was soaked. Clifford's snout was in his face.

'Quit hasslin me. I'm movin, can't ya tell?' He tugged on Clifford's ears, pulling the dog closer to his chest.

Daylight oozed into the room through the thin wedge between the blind and the wall. Stepping around the dog, Christopher went to the window and pulled up the blind. Fog. Thick, silent, close-lipped, heavy with classified information.

'Check this out man, a wall of steam obscurin the distance. I can vanish into the nothingness.' He snapped his fingers. 'Just like Merlin.'

He'd told Lola everything she needed to know. Best that he got an early start and be out of the country before the spooks came looking for him. As he tidied himself up, he thought about leaving her a note. He decided it was best not to. Safety lay in vigilance. He surveyed the room – no papers on the floor, nothing behind the chairs or bench. He double-checked between the cracks of the couch, finally tucking his shoes under his arm. He half-turned toward the bedroom, considering a quick fingertip stroke of her face, but stepped into the lift.

He got out the floor below and took the fire-escape stairs. The air howled, a lone wolf in a wind tunnel. He was grateful for the chill. The concrete steps were like slabs of ice and shot the cold through him. He leant on the wall of the stairwell, his head throbbing, cursing as his frozen fingers clumsily tied the laces.

'Motherfucker shoes.'

In the basement, he fumbled with the key to the hire car, flung himself in, turned on the engine, the heater and the phone, and pressed the redial button, reminding himself to delete the number after the call.

'She's asleep. Go to her apartment first, make sure there's no-one waitin for her. Give it another thirty minutes, head for the silo. I want you to be there when she wakes up. Take her home, tell her nothin.'

He hesitated. 'Thanks, man.'

In that bleak instant he knew he'd been closing down for his own death for so long, he couldn't find the hole in the wall he'd built around himself to come back through. The pills gave him relief, they continued to impede the virus. But the pain remained; that stupid fucking hollow creased up, came in waves, right to the core of him. Pain.

She'd feel betrayed.

He sat with himself. When he'd run through all the information, scanned, analysed and itemised every detail and finally filed it away, clear that she had everything she needed to screw Dupleix, he released the hand-brake and accelerated.

I open my eyes in the embrace of the sandman. I remember leaving Christopher on the couch, removing my bottoms but not top. I think about the missing hours. Involuntarily, I flush hot. He's on top of me, on top of the hand-woven Mexican bedcover. His chest beside my head. I listen for a heartbeat but hear the ocean. The smells collect in my nose like stacked dishes on the sink. Fish funk fills my nostrils. I take a deep breath and dive back into the surf. I tear at his white overalls with my teeth. Four sets of studs split apart, click, click, click, click. I disintegrate like a cocaine pile inhaled too enthusiastically.

'Condoms, they're in my satchel.'

He laughs and swallows the whole of my face with one gulp.

White gumboots are my horizon. On his knees, he pulls the bedlinen down with one hand, and me up, over and on top of him with the other. I'm tangled up in my bra and T-shirt. With Olympic dexterity, he's dragged his overalls to his ankles.

'Condom!' I shriek, parting my legs wide enough for Moses, the Israelites and Egyptians to pass through as a mob.

Divine intervention. He wraps his arms around behind me to unfasten my bra.

'Long way home yet, still got clothes on, mate.'

I'm fixated on his chest, pectoralis major and minor. I fingerpaint the deltoid and trapezius, my legs wrap magically like Gumpy around his lean hips, locking at the ankles. Inhaling, I gaze down and behold, finally, his uncircumcised, Greek god-like bazooka. I'm confused by the extra wardrobe. Why can't they all be the same?

In the morning light, this penis is erect and enthralling, numinous, like a magic wand.

'S'OK if I slip ya bra off?'

I'm touched by his seeking permission.

'Go ahead.' I slither backwards, away from him and his high intelligent forehead. Arse up in the air, I remove gumboots and overalls.

'What the fuck?' I howl like a cat being hosed down.

Someone else is in the room. A fetishist, lurking, waiting till that moment to chomp at my buttocks. Stupefied and scratching with lust, a simmering hormone minestrone, I tumble off the bed and stand with my back to the wall ready to smash the gnasher in the groin. I let out a graveyard shriek. Eros leaps off the bed like a winged Adonis to save me. I hadn't managed to fully remove his overalls. He crunches his nose back into place like a butcher tugging on a lamb shank.

'Is it broken?' I ask, not really giving a shit any more.

'Like I said mate, itsa work in progress.'

'There you are!' I saw him out of the corner of my eye. 'Right! You're dead.'

Clifford. Slinking around from behind the bed. I flew at him, grabbing his neck and one bent ear.

'You bit me, you bastard!' I thumped him pretty hard across his hindquarters.

He goggle-eyed me till I felt my nakedness and I had to let him go. Triumphant, he spun around, kicked up his heels, did a paw-stand and moonwalked out of the room. Eros and I, anticipating heartbreak and rejection, stayed on the floor licking each other's wounds.

CHAPTER TWENTY-SEVEN

Fear arises when we view everyone else with suspicion.
– His Holiness The Dalai Lama

DEAD GIVEAWAY

'Take a look at this crap! Fucking piss-weak attempt at a media stunt.'

Dupleix, pointing his beer at the television and waving his free arm broadly like a tap dancer, bellowed across the room to Bruce Price. 'Pricey, come and see the puppies drowning.'

Price crouched in front of the fridge, his head and hands stuffed deep into its chilly womb, stacking tinnies. He heard Dupleix but didn't bother replying.

'Pricey!' Dupleix ordered this time, Nazi-style, giddy with his own power, nearly dropping his drink. He holds grudges better than anything else.

Don Turron, the newly appointed Opposition leader and Joe McNicol, Shadow Health Minister, were hoisting a giant auction sign out the front of Springfield's main gate. They were launching the party's new health policy.

The auction sign was the symbol for what the Opposition described as Dupleix's sell-off of public hospitals. Turron, a looming menace of a bloke with exotic features and the gloss of novelty, was being greeted warmly by hospital staff who'd gathered around him to shake his hand. But no-one was really paying attention. He talked about 'building a bridge to the twenty-first century'.

'What's the point of new technology, the Internet, cable and satellite television, decoding the human genome if we have hospitals that are technically bankrupt. And the only solution being put forth by Dupleix's government is to take bids from the private sector who rebuild, if we're lucky, with whoever offers the cheapest tender. And it's them that get to control the running and destiny of the hospital.'

Dupleix had asked Bruce Price to meet him at the Windsor Hotel without giving a reason. They were standing facing the television, in front of a chinoiserie table. The room was spacious, a huge beige wool rug separated the couch and four grandiose studded oxblood leather armchairs, worn with time and ferocious egos.

'What do we do about him, Pricey?'

Price rattled a six-pack of VBs at the screen. 'For crissake, forget about him. *Nobody* gives a shit. Just some bloody artsy fartsy lezzos and poofter nurses.'

He hooked a thumb in the direction of the fridge. 'Black Label and ice, mate?' But stopped midway between an armchair and his future when he heard Turron make a statement that made him fling the beers across the floor and dent the skirting board.

'For six years we've endured a government that's a threat to the people it should be protecting. In its hunger for fiscal discipline and a promised surplus, education and health care are at a never-before-seen crisis point. A leaked document downloaded from one of the department's computers and received anonymously by my office late yesterday afternoon confirms that the Premier is trying to aid a foreign power to establish a privately-run prison in this State. And we have reason to believe that this hospital is the proposed site for the project.'

Dupleix had the shit-eating grin smeared across his face. 'I'm going to ratfuck that bastard Dixon till his nuts slide down his legs like pulped fruit.'

Bruce Price swallowed hard. 'Dixon?'

'That friggin nerd has to be the leak, he's the only bastard that could access those files. It was his job to secure my computers so they weren't vulnerable to hackers. Get your shit together, we're going back across the road to my office.'

Price cleared his throat of any paternal scraps he may have had and considered only what was integral to his government's vision. 'Maaaate! Slow down, it's a beat-up, it's bullshit, *that's* the fair dinkum stunt, not the bloody *pretend* auction. He's trying to get it up ya, can't ya see what he's up to?'

'Shut ya face and follow me.'

In his office, Dupleix handed Price a pile of A4 envelopes.

'Shred the whole lot of them, then burn what's left.' He crouched in front of his computer and started deleting files. When Price tried to speak to him he leapt at him like a doberman.

'Fuck off and get rid of that shit, *now*!'

'Where do I find an incinerator?'

'Go back to the hotel and use the fireplace.' His eyes were fixed and cruel.

As soon as Dupleix was alone he locked the door, pulled out a shoe-box from the back of the last drawer of a filing cabinet, removed all the disks from the box and tried to reformat them so they'd be erased. It wasn't working so he paged a department techie. He was crushing the empty shoe-box with his foot when his phone rang. 'Yeah mate, this heap of shit won't delete files . . . I've gone to control panels . . . hold your horses, I'll get in front of the bastard.'

He faced the computer, pulled up a chair and continued to abuse the techie. 'I've done that, yep, yep, software update . . . still comes back the same . . . fuck this mate, fuck you!' The techie vanished, leaving only the dial tone.

He shoved the rest of the disks in his pocket and punched the directory search button on the fax/phone machine. He was rigid with wanting to take a leak. He put the phone on speaker, unzipped his trousers and stood legs apart facing the filing cabinet.

A man's voice answered, kind of frenzied. 'Hello?'

Dupleix barked angrily. 'No more fucking yakkety-yak, mate.

You've got twenty-four hours to sort this out, nobody's going to take this away from me! You understand that? What the fuck was Turron mouthing off about on tonight's news?'

He listened for half the time it takes to blow out a match. 'I know this might be way above your grade of pay to understand, but I've never had a setback that I couldn't deal with. I don't give a rat's arse about popularity polls. You should've got that message loud and clear from the ambulance deal. Now, you better come to grips with the fact that you're one phone call away from being the subject of a kinky rumour to a front-page headline. You might even end up in jail.' He laughed like a loon. 'You got it, boy?'

He hung up, took two steps back and swivelled his head around the room to check that the door to his office was locked, then aimed his penis into the bottom drawer of the filing cabinet and depreciated its value considerably.

'Boss, let me in.' Price returned and asserted himself immediately. Dupleix opened the door. 'Those bastards will be screaming hard for an inquiry, I reckon we should prepare for a news conference, head them off at the pass. Why not call up a few media mates and laugh off the prison bullshit?'

They were in the hallway, Dupleix hadn't allowed Price to come into his office. He locked the door and strutted ahead, relieved at the prospect of action. 'Nah, won't bother with those scum, I've got another plan. Fix me up with a radio spot tomorrow morning. I'll work the story on air.'

Bruce Price made no attempt to keep up with Dupleix. He'd started coughing back at the hotel while burning the shredded letters. He hadn't yet fully comprehended his son's complicity in the leak. It made him feel queasy to think that the kid with the giant chip on his shoulder could show such guts or no sense at all, depending on which way he looked at it. He took a sideways step, pressed his back against the wall and coughed hard to shift the bit of phlegm that was choking him.

Dupleix stopped a few steps short of the exit and cocked his head toward Spring Street. 'Get yourself outside, face-ache, you need some fresh air. It stinks in here.'

'Bundy and a good night's sleep, I'll be right as rain in the morning,' Fillet wheezed.

The driver stood by the passenger door, poised to close it. Dupleix flung himself in, threw back his head and howled like a wolf. The driver, who'd never been comfortable with the job, observed Dupleix in the rear-view mirror. Dupleix controlled the speed and nominated the route. There was no choice. The car stopped outside Dupleix's home.

'Be here tomorrow, Greg, 7 a.m. on the dot. I'm on the wireless first thing.'

Greg nodded like a dumb brute and dreamt of never having to see him again.

They were in a tree-lined boulevard in Heidelberg, parked in the driveway of a nouveau-Greco draconically oversized building. Chubby Iceberg roses lined the freshly graded path to the front door. In the moonlight they gleamed and jiggled like marshmallows.

Dupleix stepped out of the car then turned back and leant right into Greg's face. 'Keep the engine running, I'll be back in a minute.'

Greg stalled the car. Endeavouring to conceal his clumsiness he revved the engine too quickly and sent a mechanised, mezzo-soprano screech howling through the discreetly mortgaged hedges.

Dupleix ran back to the car on tiptoe and leapt so far into the front seat his head hovered an inch above Greg's lap. 'Don't give me that look. Save that for your wife when she finds out you're rogering Rochelle in Fleet Services.' Greg drove off and concentrated on deflecting rage.

Dupleix settled back. 'Head to East St Kilda, down Burke Road, Toorak, steer straight up Hotham Street.'

When they arrived at Mimi's block of flats the darkness of the building was relieved only intermittently by the winking of a soon-to-expire outdoor light above the front door. Dupleix looked out his side window and saw Mimi's giantess silhouette sauntering around the entrance. She ducked inside as soon as she spotted his car. At that moment Dupleix heard another sound and sensed danger. He looked ahead, a pair of headlights came on, gripping them both in their high beam. The car reversed and accelerated into a U-turn.

'Get the number plate, Greg. I can't see it from my side.'

'There isn't one.'

'Follow him, you idiot . . . go . . . go . . . go!'

Greg stalled the car. 'It's gotta be a blocked fuel filter or carby. Only take a minute.'

Dupleix steamed. 'Forget it, go back to my place.'

'Any particular way?'

'With your foot on the accelerator would be handy!'

Greg shrugged. Anything to avoid conversation.

CHAPTER TWENTY-EIGHT

As one door closes another slams in your face.
– Rachel Heyhoe Flint

a BAD EGG

We arrived at my flat. Eros jumped out of the van and walked around to open my door. I pushed down on the door handle with my elbow at the exact moment he pulled. I fell out into the gutter. (I have submitted to the idea that I am clumsier than most.) He helped me up, peeling off the damp litter stuck to my clothes, and fluffed hair back off my face.

'I apprenissed as a hairdresser, ya didn't know that didjya?'

'How could I?'

'Exactly, how couldya?'

'Hang on a minute.' I turned up the radio. 'That's Dupleix.'

Dupleix was speaking in full volume, sounding aggressive and energetic. 'The letters are fake. The signatures were forged. No-one can say unequivocally where they came from.'

I bent forward to check the station. Eros cupped my right buttock with his palm. I felt the tingle of hormone whiz-fizz but this was no time for wish fulfilment.

Eros held on eagerly. 'Just checking ya don't get giddy and fall over.'

'The woman on this breakfast slot, whatshername – Jane, Tracie – her husband works in Dupleix's office.'

The presenter sounded like most breakfast-show presenters – forced. 'Mr Premier, are you saying you've never seen this correspondence?'

'That's correct, as far as I know. Some days there's a lot of paper flying around and maybe I was busy, I signed something without giving much thought to it. I cannot remember viewing this material before.'

'With respect, Mr Premier, you're aware that many people would find that hard to believe.'

'That's their problem.'

Eros interrupted. 'I got fish to deliver. But I got my eye onya. Everytime you land on your arse someplace, I hope to be there.' He raised a hand to wave goodbye. I grabbed it quickly the way some people snatch mosquitoes out of the air.

'What happened to Pillar?'

The silence lasted long enough for me to repeat the question.

'What happened to Pillar?'

'Who?'

'I left him sleeping on the couch last night. He had a fever but wouldn't let me call a doctor. As we were walking out of the apartment I noticed one of the cushions splattered with blood. Eros, I'm worried about him.'

He grinned at me as if the two of us were in on some joke. He used one arm to lift his body up into the van, slammed the door and wound down the window. 'Dunno no-one called Pillar.' Not one muscle flickered in his Hellenic cheek.

'I understand I have no prior claim on what's going on here, Eros, I don't really give a fuck any more. But I'm not good at cloak and dagger, I'm the wrong blood type. So enough already, where's Pillar?'

For several tense seconds I maintained an aloof distance. I had no doubt at all about the fan-hitting shit rain spraying into every corner of my life, but without information I was useless.

Christopher and I had collided, leaving the scene of the accident without properly exchanging details. From where I was standing things were looking very skewed. Especially Dupleix. If the truth was out about Springfield there was no way he could survive the brutal media response. Then again, Dupleix would go only low enough not to get bogged in his own shit. I had no idea what he'd do. Christopher was a gentleman; he'd given me some slack, but not enough to hang myself with.

Eros revved the motor. 'Relax, you're safe as houses for the moment.'

I laughed despite myself, nodding reluctantly.

He drove away. I was hungry. I hadn't eaten for . . . god, I couldn't remember, which was a first. I headed straight inside and clicked the door shut behind me.

I was sure the answering machine would be into full-swing cha-cha by now and dashed past, making sure it didn't spot me. I opened the refrigerator door to silence, a refrigerative death valley. A saggy carrot lay seductively across the middle shelf, believing itself firm like an ageing starlet. A fading pawpaw kept up appearances but I could tell it was rotten on the inside. Only the chorus line of eggs in their egg-shaped caravan were still in full make-up, on standby for their three-minute call.

Secure in the knowledge that I couldn't stay in there for longer than it takes to boil an egg, I stepped into my study. Wrong! It was a minefield, with every step in demanding courage. Fax shrapnel littered the floor – my antique doesn't cut the pages.

Sixteen pages. I tore them out and dragged them back into the kitchen like a jilted bride with a second-hand veil and used the Staysharp knife to slice them. The message from Lawrence, handwritten in thick jumbo texta, stood out like dog's balls. He'd faxed yesterday at 6 p.m.. My knees fell away, I was having a libido flashback. Precisely the hour I met with Eros.

LISTEN! LISTEN! LISTEN!

The Press have lobbed at the AIDS Council, asking more questions about the benefit than a drag queen solicits about her wig. Joshua's giving a squillion interviews about the hospital closing and it's like the whole crew have accepted the battle's over, a fait-accompli chi-chi. ARGHH! MUST MUST MUST call me as soon as you get this, I've left forty trillion squillion messages.

Kiss Kiss.

L

'Just sit there for a minute,' I ordered the balance of faxes.

Very spooky. I was sitting at the kitchen table with my back to the window, stove and sink. I could hear a menacing, low-pitched rumbling sound. Without moving one unnecessary muscle, I stretched out my arm to pick up the Staysharp and spun round, bent on evicting whoever had entered my kitchen.

The eggs. The boiling water in the saucepan had reduced enough for the eggs to gently rumble against the sides. I cut off their heads, in no mood for pranks.

I ate quickly and phoned Lawrence. He breathed a sigh of relief. 'I'm in shock. It is you, isn't it?'

'Knock it off, wait till I hit you with the last twenty-four hours.'

'It's not over yet darl, not till the fat lady sings, *I did it my way.* But I'd rather we talk alone.'

'We are alone.'

'Hate to disappoint, but I think it's a party-line.'

'Right now I've got the attention span of a gnat. I'll come over in a couple of hours, lunchtime-ish.'

'Lunchtime-ish, perfect. I'll grab Smokey and Freddy.'

I flashed through the remaining faxes.

CONFIDENTIAL
MINISTER for HEALTH, the Hon. William Lisbon

Lola, sincere apologies for leaving the restaurant while you were out of the room. I attempted to call you several times during the afternoon, but your phone was turned off and I felt reluctant to leave a pathetic apology on your voicemail.

Re: Springfield, I spoke with the Prime Minister late yesterday. We may be able to intervene via legislation, if certain recommendations could be met. I would suggest that we meet as soon as possible. I've alerted Joshua Newbroom, whom you know. A Press Conference should be organised with the three of us in attendance. The media will adore the juxtaposition of this troika! We must act quickly.
Regards William

How could William make such a U-turn? If Christopher was right, William was a razor's edge from being exposed and had to have accepted that fact. He didn't have the balls to make that kind of sacrifice. This was some kind of deliberate decoy crap contrived back at Dupleix's compound. I had to talk to William immediately or avoid him forever. I didn't bother listening to any messages or contacting William or Joshua.

The AIDS Council foyer was a swarm of buzzing phones, the perfect audio frequency for my internal theatrette: replays of Mimi in lingerie with the book of fairytales, the killer budgie, white gumboots, Christopher's coughing. An arm wrapped around my shoulder and pulled me into another space.

Joshua.

'William Lisbon called an hour ago, he says you haven't responded to his suggestion of a combined press conference. He's keen to chat up the postponing of the closure. You did receive the fax?'

I couldn't breathe. I nodded so he'd tell me what he was thinking.

'Lisbon's digging a hole for himself. He's not playing clever politics. My feeling is that joining him to address the media could do the Council and our hopes for the relocation of Springfield a great deal of harm.'

'If he reckons he can stop the closure, why not go with it?'

'Because it's about political point-scoring.'

'Who gives a shit if members of one team think their dicks are bigger? We get the hospital.'

The veins on Joshua's brow squirmed under the pressure. I found myself wondering if it worked for his own political future to go along with Dupleix. He sat back in his chair. 'Dita Nobb is mightily pissed off about this.'

'Who cares?'

'Part of her health policy is the restructuring of the current system. Her office has had a committee working on the planning and management of the new system for nearly a year. The first step is that Springfield has to close.'

'Maybe I'm slower than the police helpline, but wouldn't the first step be to find out what the community needs? Rather than slash and hack away and then oops, sorry, all we can offer you is a packet of Bandaids and some codeine past its use-by date.'

He was silent for a moment then continued in a restrained, formaldehyde voice.

'Lisbon's response to save the hospital by reducing beds and staff and collaborating with a bigger hospital is about headfucking the State Government. His people haven't properly investigated the figures.'

'Makes sense to me.'

'It'll cost the Federal Government over three million dollars to implement these recommendations, two million for redundancies alone. In the big picture it's far more economical to relocate.'

'I'm meeting with Lawrence about the Benefit. It's tomorrow.

Can I talk to you about the press thing later? Lisbon can't confirm without speaking to you again and you're not really interested anyway. I have to go.'

He gave me a lapsed-Catholic wave, limp and guilty. I pulled open the door and made a beeline for Meeting Room Two.

'Lawrence?' Freddy, lunatic-eyed, balancing a plate of chocolate-chip cookies and a skinnycino, lunged into my path. The cookies crushed on impact. Freddy lay in a biologically impossible contortion across the boardroom table. I was wedged between two chairs.

Smokey pulled the chairs apart with one hand, I slumped to the floor. With the other hand, she peeled Freddy off the table by his shirt ruffles.

'Looking gorgeous, darls,' said Lawrence. 'Tea-towel?'

Freddy grabbed the tea-towel grudgingly. 'What happened?'

'Sorry, sorry, sorry . . . had to get away from Joshua . . . I haven't had any sleep. My motor neuron hand–mouth action is fucked up.'

Smokey inhaled, exploiting all the oxygen in the room.

'Hand–eye, not hand–mouth.'

'Exactly!'

'So what's happening?' Smokey insisted.

'Plenty. Can we leave the building?'

Lawrence nodded. 'Sounds good to me. Let's go to the new politically-correct pizza place across the road.'

We flopped in and were led to a corner table in an almost empty room. The walls were glazed in a pale pistachio, apparently very soothing. Ergonomically designed tables were strategically placed for peaceful digestion and food meditation. One wall was a mammalian relief; several female patrons had plunged their breasts into soft plaster to create a maternal ambient space. A boy-man and his silver dolphin nose-stud hippie-hippie-shaked over to take our order. He was badly in need of decongestant.

Freddy frisbeed into a chair and lit a cigarette. He was unsympathetic.

'He's givin me a gut-ache.'

'He's probably having an allergic reaction to something.'

'I'll give him an allergic reaction –'

'Cool it. Look at the menu.' Smokey distracted him the way one would a child.

Lawrence twitched as though he were negotiating some internal trauma.

Dolphin boy hopscotched back into our circle.

'Today's special is Say-No-To-Candida-Pizza. No mushrooms, no sugar, no spices, no olives, no cheese –'

'Look buddy,' Freddy stood rigid. 'Who asked ya?'

We ordered assorted dips – guacamole, hummus, eggplant – and tempeh burgers. When the food arrived, nothing looked like the food group it belonged to.

Freddy didn't eat. 'Smells like horseshit.'

I needed to purge. To upchuck the entire devilled Dupleix turkey before it had a neuropsychological effect.

I proceeded to tell the gang about my last twenty-four hours. Smokey belched, 'Why the fairytales? I understand the whipping, I respect any individual's unique sexual *pen-chant* but *that's* a freakish combo.'

We all nodded in agreement. Freddy held a tempeh slice over each ear while I repeated Christopher's spin on Lisbon. No-one asked where I got my information; if they had I'd have said it was Mimi. I never mentioned Eros – that was my business. I had a pounding headache. It'd started on a low simmer this morning but now it was steaming. As I watched Smokey preening, I remembered Eros fixing my hair.

'What's with Dupleix on the radio this morning? The correspondence they were talking about?' Freddy rubbed his thumb against the outline of his mouth.

'We're not one hundred per cent certain for sure, but I'll bet it's Geraldo's letter.'

'The same one he gave us?'

'Probably.'

'Why would he leak it?'

'Because sometimes,' Smokey interrupted, 'people don't plan ahead when they're going to fuck someone over.'

I was confused. 'It doesn't make any sense for Geraldo to make it this easy for Dupleix to deny it. It's looking so badly like a B-grade political stunt, enough bad to create a turnaround for Dupleix if people believe that Turron is this much of a jerk.'

Lawrence was brooding. He'd sat mute until Geraldo's name came up. 'Who d'ya think recruited him?'

I didn't hesitate. 'Frank Dixon?' It seemed an irrelevant question. 'Why is it important?'

He twisted free from the question, returning to his usual style. 'Well, darls, Nanna always said two dicks make a huge cock-up.'

CHAPTER TWENTY-NINE

He who hesitates is not only lost, but miles from the next exit.
– Anon

the RALLY

The rally was Freddy's lightning-bolt idea. A public display of outrage through the central business district. We'd finalised production details for the fundraiser cabaret. Lawrence had volunteers on standby to help with ticket-selling, front of house and merchandising. Posters were up all over town.

Freddy grandstanded. 'No tickets left.' He opened his eyes as wide as they'd go and clicked his fingers. 'Baby's already sold out!'

The idea germinated after a phone call from Deidre. We were still in the restaurant. That something bad was about to happen felt as real as the stench of burning sesame oil.

Dolphin boy pirouetted from across the room to remove the plates. I asked for doggy bags.

Lawrence turned up his nose. 'You're not seriously taking that crapola home?'

'They'll make great face masks – hummus is very astringent.'

'Just like you! *Whaaaat* exactly is your problem?'

Smokey squinted at Lawrence. He responded with his sore-tooth expression. Her mobile chirped from its nest in her clutch bag. 'Hey

Deeds, what's curling up? Need more lippie, bigger earrings, is there anything you want us to bring you?' Turning her back to us, she shoved a huge knuckle in her ear but still kept barking down the phone. 'Speak up love, I can hardly hear you.'

Freddy, Lawrence and I sat like pie-shells waiting to be filled. Our individually designed pizzas arrived. That was the big pitch of the restaurant, DIY pizza, to encourage your inner child. And non-alcoholic sangria that doubled as cinnamon-and-spice bathroom deodoriser.

Freddy hissed under his breath. 'Toilet Duck-in-a-jug.'

Lawrence gave him a peck on the cheek. 'Sangria. You wake up in the morning, your head feels like a Mardi Gras dance-track playing really, really loudly through a dustbin.'

Freddy winced at the thought. 'Never heard of it.'

'It's foreign. Spanish, actually.'

'I flunked foreign at school, hated the teacher.'

Lawrence poured a drink, pushing the handmade goblet across to Freddy. 'Get your slurpies round that.'

Smokey was the colour of the walls. 'She's about to leave the hospital.'

'Fantastic!'

'She's *not* ready to leave. They're being forced to go.'

'Whaddaya mean, forced to go?'

Freddy's ears grew chilli red, at least two shades darker than his neck.

'Yesterday, certain patients – some of them have been in there for years, like Trevor on the lung machine – were transferred to other hospitals. None of them was consulted, no announcement was made.'

She extended three fingers, holding them parallel to her chest. 'Three guys have died. Deed reckons prematurely, because of all the uncertainty and confusion.'

Smokey's voice disappeared down her throat. Her eyebrows crumpled. Mascara, eyeliner, lipstick, a domino effect of grieving and sobbing. Five fluorescent-pink nail extensions covered her face. We floated on her raft of tears.

She used all the paper napkins to blow her nose. 'Because of the rumours of an early closure, they've started moving people weeks ahead of the agreed timeline.' With each sob her voice climbed to a higher frequency. 'And because of work bans, they've only been getting one hot meal a day. The volunteers can't sustain the load. Two days ago, Simon and Jimbo were woken up around 5 a.m., fed, washed and transported to Prince Andrew's before daylight.'

'That's gotta be illegal! They were in the final stages.'

Grabbing hold of Freddy's shoulders, Smokey collapsed in a nylon heap into his chest hair. Her voice reverberated through his body. 'Jimbo died this morning lying on a trolley at Prince Andrew's. The bastards hadn't found him a bed.'

Freddy scratched the crest of his chin. 'Your hair spray's givin me a rash.'

'Fuck you.'

Freddy rubbed his fingers together, laughing bestially. 'Drag queens in fairytale costumes . . . '

Smokey slapped him. 'What are you like?'

He leapt out of his seat. 'Strutting down Bourke Street to Parliament House. Dupleix's not expecting nothing. Another day, another rally . . . he comes outta the building and the gang is cracking their whips, baby. Roll 'em out, head 'em on . . . rawhide! Yeefuckinha! Sleeping Bewdy, Cinderella, Snow White, little piggies, Hansel and Gretel, wicked fuckin witches. We'll have ourselves one squealing Premier.'

I loved it.

Smokey shook as though she was suddenly battling alcoholism. 'I love you.'

Channelling Michael Jackson and squealing like a pig, Freddy licked his forefinger and touched himself. 'When there's scum to trash, I'm on fire.'

Smokey blitzkrieged him with cheek-pulling. 'I'll get a bootload of cat-o'-nine-tails from the leather boys. We'll have us a leather crusade, fling down our gauntlets and make him bend over. We'll bear arms. Fuck it, we'll bare arses.'

Smokey spoke in urgent.

Lawrence was subdued. 'I'm not sold on overstated drama.'

'Whaaaaaaat?' Plasma oozed out of my ears. 'Did you forget your medication today?'

'A bunch of screeching drag queens could be an anti-climax. And anyway, how do you know Mimi isn't bullshitting?'

I was uneasy with Lawrence's increasing tension. He walked toward the door, shaking his head. I followed him talking to the back of his vest. 'Thousands of people will turn up from across the whole community. It won't be *just* drag queens.'

He kept moving. He wasn't listening. 'I'll pick Deidre up and bring her over to Smokey and Freddy's in a couple of hours.'

Freddy was aglow. 'What? We should sit around scratching our balls with so much at stake?'

I followed Lawrence out the door, grabbing his arm to stop him. 'Is there something you need to tell me?'

Perspiration leached through to his leather vest. 'Don't wear flats, darls, a girl can always do with a little elevation. Ciao!'

I wanted to speak to Joshua before the end of the day. It was 4.30. Toorak Road was crammed with drivers honking horny, rut-tish for the five o'clock peak.

The benefit was tomorrow. We'd decided the rally would be two days after that. There wouldn't be another opportunity. I went back inside.

'Here's my share for the food. I want to catch Joshua before he leaves. Call me at home later.'

I cradled the parcel of dips, neatly stacked in plastic containers and alfoil. Smokey and Freddy lifted their faces from out of tall glasses of sangria.

Smokey didn't make eye contact. 'You look worried.'

My intestines yodelled for Alka-Seltzer. 'I need some elevation.'

Joshua sat cross-legged in an ergonomic chair behind an industrial-design desk. His neck threatened to burst the collar of his self-imposed leash. He stared out the window.

'What do you expect me to do?'

'Can't you negotiate a deal between the union and management, something temporary until everyone knows what's happening?'

'Management decided to close the hospital because they couldn't guarantee volunteers to staff the plating of food and cleaning.'

'THAT'S BULLSHIT – the volunteers in the support program are committed to seeing this through.'

'Maybe, but it's taking its toll. Every day the situation gets worse; the more demands are placed on them, the less they're able to sustain the required level of care. So far, union members haven't been able to resolve the terms of their redundancy packages because these packages were designed for people who chose to leave on a voluntary basis. These are forced redundancies. Can you understand their position?'

I stopped pointing my finger. 'Nobb gave her word that the hospital's closure wouldn't adversely impact on patients.'

Joshua grinned, displaying all the cynicism of a prisoner of war. 'Haven't you seen today's headlines?'

He didn't wait for a response. 'The Supreme Court released a police report that found Dupleix's gang had illegally suppressed politically damaging briefing notes over the ambulance contracts scandal.'

'Exit stage left, Dita Nobb.'

'Among the documents there were references made to the Springfield closure. The Opposition are loving this. They're pushing for a new inquiry into the whole affair. Naturally, she denies seeing any briefing notes. She's claiming that she's never misled

Parliament and it's the police justifying the two years they've spent on the investigation.'

'What's Dupleix's reaction?'

'Laughed it off. Said it was a beat-up. The Opposition having paranoid fantasies. He even denied signing some of the documents.'

'They've been trying to get a hold of those documents under Freedom of Information for two years. This is bullshit. You know it, everyone knows it.'

'But it changes the political landscape. It's no longer about saving money or Nobb's arse. It's about saving Dupleix and the election. At this moment many people think he's invincible. But things can change in a matter of hours; Dupleix doesn't have a lot of time to turn this one around. He's going to stall for as long as he can. My bet is there'll be a huge swing to the Opposition. He'll get his butt kicked but still remain Premier. If we're lucky he might do a flip on the closure.'

I corrected him. 'If we're lucky, that sonofabitch will get trashed. That's the only thing that will stop the sell-off.'

'You believe the sell-off story?'

'It looks and smells like a Dupleix dinner to me. How many S's in sell-off, Joshua? Squillions!'

Six-thirty: time to go home, have a bath, get a decent night's sleep.

Where did I leave my car? The market carpark. I walk up the ramp and stop. I'd believed Lawrence's story about meeting Geraldo at the tubs. Addicted to my bad habit of trusting at least one person unquestionably, I'd relinquished the usual self-interrogation. I was now aware that Lawrence maintained close contact at all times. I'd shared every detail about Pillar and in spite of my initial hesitation about Geraldo's intentions, I accepted Lawrence's explanation. It was possible that I'd walked into a plan well set up to keep me under surveillance.

It was too late to do anything about these paranoid fantasies. I didn't have enough adrenalin to have an anxiety attack. Thoughts of Dupleix as a deadly virus crept in: *HIV works by destroying the very cells which are responsible for mounting a fight against the infection itself.*

My car finds me. I do foreplay with the engine and make sure it's warmed up enough to get me home. I blink. The Vasilis Fish Supply van is blocking my path. My foot slips off the accelerator. I smell cod. I pause to consider my next move and in that space between chaos and complexity, the van does a U-turn, flashing its headlights, manoeuvring into the space on my left. The face is in shadow. No exchange. He keeps the engine running, then moves off.

I'm shallow-breathing. I take a zigzag route home. Chapel Street, window-shopping in the twilight, onto Toorak Road, down Domain and into the drive around the Botanical Gardens. I stretch my jaw, open my eyes wide in an attempt to straighten up and concentrate. The sky is a scalloped black lace edge on a blue satin chemise. I think about driving home naked. If I crash into a tree that's how they'd find me. Fuck it. I slide out of my clothes and keep well within the speed limit.

CHAPTER THIRTY

Hope is the feeling you have that the feeling you have isn't permanent.
– Jean Kerr

the FUNDRAISER

The theatre was packed. The pulse of a thousand people feeling ripped off snapped the elastic lace strap of my push-up bra. I walked on stage, my throat as dry as a week-old slab of meatloaf, one breast lower than the other. I'd slept fitfully. Each time I woke up my nose was more clogged. My memory cross-referenced one incident with Lawrence to another. Like a schizophrenic filing system, it delivered memories at once both clear and confused. I found it difficult to distinguish between what I believed to be fact and my escalating paranoia. I looked for him backstage before I went on, but there wasn't enough time.

A room of flared nostrils. Union members, public servants, hospital staff, mums and dads, anyone affected by the hospital's closure and every patient who wasn't dead and could be there, were present. I felt myself the focus of countless bloodshot eyes. Memory leap-frog: Deidre's eyes in the hospital. The drive there, Lawrence rolling joints on his knees using a sliced-up magazine for a flat surface. The cut-and-paste warning letter delivered to my door in Canberra. I'd been impressed by his finding me there at that hotel.

I ransacked my memory in vain, trying to recollect that conversation.

When the clapping subsided, I leant into the microphone, opened my mouth, but nothing came out. The audience laughed. Smokey strutted on stage with a glass of water and got applause that bordered on religious fervour.

'Poor love, I warned her not to let them shove the butt-plug in too far.'

She handed me the glass. 'Swallow hard.'

I gulped the water, my heart beating slightly out of tune.

Take two.

'Ka-ching, ka-ching! Ladies and gentlemen, the latest Victorian number plate. It's the sound of buying and selling.

'I've always been fascinated by the supernatural – ouija boards, seances, feminine hygiene spray. Although I find it difficult to make contact with the dead since dead people generally don't speak, I recently participated in a seance. Mahatma Gandhi appeared in the room wanting to know if anyone had seen his rubber-grip biro.

'"Someone's always walking off with it" was the message he left us with.

'I've read that people have experiences of poltergeist after severe emotional shock. This is incredible because a scientific paper presented to the Victorian Government several months before Dupleix was voted in warned of various poltergeist events about to erupt. Victoria would be cast into an era of unexplained phenomena.

'Parents will picket and barricade themselves in primary schools, fighting with police over the closure of schools.

'Mothers will leave hospitals minutes after their babies are born, tying umbilical cords as they're running through the self-opening doors. Imagine! A whole generation of babies with weird belly buttons tied in slip knots for speed.

'Proper health care will be available only for the very rich or politicians with penile dementia. Medicare will stay, but just like wearing one of those hospital gowns, you'll think you're covered all over but there's that split down the back that doesn't quite cover your arse. Unemployment will reach never-before-seen peaks and women will dance naked on tables in inner-city pubs only minutes from Parliament House. Auditor-Generals will combine art and black magic in an attempt to maintain their jobs as performance artists.

'At Parliament House, recently relocated to the new casino, there'll be unexplained phenomena such as stone-throwing, out-of-body experiences, levitations, hair-pulling and diarrhoea. A kind of mass primal event attracting corporate sponsors keen to be seen as promoting the arts. Exorcism will become a free item on Medicare for unemployment card holders and our new national anthem will be "Who wants to be a millionaire".

'We know that Springfield shouldn't have to close . . . '

Someone heckled, 'We won't let that happen.'

I continued. 'Yes, there are problems. The biggest is that it's a sensational piece of real estate. You would've heard the news that Springfield Hospital is being proposed as a site for an American private prison. America, where they're trying to make capital punishment more humane by developing an ergonomic electric chair. No more backache while you wait for the switch to be flicked. The Premier strongly denies this and wants us to believe him. His part-time job is at the weather bureau.

'The organisation – let's call them Ball and Chain Incorporated – plan to negotiate a deal with our State Government. They'll redevelop the site into a prison, contract out services like prisoner transport, education and food, and hey presto! someone's mates get to retire early in Majorca.

'We can't let that happen. The few patients left at Springfield are too worn out to make a loud enough noise. It's up to us to make sure the government hears them. Thank you for your support.'

Down the back, pennies dropped. People began to applaud and gradually everyone joined in. The perfect cue to bring Smokey on stage.

'Ladies and gentlemen, go feral for the one and only . . . Smokey Topaz.'

The curtain opened with a blast of flashing cameras. Smokey doing Marlene Dietrich: cigarette dangling from blood-red lips, leaning on a cardboard cut-out lamp post.

Joshua arrived backstage with the biggest *oh fuck* look on his face. 'Lisbon's cancelled the press conference. I'm presuming the Prime Minister reconsidered because of upcoming State elections.'

'I wouldn't count on that. I don't reckon he ever seriously intended proceeding with the press conference. It was a stunt to divert attention from Dupleix.'

'I know you think he's . . . '

'Toxic. And like any dangerous chemical, needs to be disposed of carefully. You don't believe he's sold off Springfield, but I've seen proof. Questions are going to start flying around like poison darts and the right one might disable the Americans for long enough to change their minds about this being a satisfactory location.'

A sinister gleam shone in Joshua's eye. 'You're leaving yourself wide open. At best to charges of slander, at worst to being perceived as paranoid and irrational.'

'I've got nothing to lose, Joshua. There's not much profit in taking the piss. There are no long-term incentive schemes for comedians.'

'Dupleix's no doubt heard about your prison fantasy. I'd be surprised if someone doesn't contact you about it.'

'I'll look forward to a visit from a couple of thugs in Zegna suits with less vocabulary between them than a fungus then.'

'I doubt it. A letter, probably, requesting you remove that material from your routine.'

'This is a democracy. At least it still was this morning when I last flushed. Dupleix's a testicle squeezer. His premiership is a series of cosy deals and slimy handshakes. He believes everyone's got their price. Fuck him, he's wrong.'

'His friends were rich before he came along.'

'He doesn't have friends, they're commercial relationships.'

Joshua looked somewhere over my shoulder. 'I think you've been overzealous and we could very well be in the shit now.'

He lifted a pointed finger not exactly at my face but close enough. 'What the fuck have you brought to this campaign anyway? Do you honestly think you can save the hospital with gags?'

'No! But you won't do it standing around scratching your balls,' I said, putting a finger in my ear trying to block out the audience applause for Smokey.

I glimpsed Lawrence helping Smokey with her costume between songs. I couldn't call out, so I waved and snapped my fingers to get his attention. It was useless. He couldn't see me or was pretending not to.

Joshua was relentless. 'The ability to see this out is based on very careful planning and scrupulous behaviour. We're operating under tough conditions as it is.'

I'd had enough. 'Joshua, risk-taking is not my area. It's just the way things have worked out. I didn't plan it this way!'

He wasn't listening. 'But you . . . '

I grabbed my load. 'Gotta go. Enjoy the rest of the show.'

I walked into my flat and got the shower steaming. Disaster stains – you have to scrub them immediately. I checked the machine. No red flashing light – I'd forgotten to switch it on. I rewound the tape.

'Howdy, ma'am.' It was Christopher, and he didn't say what day it was. 'Being commitaphobic, part of my twelve-step program to recovery is to call someone I care about at least once every six months . . . ' His voice fell away.

Beep.

'Eats your mudder. I need to talk mid you ergent. I said sometheeng, but dey mix me up, I'm not shure exactly what I sed. I must to go because I ate a slice shrtudel and I got gas. Call me pliss.'

Too late now. Under the shower, hot water massaging my back

and shoulders, I stretch my neck. Stiff from optimism. I sit on the edge of the bed, the sag of my arse pulling the pillow closer. The fridge hums me to sleep. The dog next door sleeps. My mother sleeps. Worst of all, Dupleix sleeps. I wake to the sound of birds discussing the NASDAQ in the branches outside my bedroom window.

The ABC radio signal announces the eight o'clock news. I cover my ears, unable to stomach the round-up of tragedy, and then:

Entertainment news this morning reveals that Lola Finkelstein, stand-up comic, is a man. Ms Finkelstein's mother, Bella Finkelstein, has recently undergone the Minimental psychiatric test for suspected dementia. It's believed her file was leaked to a tabloid publication by someone from the clinic. In it, Bella Finkelstein admits she's never been able to accept that her son, Leonard, underwent a sex change in Hong Kong without consulting her twelve years ago. On his return to Melbourne, with a new body and identity, according to Bella Finkelstein's account, he phoned her and told her that Leonard had died during surgery but she had a daughter, Lola. She believes this shock provoked her dementia.

My head filled with whipped cream. I got to the bathroom and took the throw-up option. A primitive instinct prevented me from returning to the bedroom. I was awake, anger giving anxiety to my day. Rage, the breakfast of champions. Habit insisted I check my answering machine. I told habit our relationship was redundant.

A fax from London had streamed in overnight. I regretted speaking to habit in a dismissive tone.

Hiya Lady,
When are you moving into the real world and getting email? I feel like Cro-Magnon woman using the fax! Not still agonising over the lanky American I hope? Enough with enabling, enough

with your intimacy crap! Thought you might find this interesting, from the Guardian. *Could it be the same guy?*
Ciao, Amanda

Despite fax distortion, the man in the photo was a double for Pillar, maybe ten years younger. The piece was about a suspected double agent whom authorities believed had information that could help with the investigation into the death of an American engineer in Nicaragua in the early 80s.

I lay on the couch surrounded by the decor of heartburn.

Where to from here? Should I have my blood pressure tested or stomach pumped? I practised squeezing my abdominal muscles and grimaced to acclimatise to the geographical extremes I'd encounter over the next few weeks – the snake-infested streams of the media, the arid wasteland of family, the swamps of political dross. No inoculations for this destination.

To confirm that advertising ruled our lives, not the sun, I tuned into breakfast television. Dupleix's face squirted across the glass rectangle.

'Is it true, Premier, that your government has sold more than $30 billion in Victorian Government assets?'

Dupleix grinned broadly at the presenter. 'There's no need for that tone, Kylie. We've brought the State out of its black hole into the black.'

Kylie positioned her perfectly pressed baby-blue lapels and fired. 'Then why are you closing schools and hospitals?'

'That's a stupid schoolgirl question.'

CHAPTER THIRTY-ONE

Queue – the procedure nowadays for minor surgery like heart transplants, brain replacements, etc.
– Paul Lyneham

JUST for FUN

The rally was a buzzing, gurgling, whip-cracking showdown. I stayed away but watched it on every news broadcast that night. The call had gone out for whips and they came conscientiously from every direction. The sheer number of people of all shapes, sizes, colours and sexual predilections was a gobsmacking spectacle. Drag queens fronted the pack. A row of almost twenty Snow Whites whipped blow-up cartoon dwarfs, followed by a clutch of bare-chested Muscle Marys in too tight jam-packed nappies and pink plastic piggy noses.

After them, a show-stopping squad of high-kicking single-booted Cinderellas. They held a banner that read, *The shoe's on the other foot, Dupleix!* Suddenly Little Red Riding Hood passed between the camera and the parade. Twenty stone of scarlet sequins and stilettoes totally eclipsed the camp labyrinth. Smokey Topaz marched triumphantly up Bourke Street in an easterly direction toward Dupleix. Grabbing fistfuls of coloured condoms from her basket, she threw them at the crowd like seed to be fertilised.

The lunchtime shoppers lining the bitumen cheered as the carnival marched by. Several joined in with the doctors, nurses and thousands of other Victorians who wanted to reinforce the fact that they didn't want to lose the hospital.

Dupleix imploded. His advisers had alerted him to the event but he could never have anticipated the chaos he'd be confronting. Cameras were banned from filming any further than Exhibition Street so no-one got a shot of Dupleix having a massive asthma attack. He's still under medical supervision. Smokey can't stop howling with scornful jubilation.

'Freddy, let's visit him in hospital and blow cigarette smoke in his face.'

Documents sought and finally released through Freedom of Information revealed that two of Dupleix's mates, one a senior politician, were major shareholders and directors of the Australian subsidiary of Shackles Inc. And they'd won the tender to rebuild the hospital.

Two months later, Labor ran a campaign fuelled mainly by spelling out their policies on health, education, open government and a promise to listen to the rural sector. It was no gourmet feast, just your basic chop-and-three-veg affair. But it filled the spot. And with the help of a couple of Independents, they got in.

Springfield Hospital had already been vacated and all patients had been moved to other locations. But controversy over the site prevented its sale to the Americans. It remains empty, but for the peacocks that roam the wards and guard with vigilance the memory of those who died and are buried there. Somewhere in the quivering jelly, Lawrence was appointed as staffer to the new Health Minister.

I didn't see him – he vanished until his appointment was announced.

I interrogated a conga-line of Nigels till it was obvious that the Bella Finkelstein leak was organised by Frank Dixon, who was working on Dupleix's behalf.

Poor Bella, they fucked with her head. Being interrogated by the specialists for the dementia test pushed her panic button. She started seeing ghosts in black shirts and answered yes to every question . . . in German.

'Do you still love me?' she kvetches.

I pause and consider. 'What's your next offer?'

I needed space and elevation from the liquid waste and synthetic conversation. I needed life to be organic. So I rang Dave and Ingrid and let them know I was on my way. They're building a house on a hundred acres of bush just outside of Cobargo, 150 kilometres across the border from Victoria into New South Wales. They're in a temporary shack, and I could use the caravan. Perfect.

Ingrid chops onions as skilfully as she chops wood. She recognises and has conversations with every creature that crosses her path. In everything she does she's practical, rational and informed, with the exception of Dave, the man she loves.

Dave's a bloke. A bloke of the brooding, grunting, hunter–gatherer species. There isn't anything he can't get to work, jumpstart, kickstart, push-start, chop, break, split or smash. I watch him insert precious seedlings with the gentlest prod of his fist.

I arrived feeling seedy after a showbag of small aeroplane and four-wheel drive. Dave lifted me up by the collar of my army disposals camouflage jacket and put me where he wanted me, out of his way.

Surrounded by tall trees and enough pests to provoke an entomologist to orgasm, we do combat with the bush. The bush wins. Dave's shoulders dominate the landscape, and on scorching days I stand in his shadow. We cook, we plant, we probe seedpods and fill empty barrels with luxurious water. One morning I wake up beside a giant huntsman spider on my pillow. I don't stir. He doesn't either. He seems baffled, as if he's thinking, *Jesus, was I that pissed?*

I returned home tanned and healthy but crushed by the brutal arachnid rejection. I rushed to the answering machine. A message from Lawrence: 'It's meeeeeeee! I know you're practising being invisible right now but peering into my crystal ball I see you'll be calling me back any day soon.'

I could hear the castanet of the snake's rattle in my head but it didn't stop me from calling his mobile number. 'Speak to me!'

'Lola Finkelstein.'

'I was only marinating some juicy chicken thighs this morning and thought of you, gorge. How's tricks?'

'I got dumped by a huntsman.'

'As in flannel shirt? Ooohaaah.'

'As in simple eyes, four sets of legs and a hairy back. And you?'

'I got myself a new job. Adviser to Joe McNicol, the Health . . . '

'I know who he is.'

'He's heartbreakingly gorgeous *and* straight. He's asked me to organise an evening's entertainment for the Department. A celebration of his appointment and an opportunity for his team to have some fun and get to know each other before the real slog starts.'

'I won't do any more freebies, Lawrence.'

'We've got a budget.'

'What date?'

'Not one hundred per cent sure. About three weeks away but I'm wanting to book the function room at Luna Park.'

'Perfect. The procrastinators can sit on the roundabout all night while the manic-depressives throw up their medication on the roller-coaster.'

'I'm meeting with the Functions Coordinator on-site later this arvo to view the facilities. If you can be there, we can walk through the proposal.'

'What time?'

'How's 6.30? Doors close at 5.30. We can rendezvous in the big mouth.'

'I'll be there.'

Uh-oh. Lawrence was serious about the job. He'd changed shape and colour to blend in with the bottom feeders. My heart sank to the ocean floor, offering a new sanctuary to marine life. For no logical reason other than to seek more therapy, I needed to know what flavour of stooge I'd been played.

I stopped the car on the Lower Esplanade near the kiosk facing the city. Tall buildings consorted with God, cloud-wrapped by another item of her lingerie.

Lawrence was waiting. He beamed at me, his smile as big as Luna Park's. 'Looking gorgeous, darl. Did we buy a season of sol at the solarium?'

'I've been bush, Lawrence.'

He shrieked and covered his eyes. 'Reee-al sun? That'll kill you, darl.'

I lunged forward and gave him a one hundred per cent pure pretend-hug.

'Congratulations on getting the gig. Are you having fun at State Government world?'

'I take the path of least resistance and then do a U-turn. I'm loving it, darl. It's grown-up, hip, hop and happening. Bullshit and cutting ribbons. It's me!'

'What about the leather?'

'I told them it's practical. Any weather is leather weather.'

A Sri Lankan woman wearing a dark green skirt and polo top approached the chained gate. Lawrence reached out to help as she began unravelling the chain.

'Don't bother, you'll only be getting in the way.'

He persisted in being Mr Friendly Pain-In-The-Ass. 'You must be Jane Sutton. I'm Lawrence from Joe McNicol's office. This is Lola Finkelstein.'

'Hyacinth. Jane's busy, she asked me to show you the function room. Move through please, I have to lock up.'

I stepped over the threshold. JUST FOR FUN, the slogan was tiled into the path as you entered in case you forgot why you came. I looked for remnants of fun in the empty grounds. I could smell it. Fairy floss, pink magically-spun fun. The entertainment parlour was sealed off with a roller door. Fun was locked in for the night, away from trouble. Fun and trouble – a dangerous liaison.

We followed Hyacinth up some metal stairs to the right of the fun parlour. She unlocked the door and opened a window. It was a giant space with a good-sized stage against the back wall, facing an entire wall of windows. Presently the room was filled with the colours of dusk: red, mauve, straw and pink, identical to my standard lighting specifications. Dusk looks good on anyone.

I stood by the row of windows gazing to the west, the direction of our dreams, allegedly. Peak-hour traffic on the West Gate Bridge, not my idea of Avalon. Unannounced, the scenic railway rattled by, one man standing solo against the sunset. I turned back to Hyacinth, who was overshadowed by Lawrence, who was revelling in a golden beam of light.

'What's happening?'

'The only time they can do any maintenance is after-hours.'

When Lawrence switched into full-swing number-crunching speak with Hyacinth, I was lured down the stairs by the eeriness of the empty hall of mirrors, now only a wall of mirrors because of downsizing. Happens everywhere.

The rest of the space had been invaded by a gallery of shooting, looting and copyright. Thankfully, fun was unplugged.

I stepped in front of a mirror and lost my head. It had run off with someone else. Someone less *mea culpa* and more *carpe diem.* My reflection spoke to me with two arms and two legs floating out on their own from a crease of nothingness. No staples. I'm transfixed and transfigured. A cubist nightmare with a porn-star chaser. Straight up.

Footsteps advanced rapidly behind me. I shifted my eyes but not my head. I know it's disappeared but I can still feel it. The mirror told another story. Eight arms and legs – the huntsman returned to kill the fatted calf? Still no head.

'Lola.'

'Pillar.'

I didn't turn around. Two arms slid past my waist, a hand cupped each breast. No moving, just breathing.

'Is it true you once owned a penis?'

'I was married, that's correct.'

'I meant your own penis, not lend-lease.'

I reached up and slid his hand down onto my vagina.

'Can't you tell?'

'No, ma'am.'

'Is it true you're allergic to rubber?'

'Yes, ma'am. But I've just been given an item imported from South Africa made from buffalo testicles.'

'But what about the buffalo?'

'They're latex-free.'

His body pressed into mine. We were still spooning. One thumb and a forefinger squeezed my marble-hard right nipple. Another thumb and forefinger dragged at the zip of my spandex and cotton-mix capri pants. He bent his legs so I was sliding down his front. The heat curdled my knees till they formed a blob at his feet.

I faced him frontwards. My face, his stiff penis. Intensity without volume.

'Don't make me come here. I'll scream and tear your back to shreds.'

He crouched to the ground. 'Yes, ma'am.'

'I need to know what happened to Frank Dixon.'

Pillar grunted. 'Greg drove him to Tullamarine and he left the country.'

'Who's Greg?'

'He drove for Dupleix for a while. Kept an eye on him.'

'That's how you knew about Lisbon.'

'Maybe.'

'He's still in his seat.'

'Not for long. He knows he's history. He'll resign before he gets busted so he can collect his super.'

Pillar was bent down in a half-squat. I took his face in my hands and kissed him slap-bang on the mouth.

'Let's try for a comfy spot under that ride over there.'

I began crawling towards a sign with the words 'G Force' painted diagonally across it in techno font. 'We can slide in between those big tyres and the two gears.'

Pillar grabbed my ankle. 'Wait a minute, you're makin me feel like trailer trash, ma'am.'

I shrugged. 'You got a problem with that?'

'There isn't going to be enough room for both of us under the axle.'

'I'll get on top, my legs are shorter. If Lawrence comes looking for me, I'll duck.'

Pillar's grin shifted into a four-wheel-drive smile for better climbing ability.

'Who do you think gave me the leather condoms?'

ACKNOWLEDGEMENTS

If the boulders are moved, even a river will change its flow.
Deng Ming Dao

Since 1981 just over six thousand Australians have died due to an AIDS-related condition. Their voices assisted my research and strengthened my resolve to complete the book.

But along the journey I relied on the following people to help me shift the boulders: Kevin Hume, Johnny Sevenoaks, Tony Keenan, Bill O'Loughlin, Tex McKenzie, John Daye, Mark Counter, David Menadue and the exceptional team at Positive Living magazine, Marilyn Wane, Trevor Marmalade, Stephanie and Rick Kalesh, Jane Lewis, Janet McLeod, Jane Cornwell and Morris Gland.

The crew at Penguin Australia: thank you to Captain Bob for taking the risk with boundless enthusiasm and Clare Forster for managing it with a cool head and matching pearls, Anne Rogan for her insightful checking and polishing and Susannah Low for cover-design voodoo.

I am grateful to AFAO and PLWHA Victoria for research material and support for my project.

My greatest debt however is to my editor, Foong Ling Kong, for her editorial acuity, intellectual rigour and Scorpio intuition.

PENGUIN AUSTRALIA SUMMER STORIES 4

Sand between the toes, soft serve ice-cream, the scent of baby oil, and the stillness before a thunderstorm – summer's here.

Twenty dazzling stories for summer reading by some of Australia's best-loved writers and hottest new voices, evoking the languorous days, restless nights and indelible memories of summers past and present.

Robert Drewe Andy Quan Helen Garner Elliot Perlman
Chris Daffey Derek Hansen Nick Earls Peter Goldsworthy
Tom Petsinis Tim Winton Kay Donovan Gillian Mears
Mena Abdullah & Ray Mathew David Campbell Thea Astley
Rachael Treasure Brenda Walker Dorothy Hewett Lily Brett
Amy Witting Herb Wharton